hKjc

MERMIN™

BOOK TWO: THE BIG CATCH

D1409104

OCT   2021

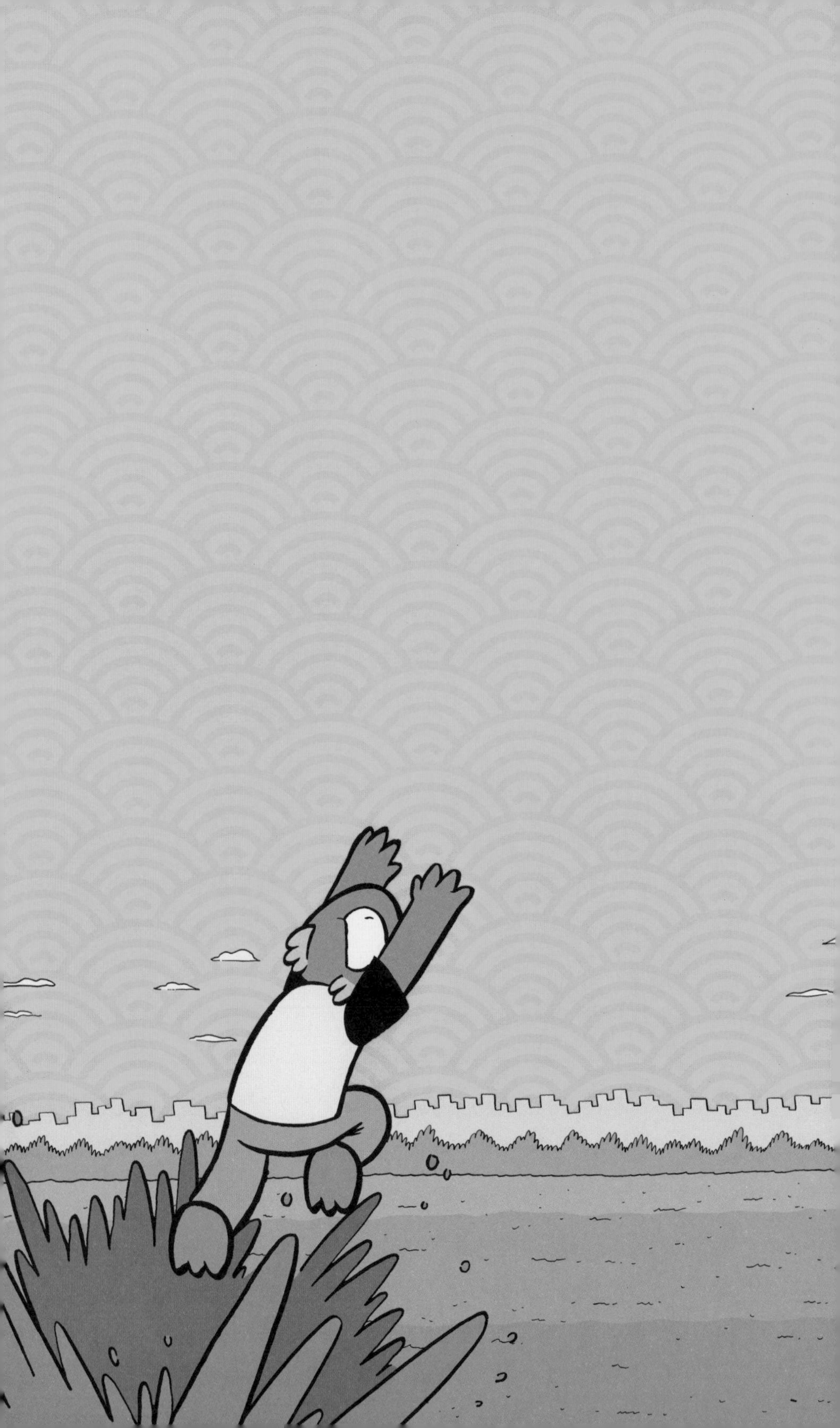

MERMIN™

BOOK TWO: THE BIG CATCH

Written and illustrated by
Joey Weiser

Edited by
Jill Beaton

Designed by
Keith Wood

Oni Press, Inc.

publisher, **Joe Nozemack**

editor in chief, **James Lucas Jones**

v.p. of marketing & sales, **Andrew McIntire**

sales manager, **David Dissanayake**

publicity coordinator, **Rachel Reed**

director of design & production, **Troy Look**

graphic designer, **Hilary Thompson**

digital art technician, **Jared Jones**

managing editor, **Ari Yarwood**

senior editor, **Charlie Chu**

editor, **Robin Herrera**

editorial assistant, **Bess Pallares**

director of logistics, **Brad Rooks**

logistics associate, **Jung Lee**

onipress.com
facebook.com/onipress
twitter.com/onipress
onipress.tumblr.com
instagram.com/onipress
tragic-planet.com

First Edition: December 2016
ISBN: 978-1-62010-354-8

Mermin, Book Two: The Big Catch, December 2016. Published by Oni Press, Inc.
1305 SE Martin Luther King Jr. Blvd., Suite A, Portland, OR 97214. Mermin is ™
& © 2016 Joey Weiser. All rights reserved. Oni Press logo and icon ™ & © 2016
Oni Press, Inc. All rights reserved. Oni Press logo and icon artwork created
by Keith A. Wood. The events, institutions, and characters presented in this
book are fictional. Any resemblance to actual persons, living or dead, is purely
coincidental. No portion of this publication may be reproduced, by any means,
without the express written permission of the copyright holders.

Printed in China.

Library of Congress Control Number: 2012953664

1 2 3 4 5 6 7 8 9 10

CHAPTER ONE

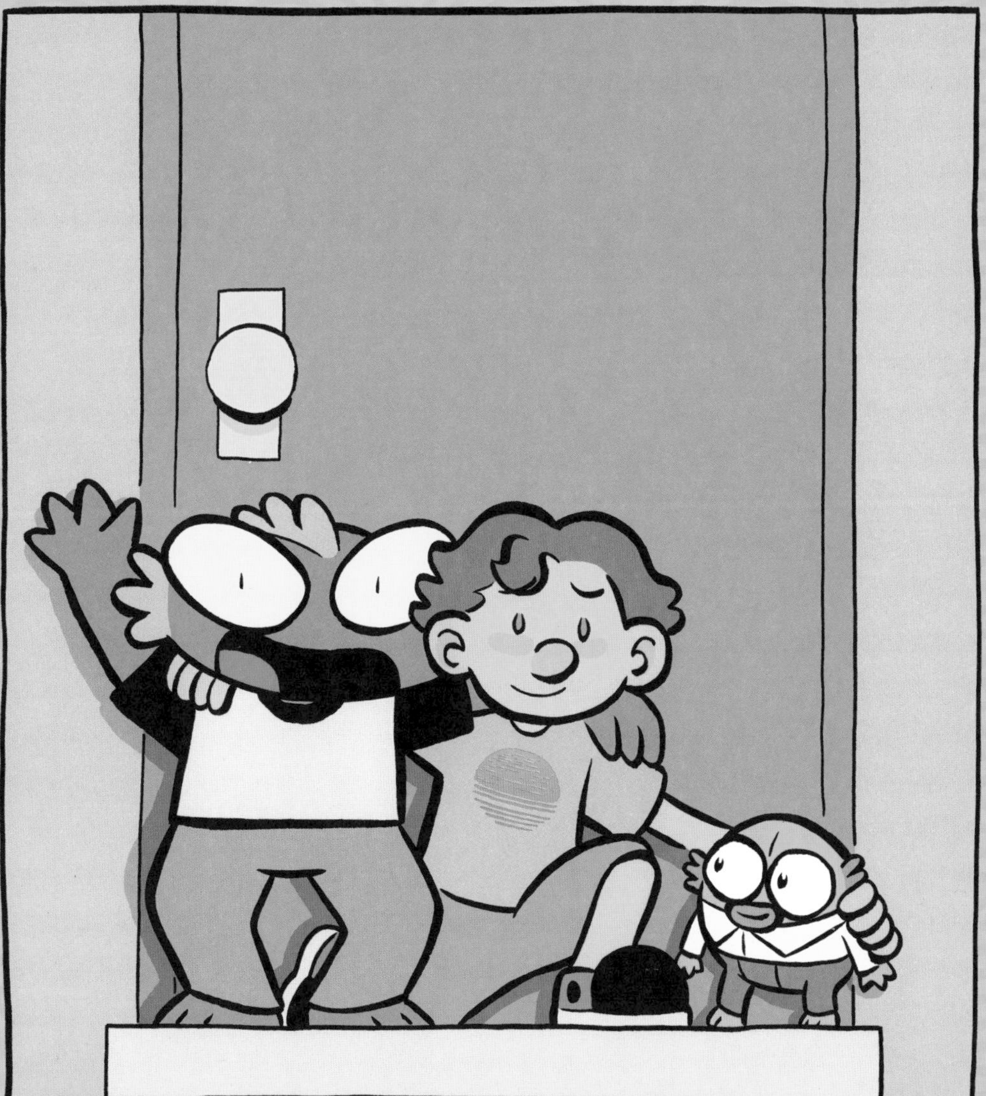

. . . BIZARRE INCIDENT AT TEAWATER ELEMENTARY LAST WEEK . . .

HM?

REPORTERS RUSHED TO THE SCENE AS WHAT CAN ONLY BE DE

RIGHT THERE!

IIPAUSE

I THINK I FOUND SOMETHING!

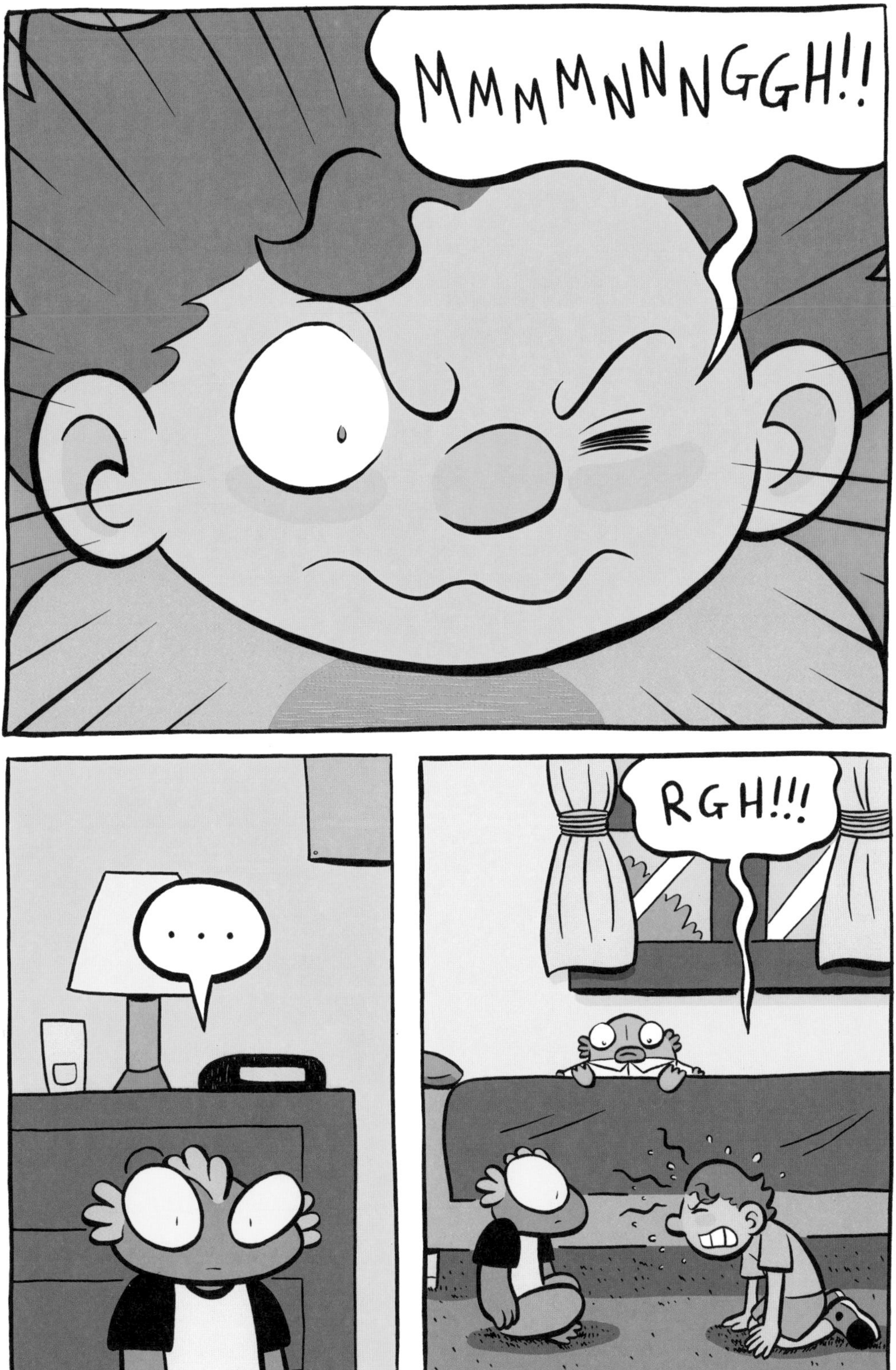
MMMMNNNGGH!!
. . .
RGH!!!

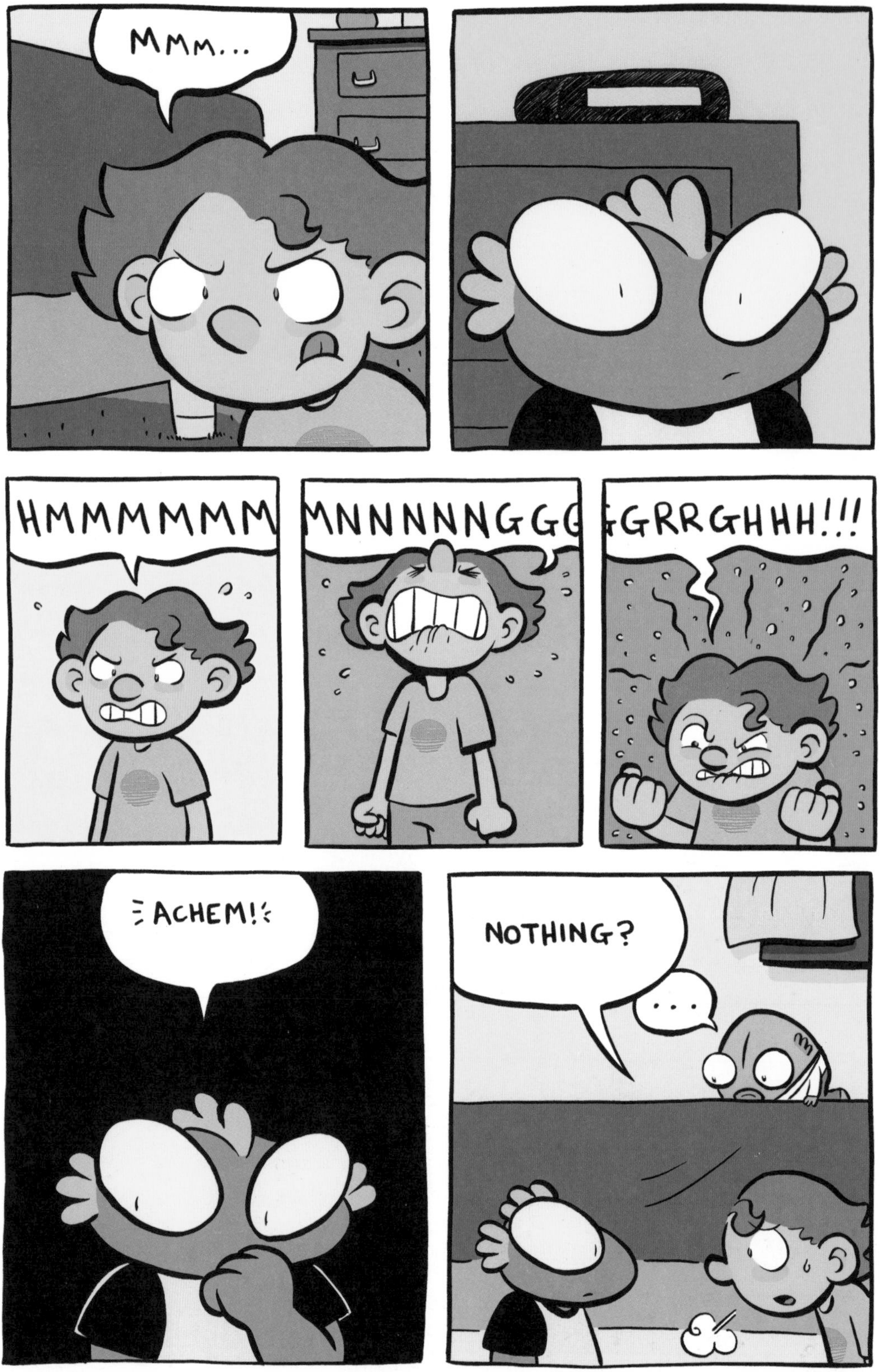
MMM...
HMMMMMM
MNNNNNGGG
GGRRGHHH!!!
ACHEM!
NOTHING?
...

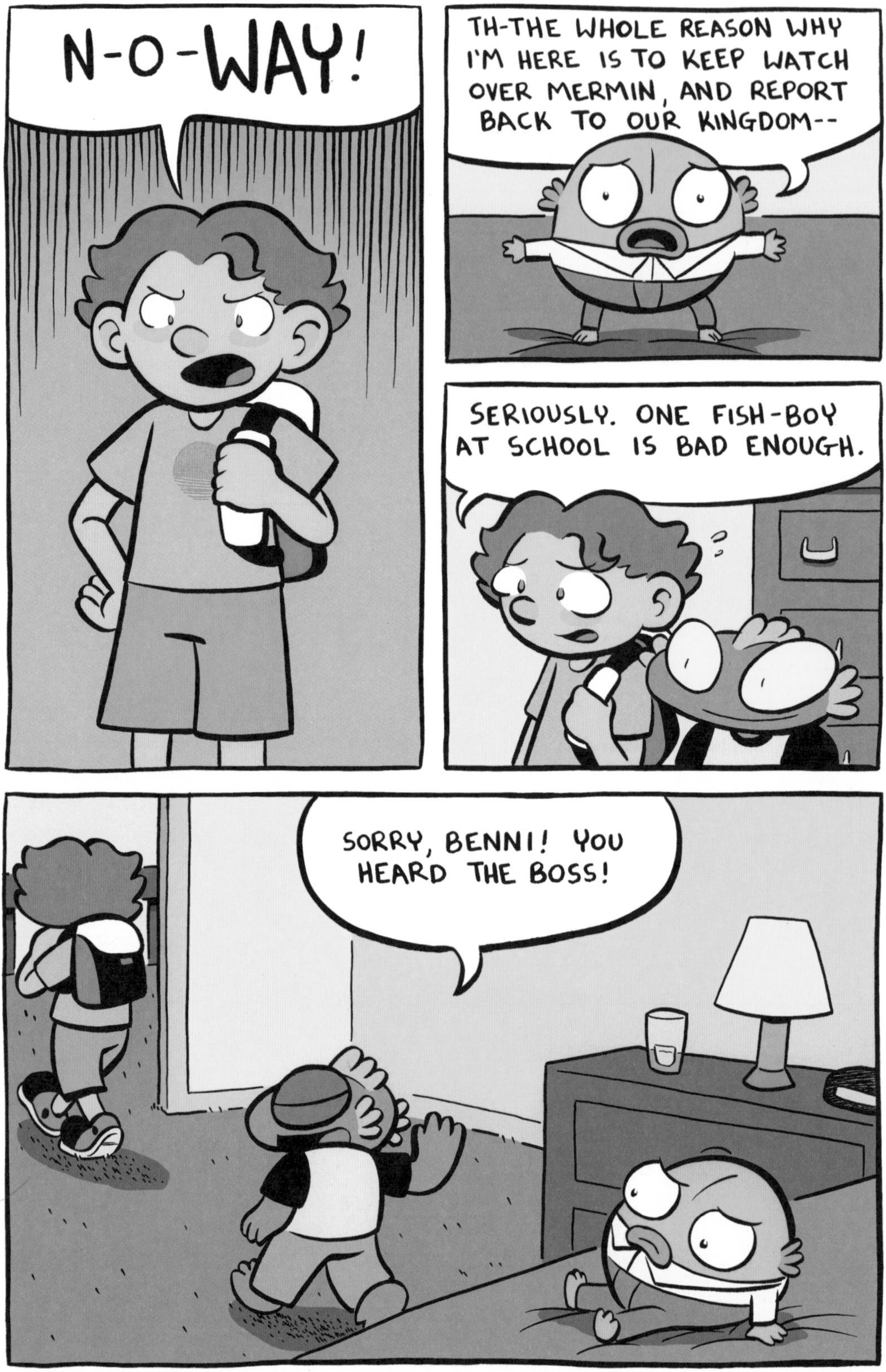
N-O-WAY!
TH-THE WHOLE REASON WHY I'M HERE IS TO KEEP WATCH OVER MERMIN, AND REPORT BACK TO OUR KINGDOM--
SERIOUSLY. ONE FISH-BOY AT SCHOOL IS BAD ENOUGH.
SORRY, BENNI! YOU HEARD THE BOSS!

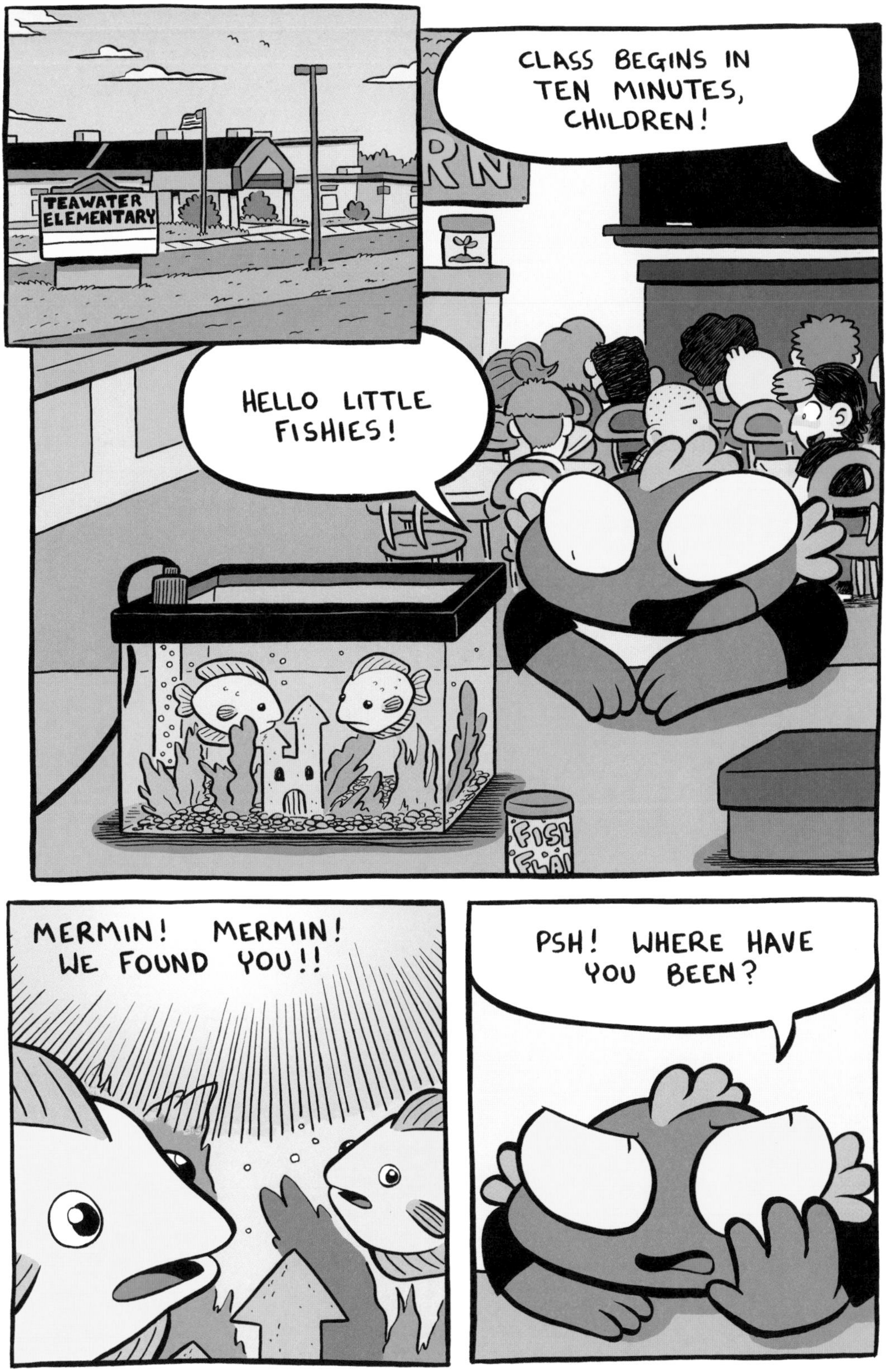
TEAWATER ELEMENTARY
CLASS BEGINS IN TEN MINUTES, CHILDREN!
HELLO LITTLE FISHIES!
MERMIN! MERMIN! WE FOUND YOU!!
PSH! WHERE HAVE YOU BEEN?

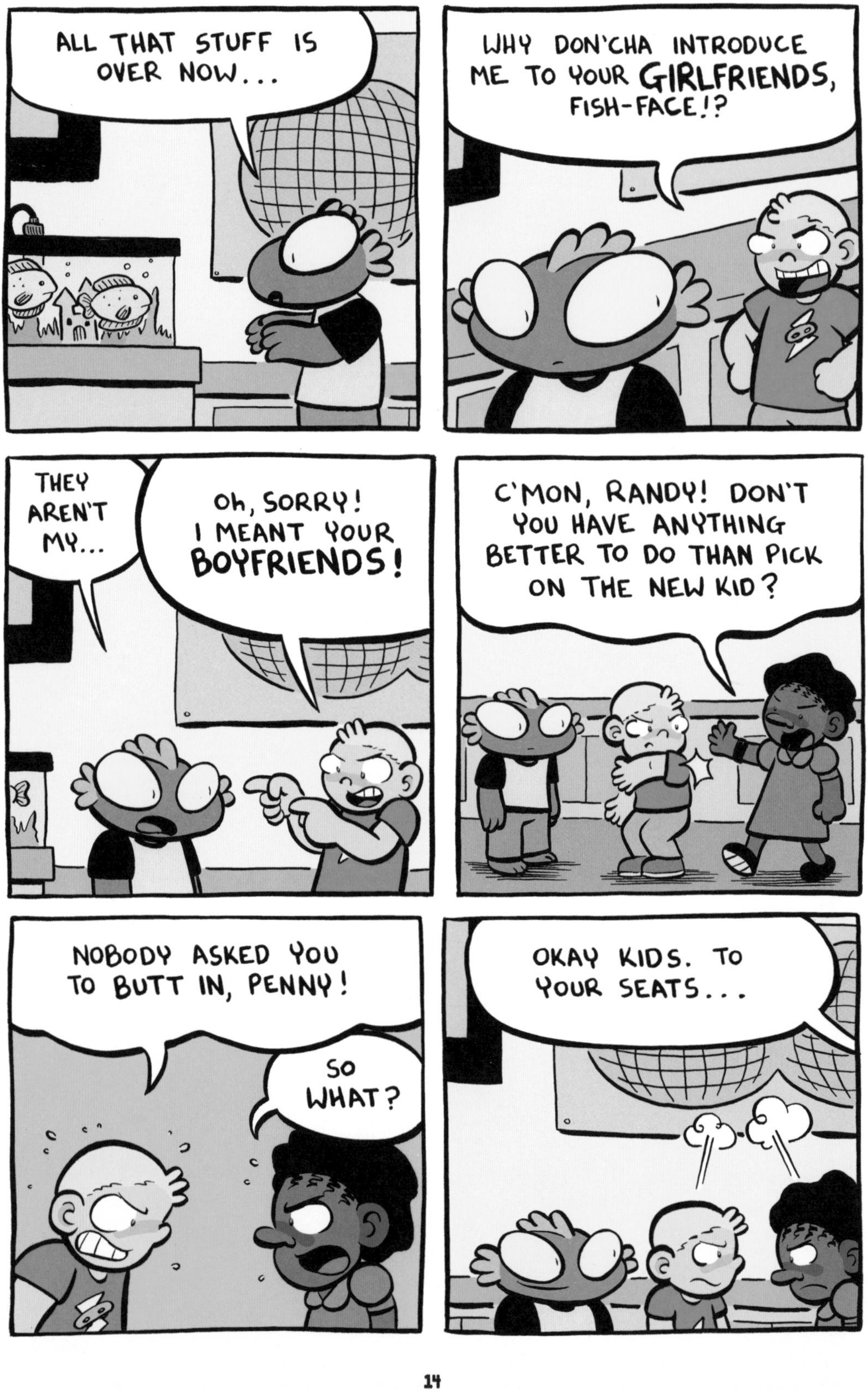

ALL THAT STUFF IS OVER NOW...
WHY DON'CHA INTRODUCE ME TO YOUR GIRLFRIENDS, FISH-FACE!?
THEY AREN'T MY...
Oh, SORRY! I MEANT YOUR BOYFRIENDS!
C'MON, RANDY! DON'T YOU HAVE ANYTHING BETTER TO DO THAN PICK ON THE NEW KID?
NOBODY ASKED YOU TO BUTT IN, PENNY!
SO WHAT?
OKAY KIDS. TO YOUR SEATS...

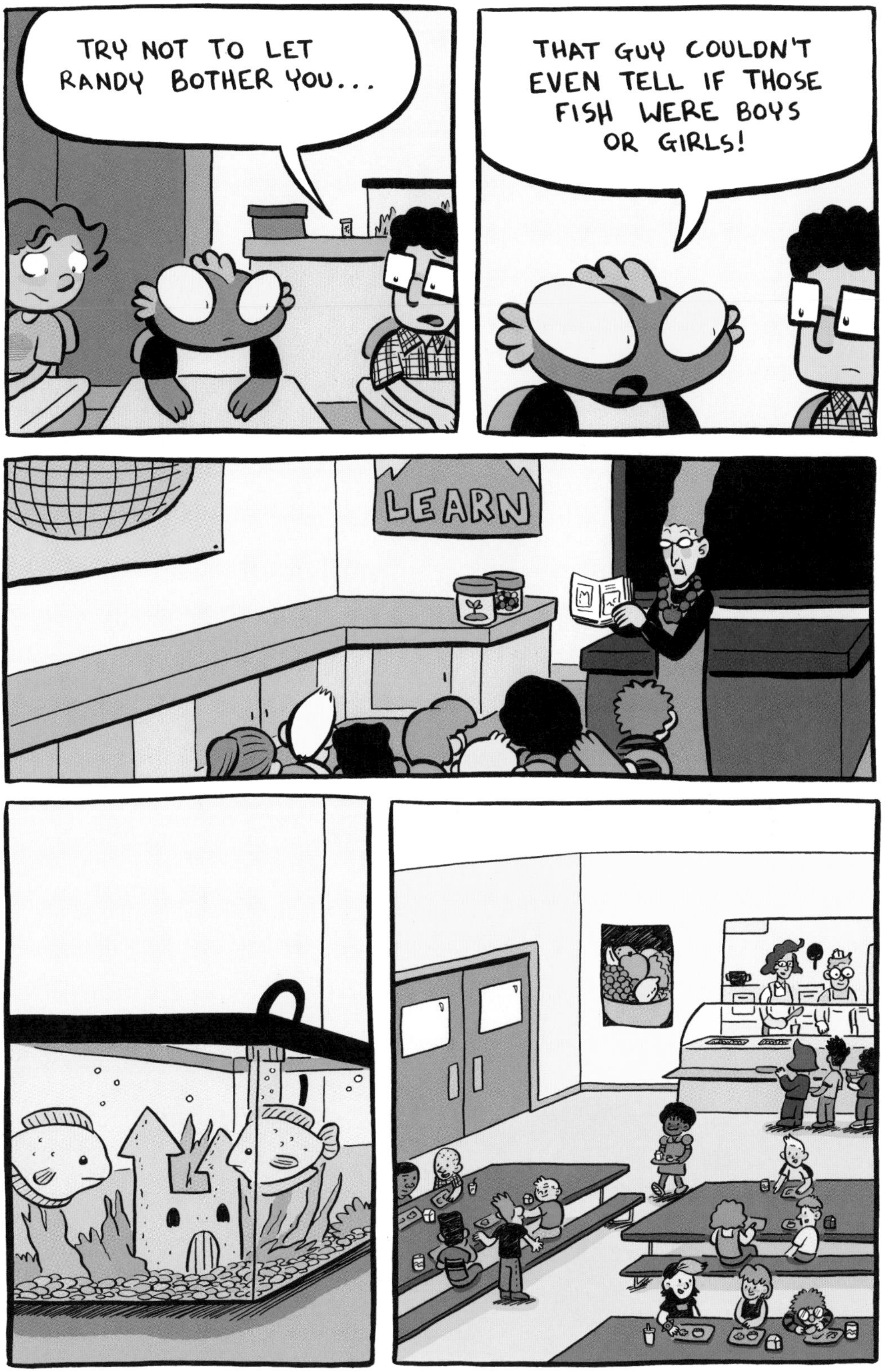
TRY NOT TO LET RANDY BOTHER YOU...
THAT GUY COULDN'T EVEN TELL IF THOSE FISH WERE BOYS OR GIRLS!
LEARN

16

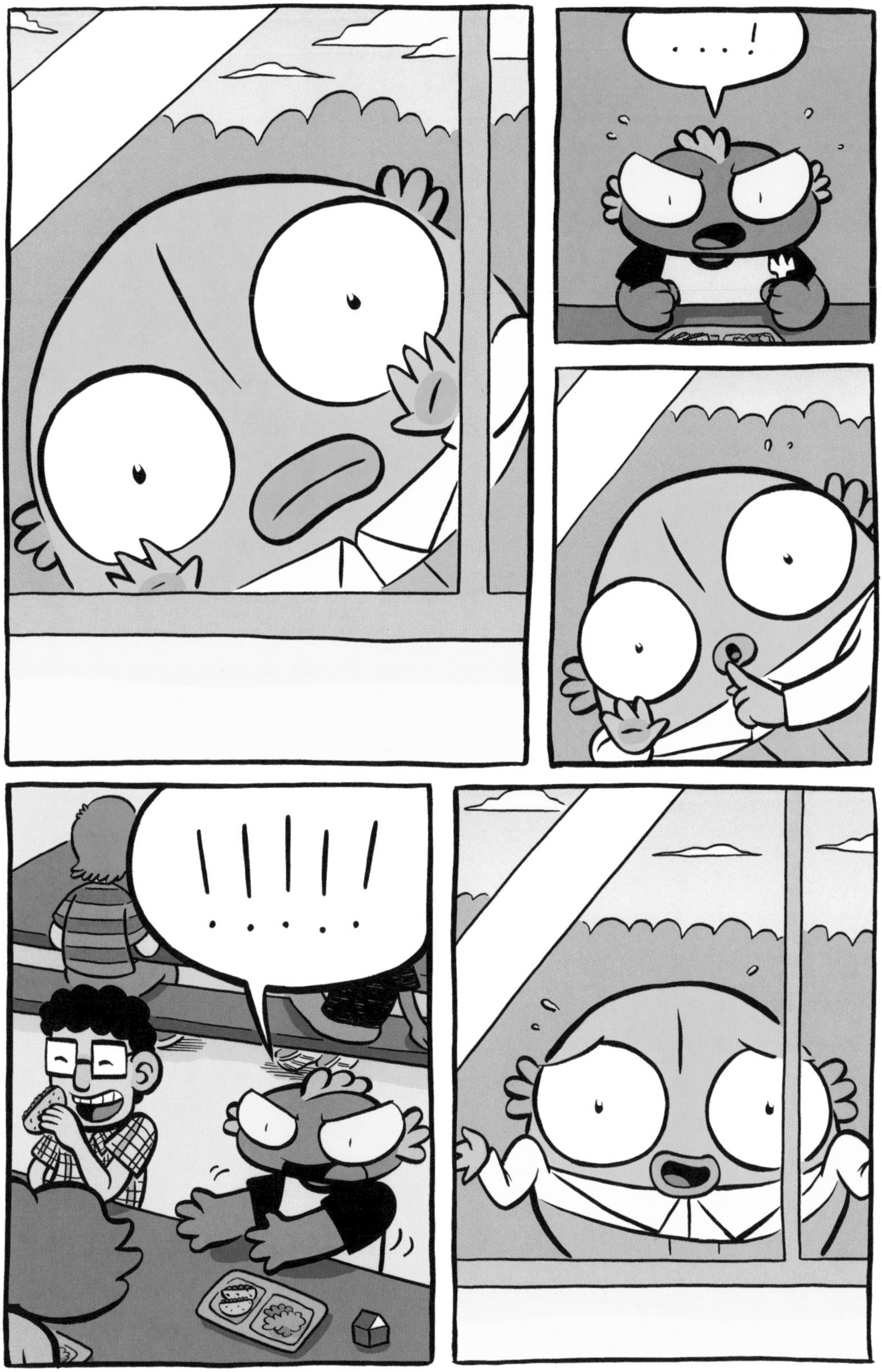

. . . . !
! ! ! ! !
. . . . .

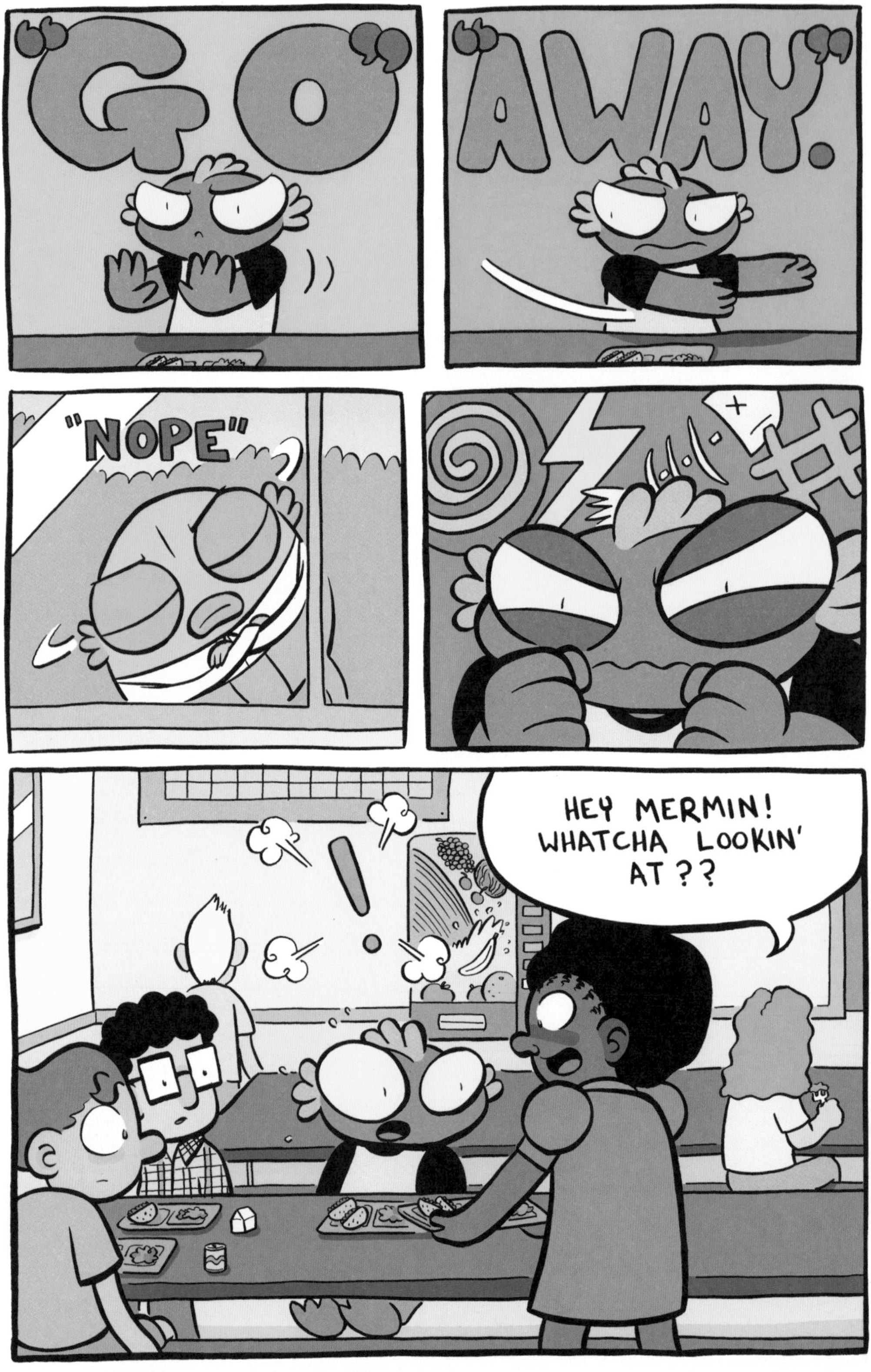
"GO"
"AWAY."
"NOPE"
HEY MERMIN! WHATCHA LOOKIN' AT??

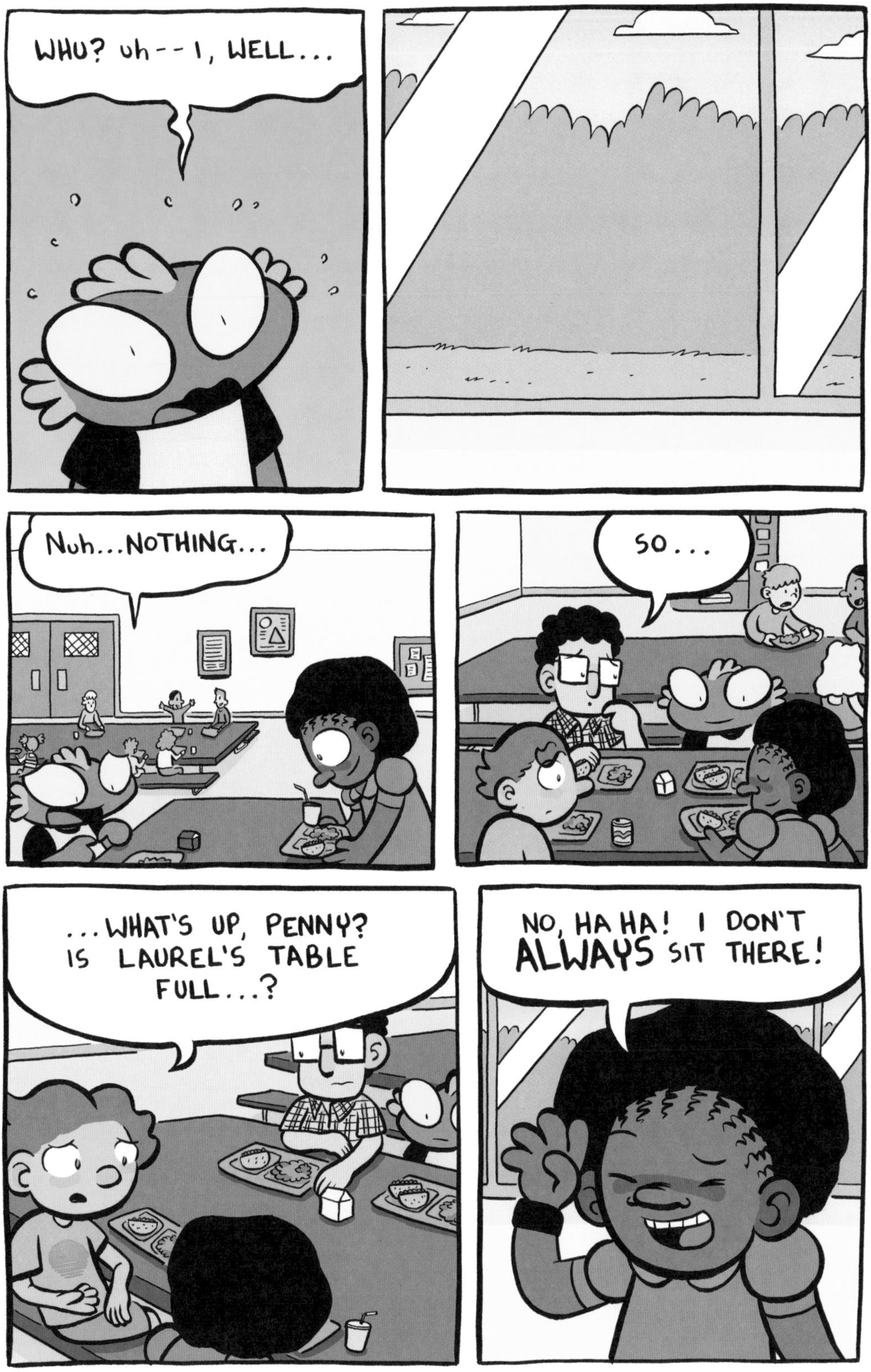
WHU? uh-- I, WELL...
Nuh...NOTHING...
SO...
...WHAT'S UP, PENNY? IS LAUREL'S TABLE FULL...?
NO, HA HA! I DON'T ALWAYS SIT THERE!

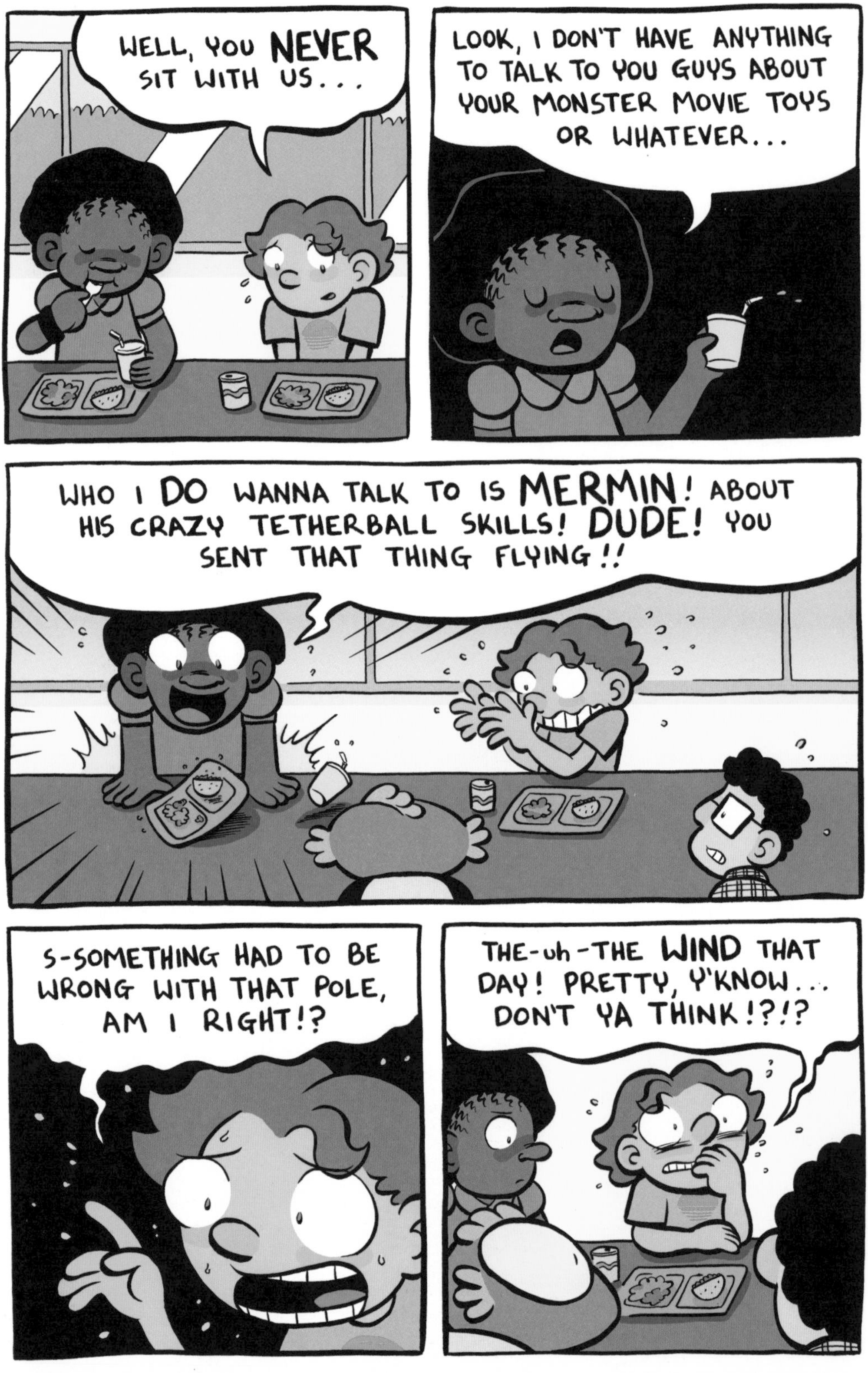
WELL, YOU NEVER SIT WITH US...
LOOK, I DON'T HAVE ANYTHING TO TALK TO YOU GUYS ABOUT YOUR MONSTER MOVIE TOYS OR WHATEVER...
WHO I DO WANNA TALK TO IS MERMIN! ABOUT HIS CRAZY TETHERBALL SKILLS! DUDE! YOU SENT THAT THING FLYING!!
S-SOMETHING HAD TO BE WRONG WITH THAT POLE, AM I RIGHT!?
THE-uh-THE WIND THAT DAY! PRETTY, Y'KNOW... DON'T YA THINK!?!?

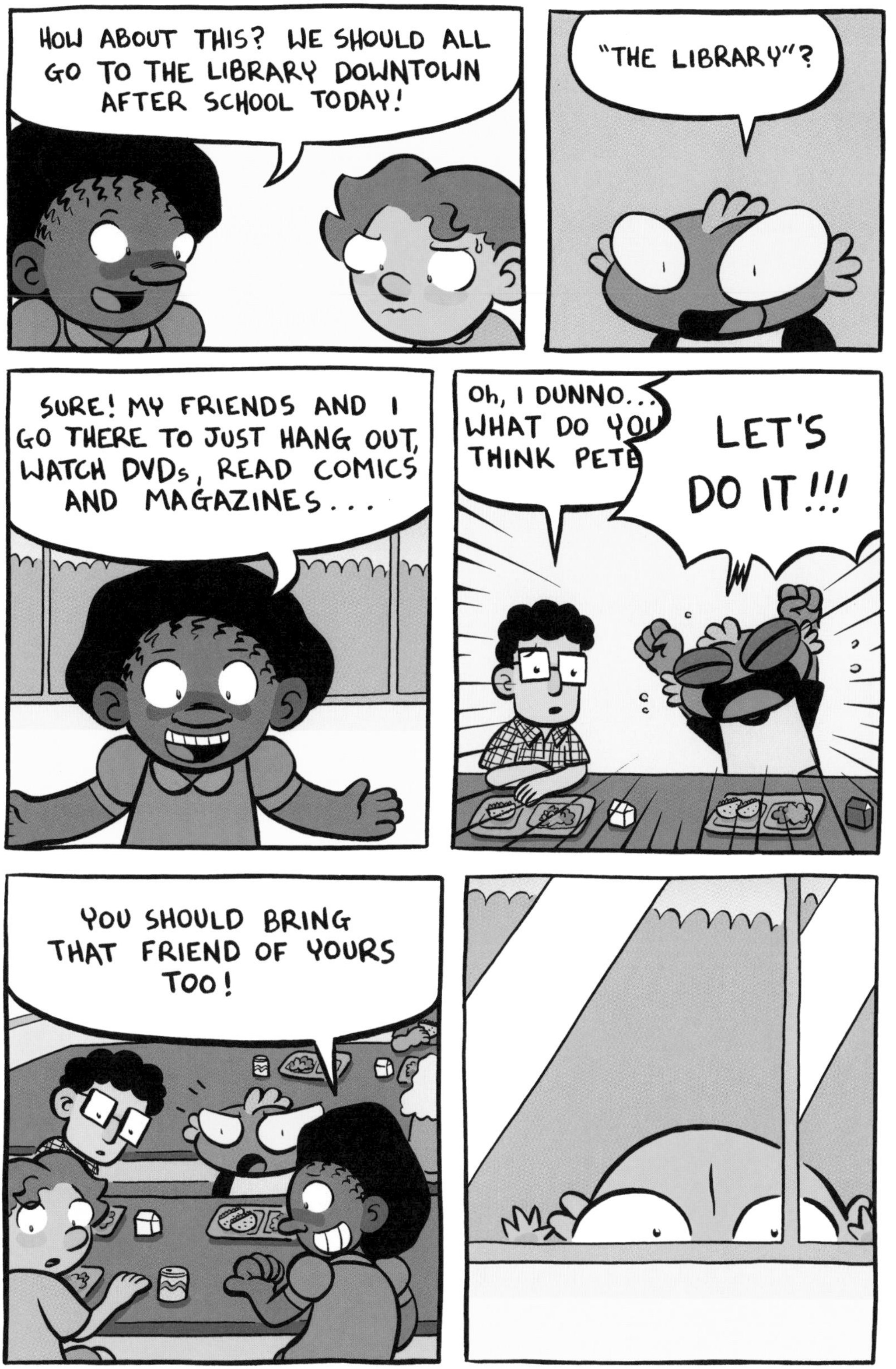
HOW ABOUT THIS? WE SHOULD ALL GO TO THE LIBRARY DOWNTOWN AFTER SCHOOL TODAY!
"THE LIBRARY"?
SURE! MY FRIENDS AND I GO THERE TO JUST HANG OUT, WATCH DVDs, READ COMICS AND MAGAZINES...
Oh, I DUNNO... WHAT DO YOU THINK PETE
LET'S DO IT!!!
YOU SHOULD BRING THAT FRIEND OF YOURS TOO!

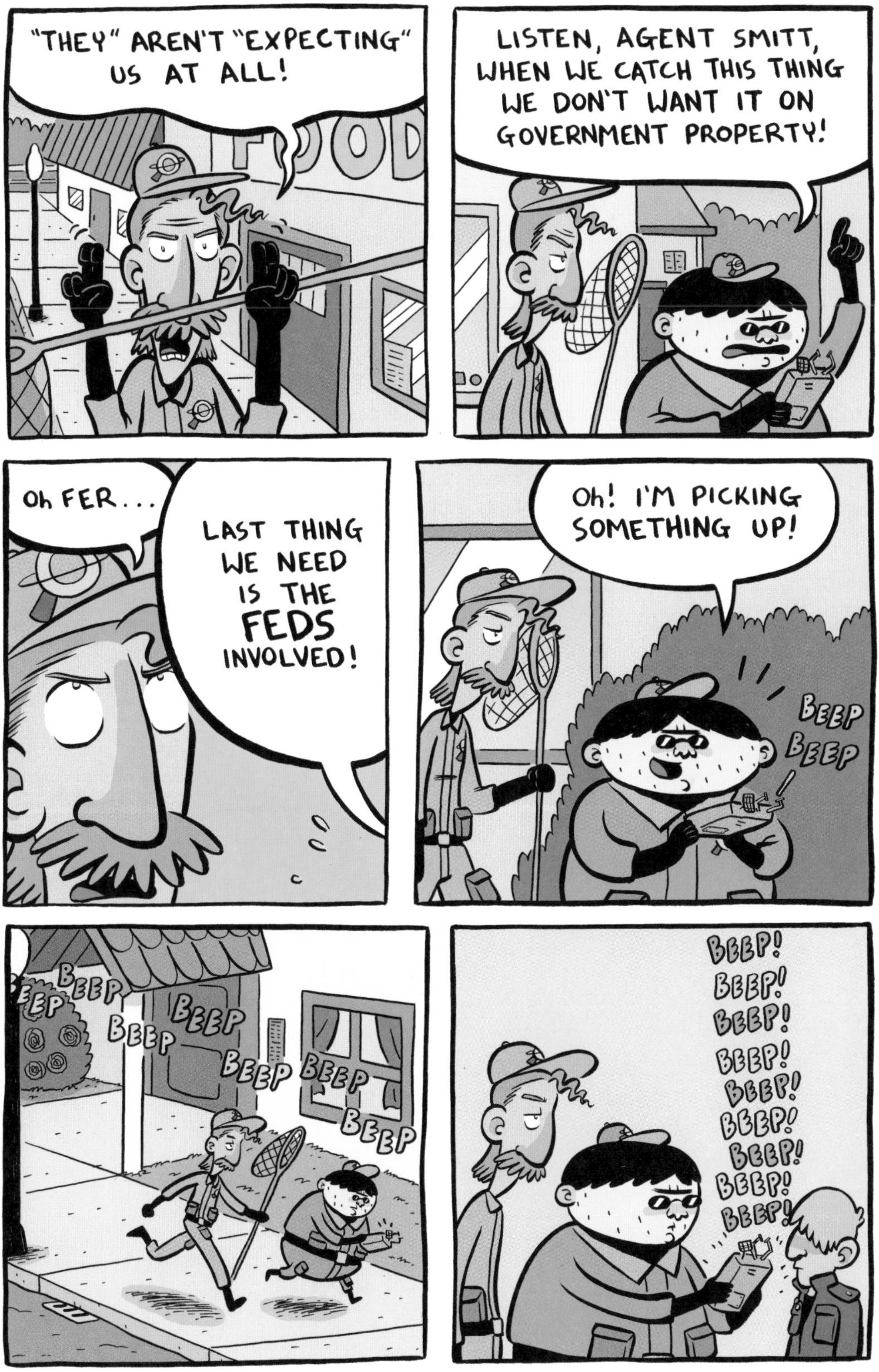
"THEY" AREN'T "EXPECTING" US AT ALL!
LISTEN, AGENT SMITT, WHEN WE CATCH THIS THING WE DON'T WANT IT ON GOVERNMENT PROPERTY!
Oh FER...
LAST THING WE NEED IS THE FEDS INVOLVED!
Oh! I'M PICKING SOMETHING UP!
BEEP
BEEP
BEEP
BEEP
BEEP
BEEP
BEEP
BEEP
BEEP
BEEP!
BEEP!
BEEP!
BEEP!
BEEP!
BEEP!
BEEP!
BEEP!
BEEP!

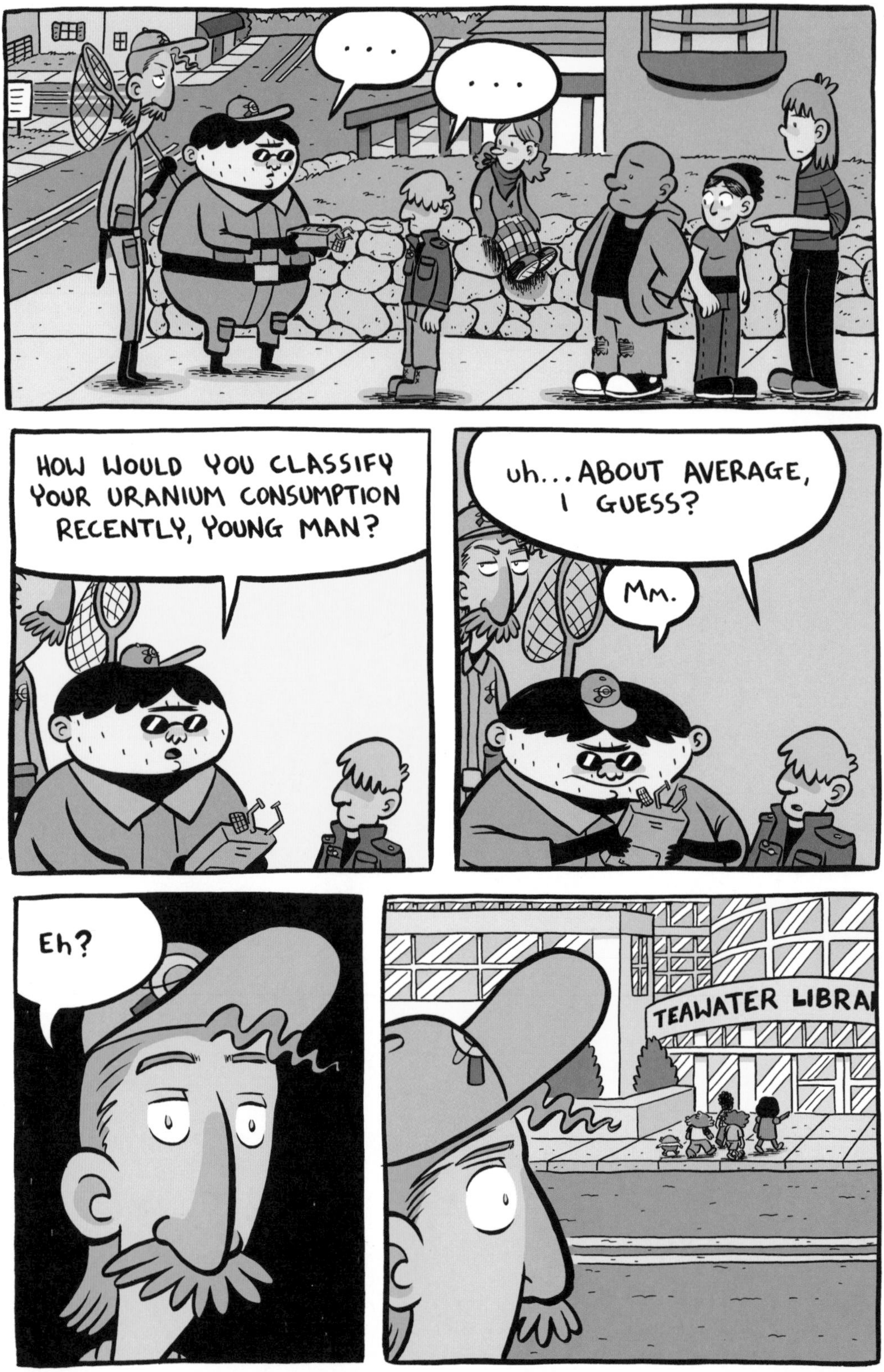
. . .
. . .
HOW WOULD YOU CLASSIFY YOUR URANIUM CONSUMPTION RECENTLY, YOUNG MAN?
uh... ABOUT AVERAGE, I GUESS?
Mm.
Eh?
TEAWATER LIBRA

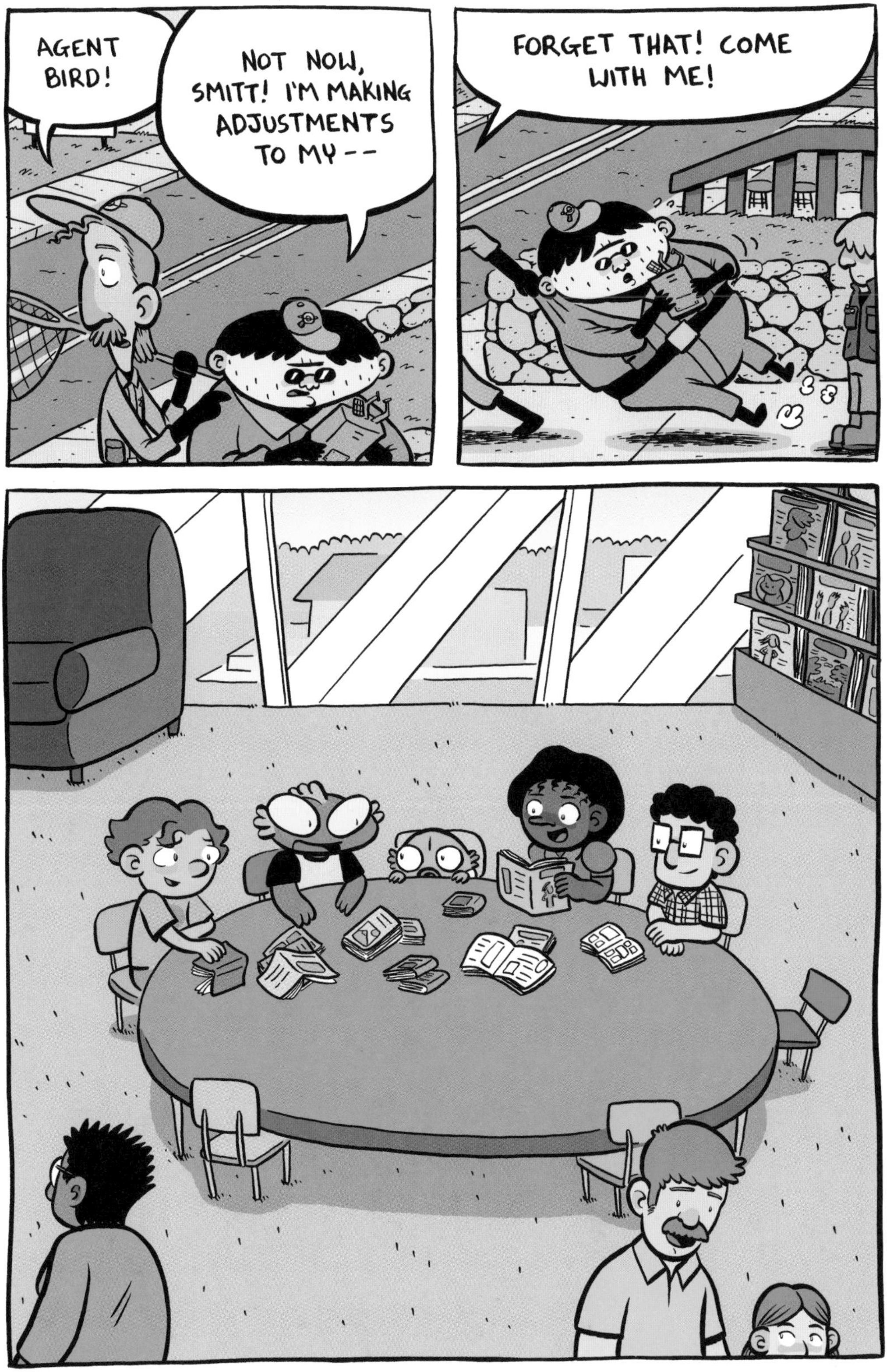
AGENT BIRD!
NOT NOW, SMITT! I'M MAKING ADJUSTMENTS TO MY--
FORGET THAT! COME WITH ME!

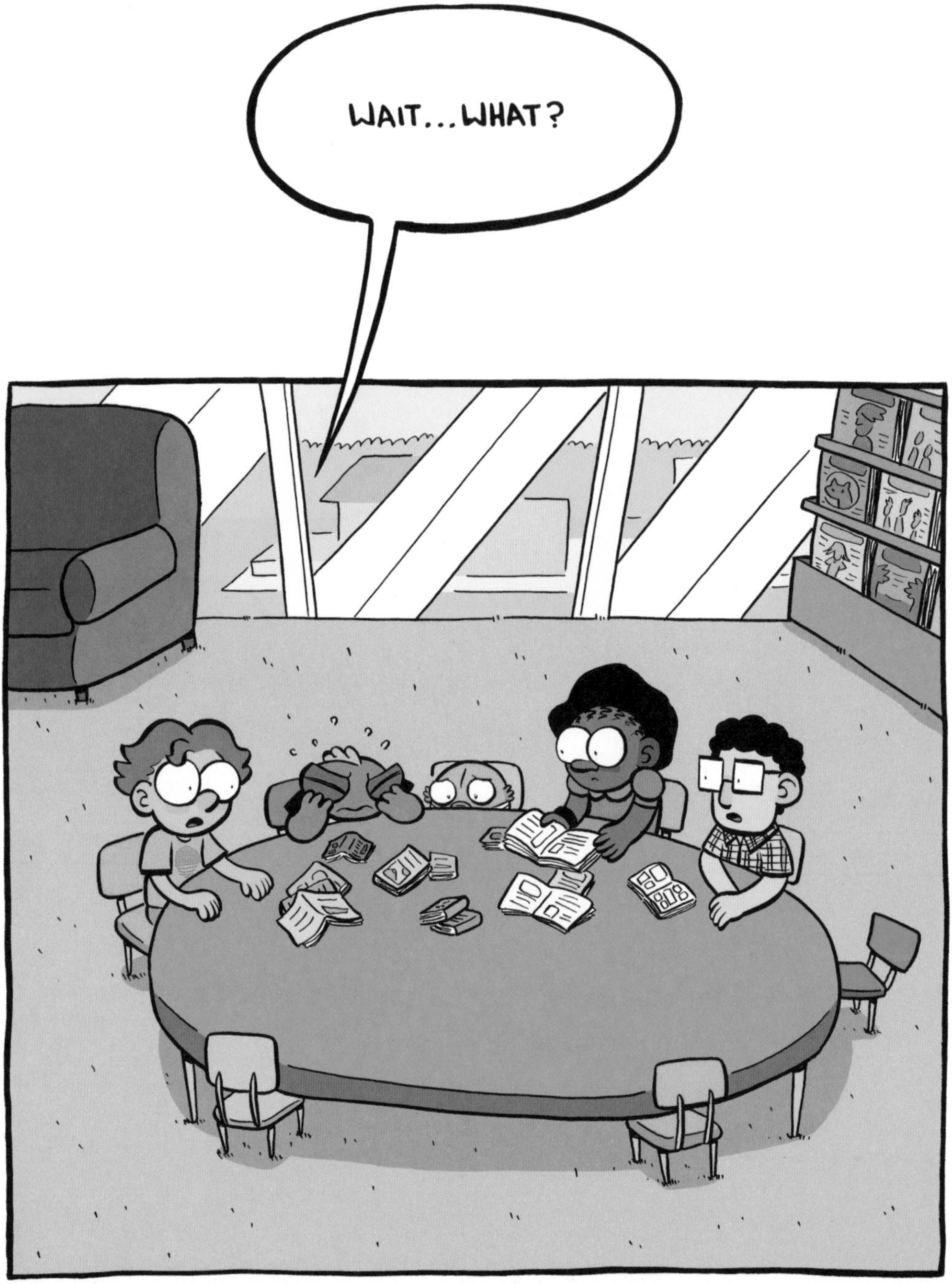
WAIT...WHAT?

CHAPTER TWO

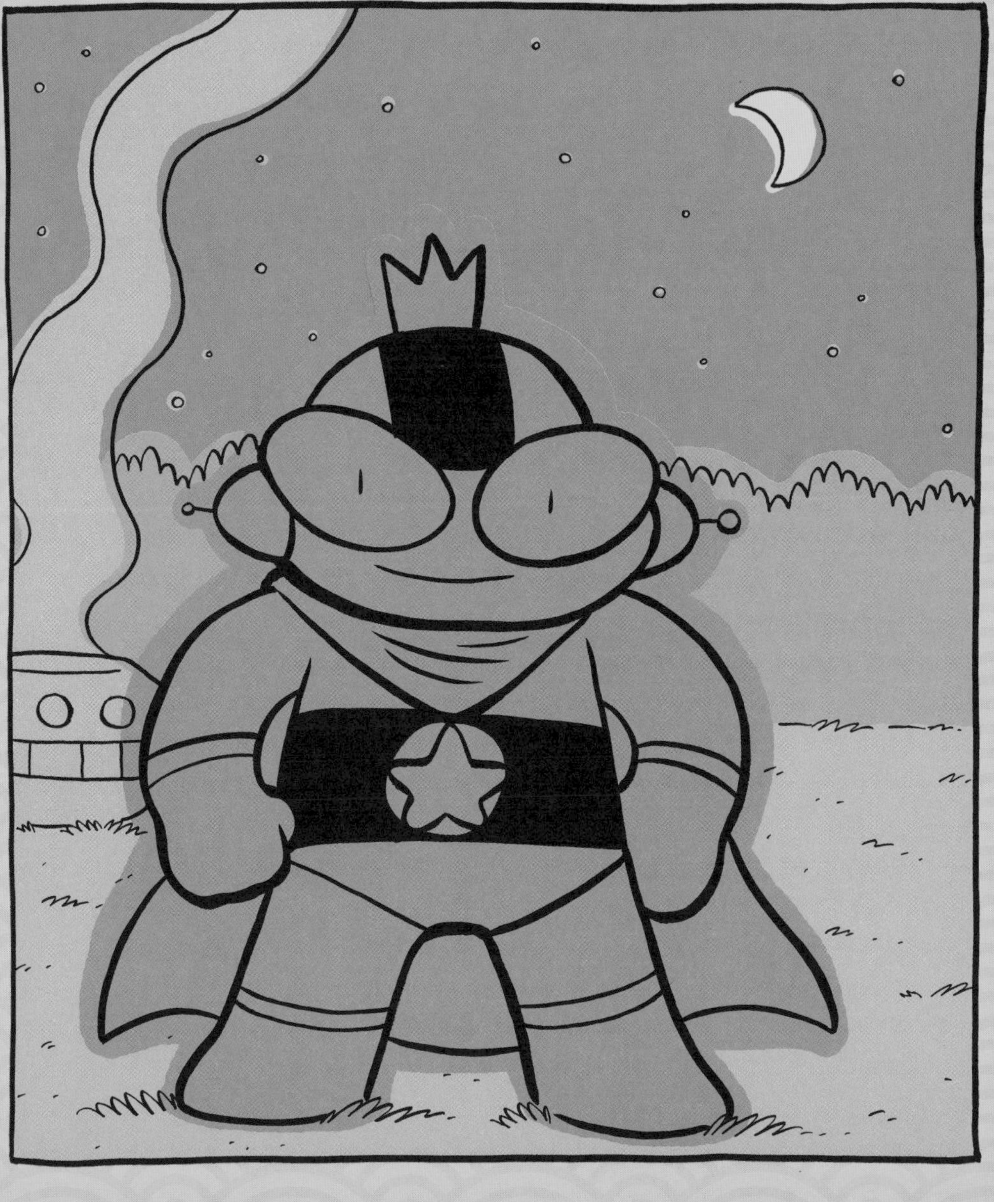

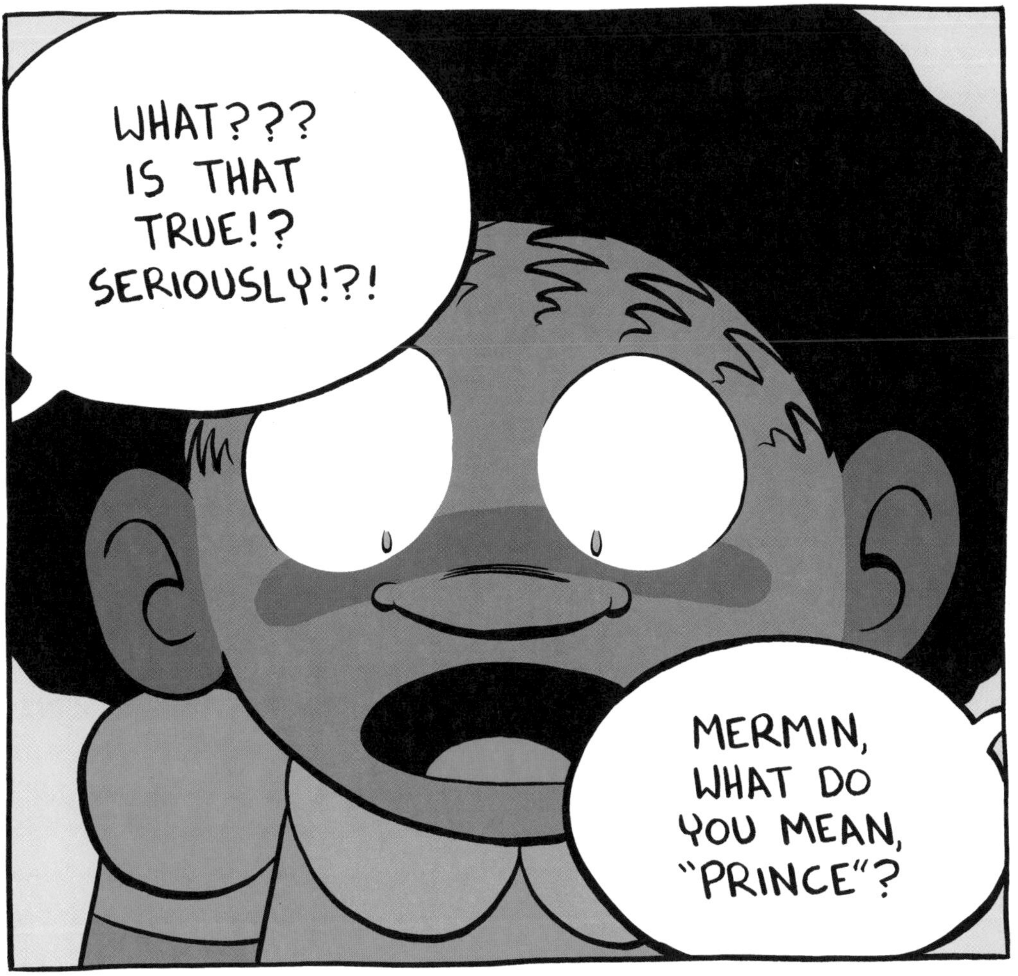
WHAT???
IS THAT
TRUE!?
SERIOUSLY!?!
MERMIN,
WHAT DO
YOU MEAN,
"PRINCE"?

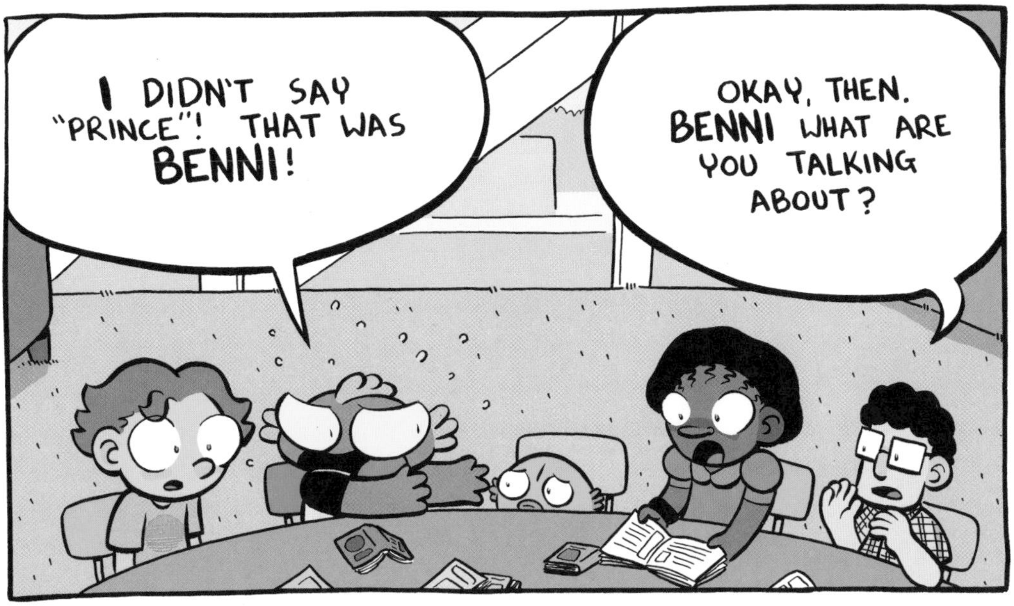
I DIDN'T SAY
"PRINCE"! THAT WAS
BENNI!
OKAY, THEN.
BENNI WHAT ARE
YOU TALKING
ABOUT?

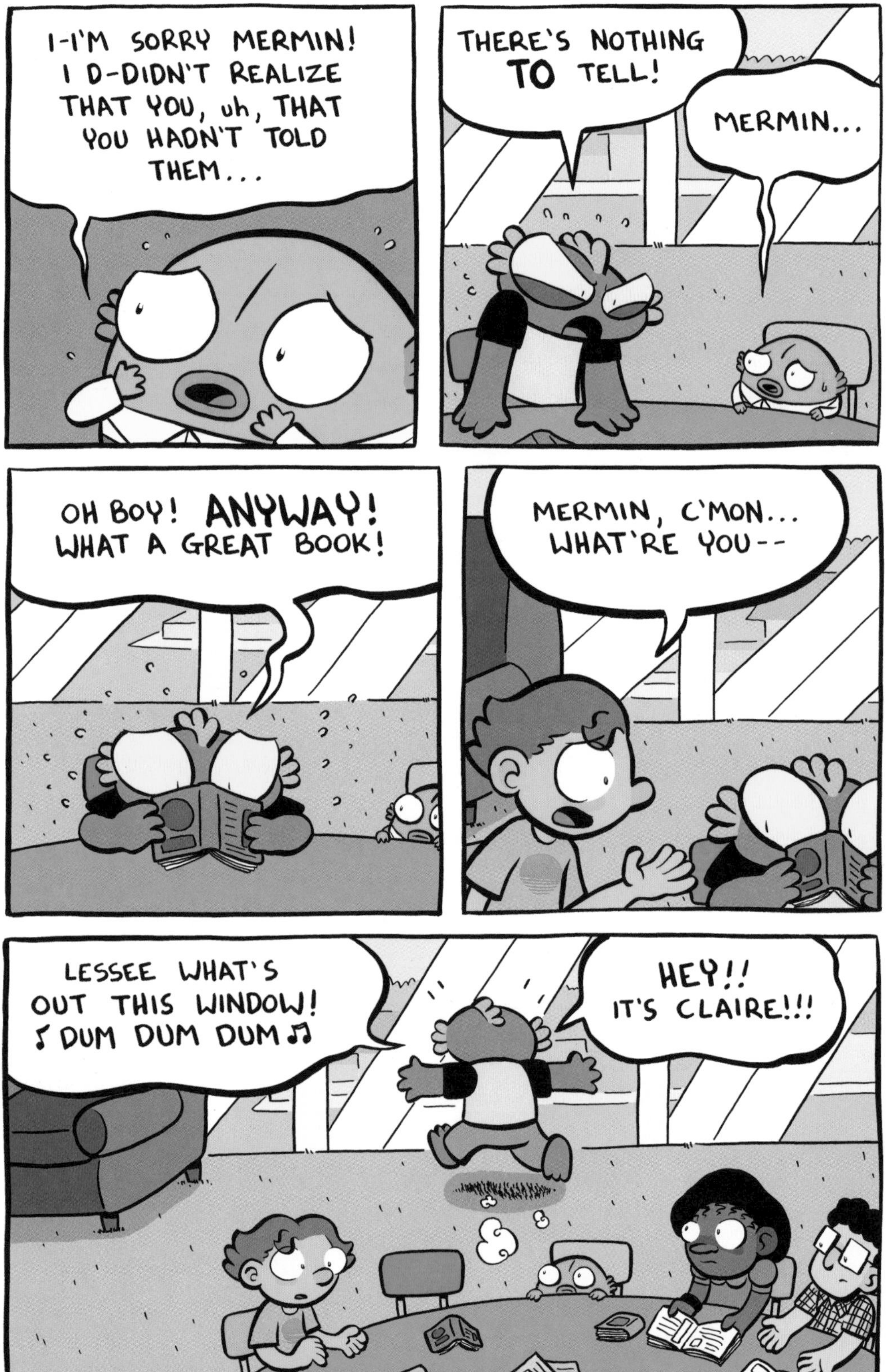
I-I'M SORRY MERMIN! I D-DIDN'T REALIZE THAT YOU, uh, THAT YOU HADN'T TOLD THEM...
THERE'S NOTHING TO TELL!
MERMIN...
OH BOY! ANYWAY! WHAT A GREAT BOOK!
MERMIN, C'MON... WHAT'RE YOU--
LESSEE WHAT'S OUT THIS WINDOW! ♪ DUM DUM DUM ♫
HEY!! IT'S CLAIRE!!!

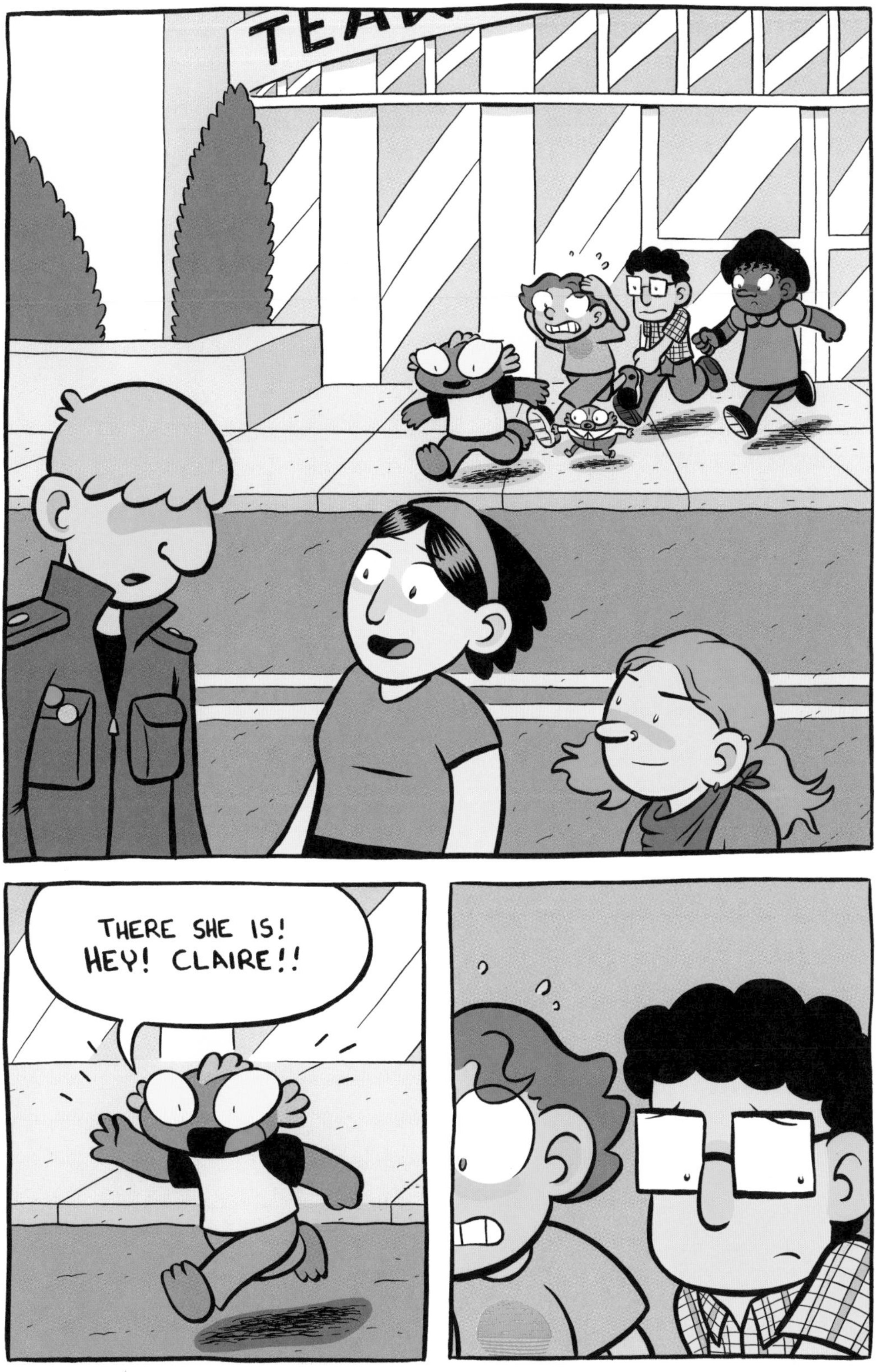
TEA
THERE SHE IS! HEY! CLAIRE!!

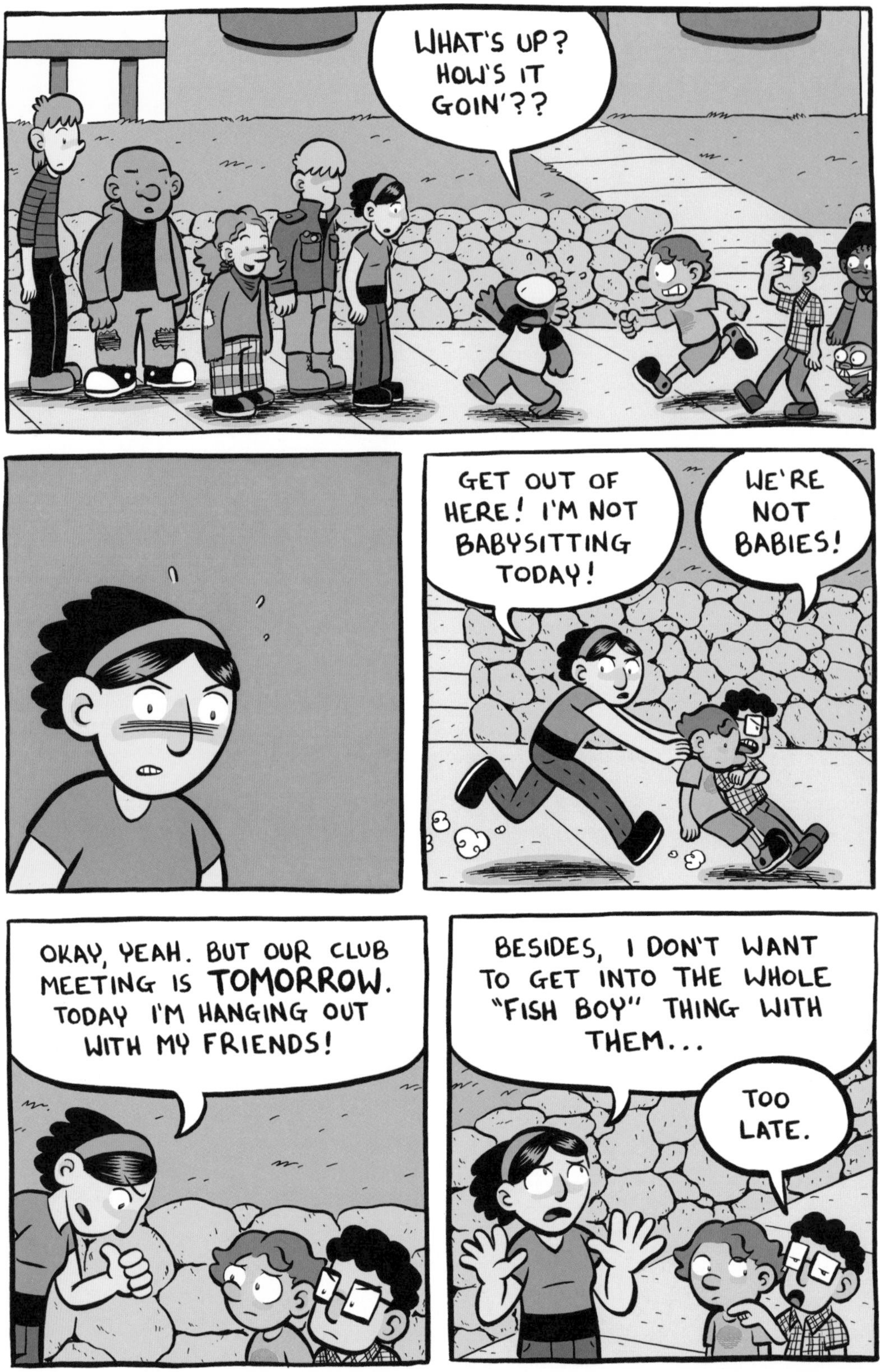
WHAT'S UP? HOW'S IT GOIN'??
GET OUT OF HERE! I'M NOT BABYSITTING TODAY!
WE'RE NOT BABIES!
OKAY, YEAH. BUT OUR CLUB MEETING IS **TOMORROW**. TODAY I'M HANGING OUT WITH MY FRIENDS!
BESIDES, I DON'T WANT TO GET INTO THE WHOLE "FISH BOY" THING WITH THEM...
TOO LATE.

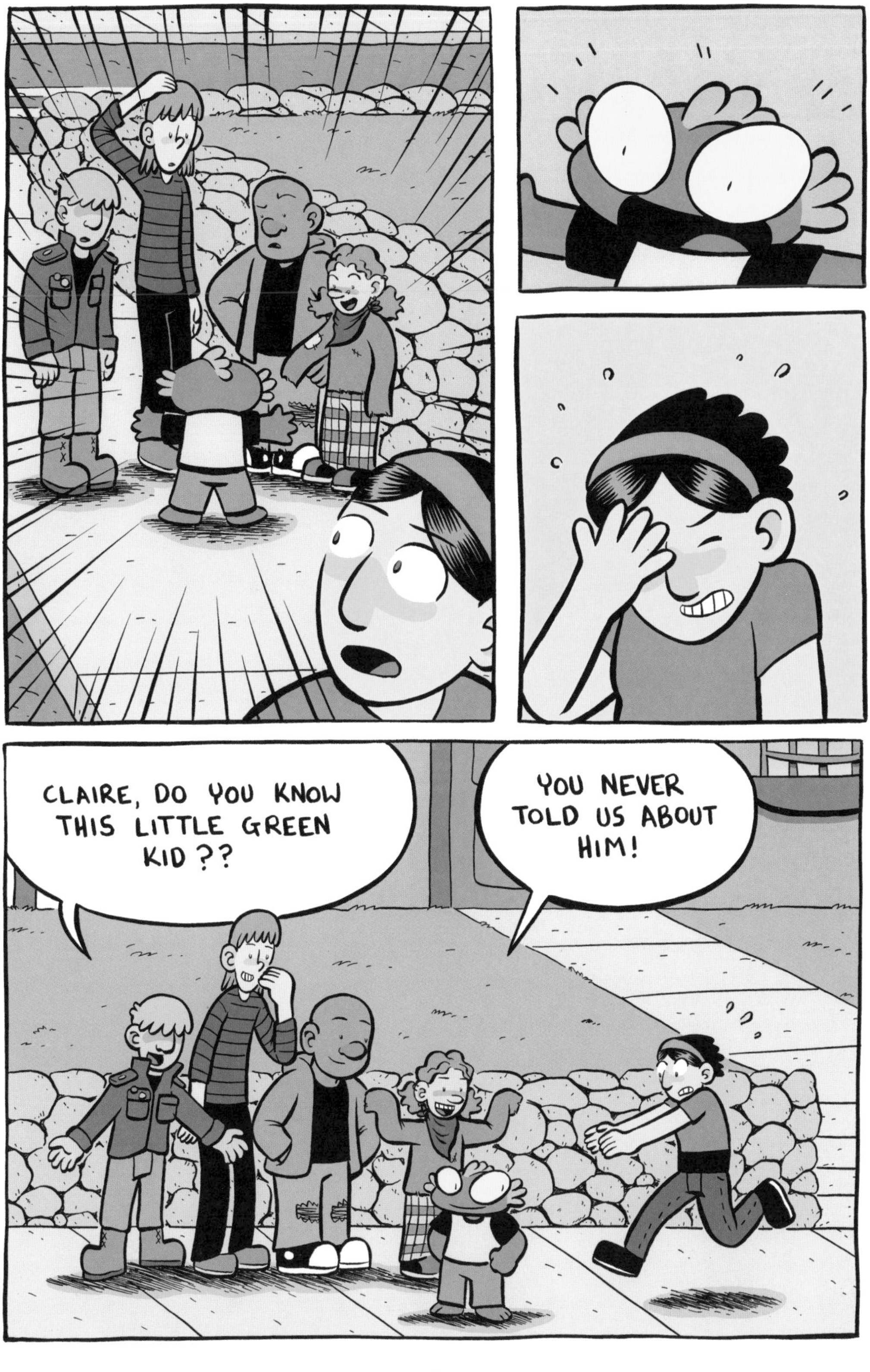
CLAIRE, DO YOU KNOW THIS LITTLE GREEN KID??
YOU NEVER TOLD US ABOUT HIM!

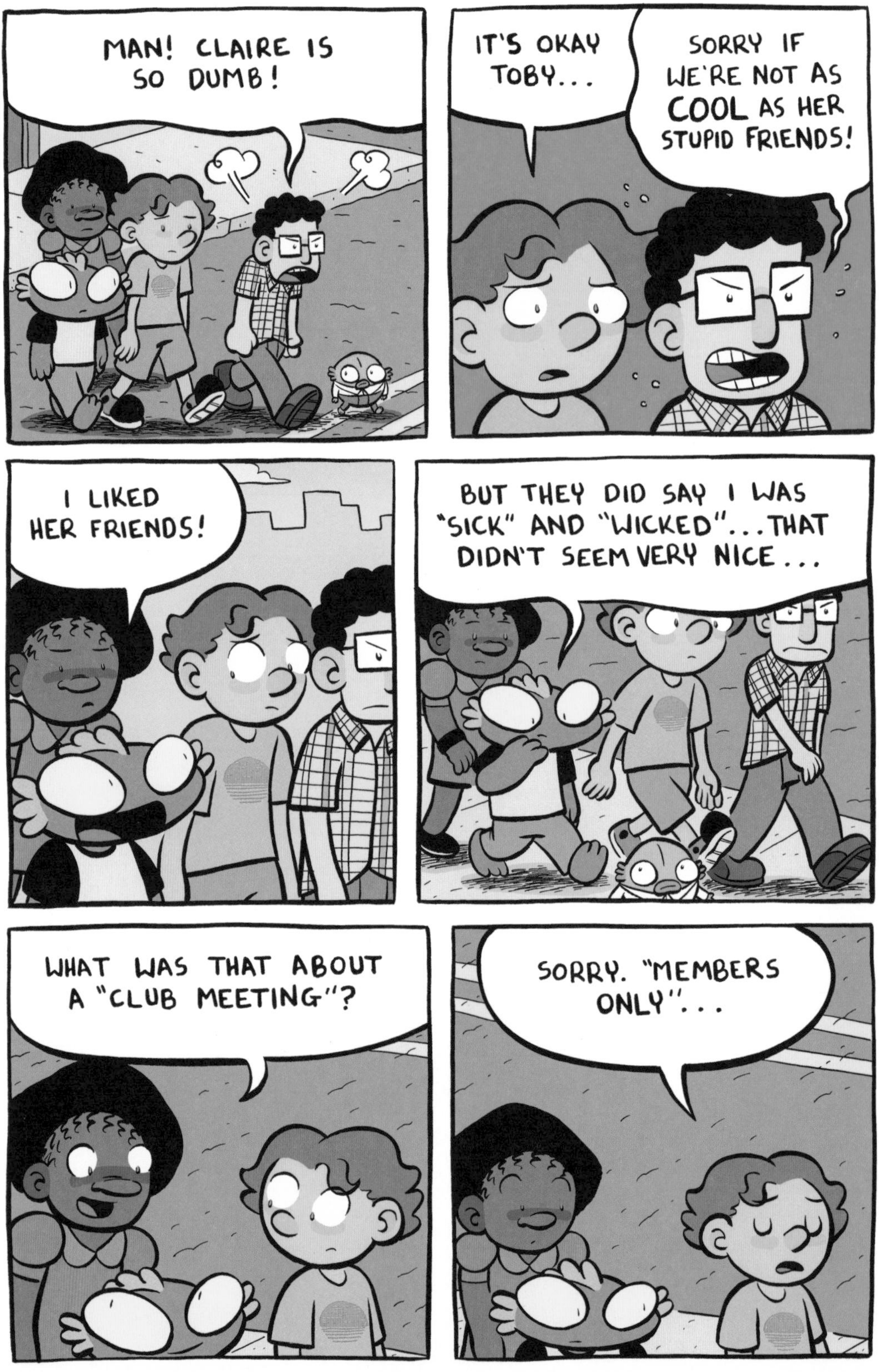
MAN! CLAIRE IS SO DUMB!
IT'S OKAY TOBY...
SORRY IF WE'RE NOT AS COOL AS HER STUPID FRIENDS!
I LIKED HER FRIENDS!
BUT THEY DID SAY I WAS "SICK" AND "WICKED"...THAT DIDN'T SEEM VERY NICE...
WHAT WAS THAT ABOUT A "CLUB MEETING"?
SORRY. "MEMBERS ONLY"...

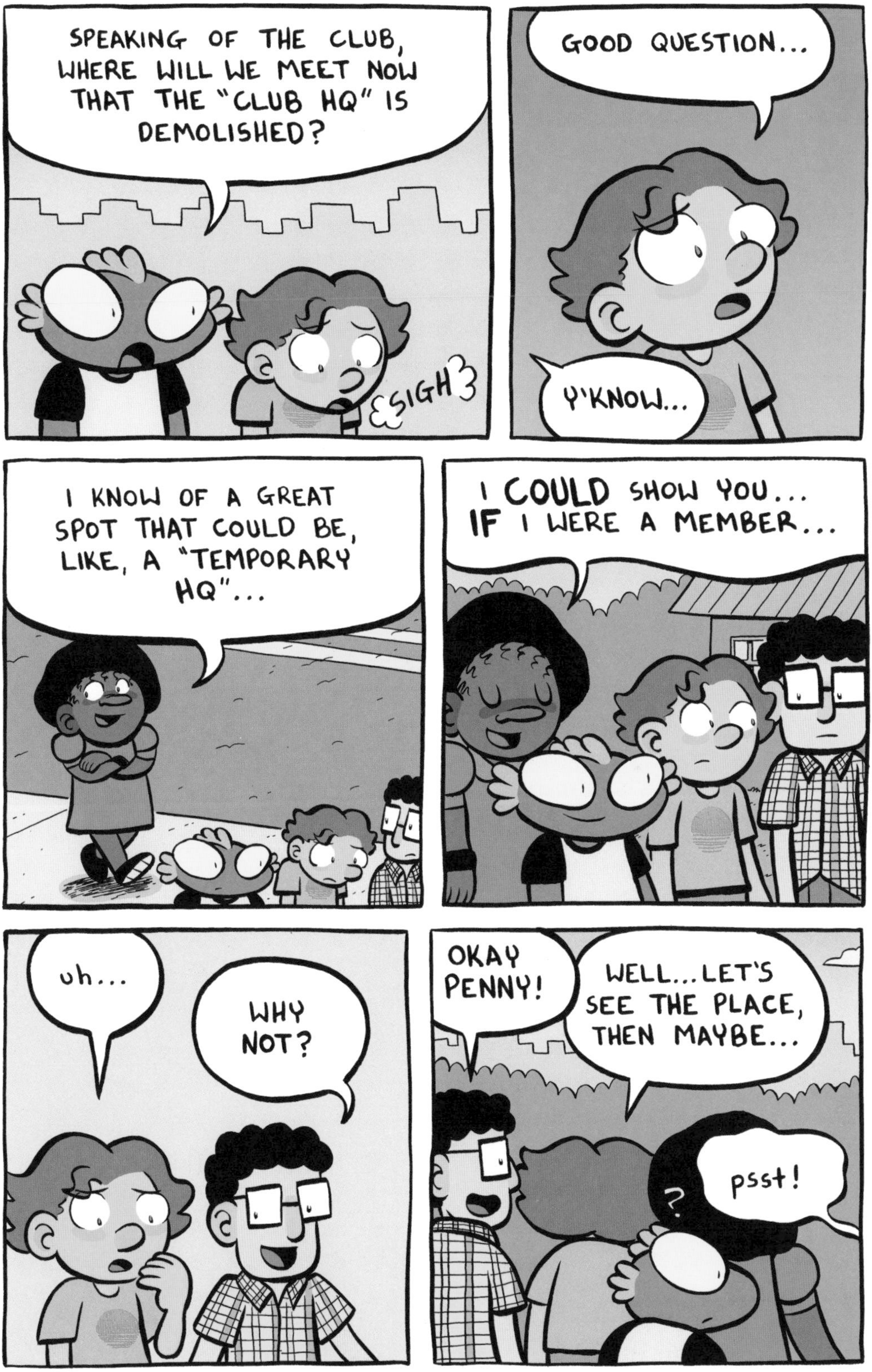
SPEAKING OF THE CLUB, WHERE WILL WE MEET NOW THAT THE "CLUB HQ" IS DEMOLISHED?
SIGH
GOOD QUESTION...
Y'KNOW...
I KNOW OF A GREAT SPOT THAT COULD BE, LIKE, A "TEMPORARY HQ"...
I COULD SHOW YOU... IF I WERE A MEMBER...
uh...
WHY NOT?
OKAY PENNY!
WELL... LET'S SEE THE PLACE, THEN MAYBE...
?
psst!

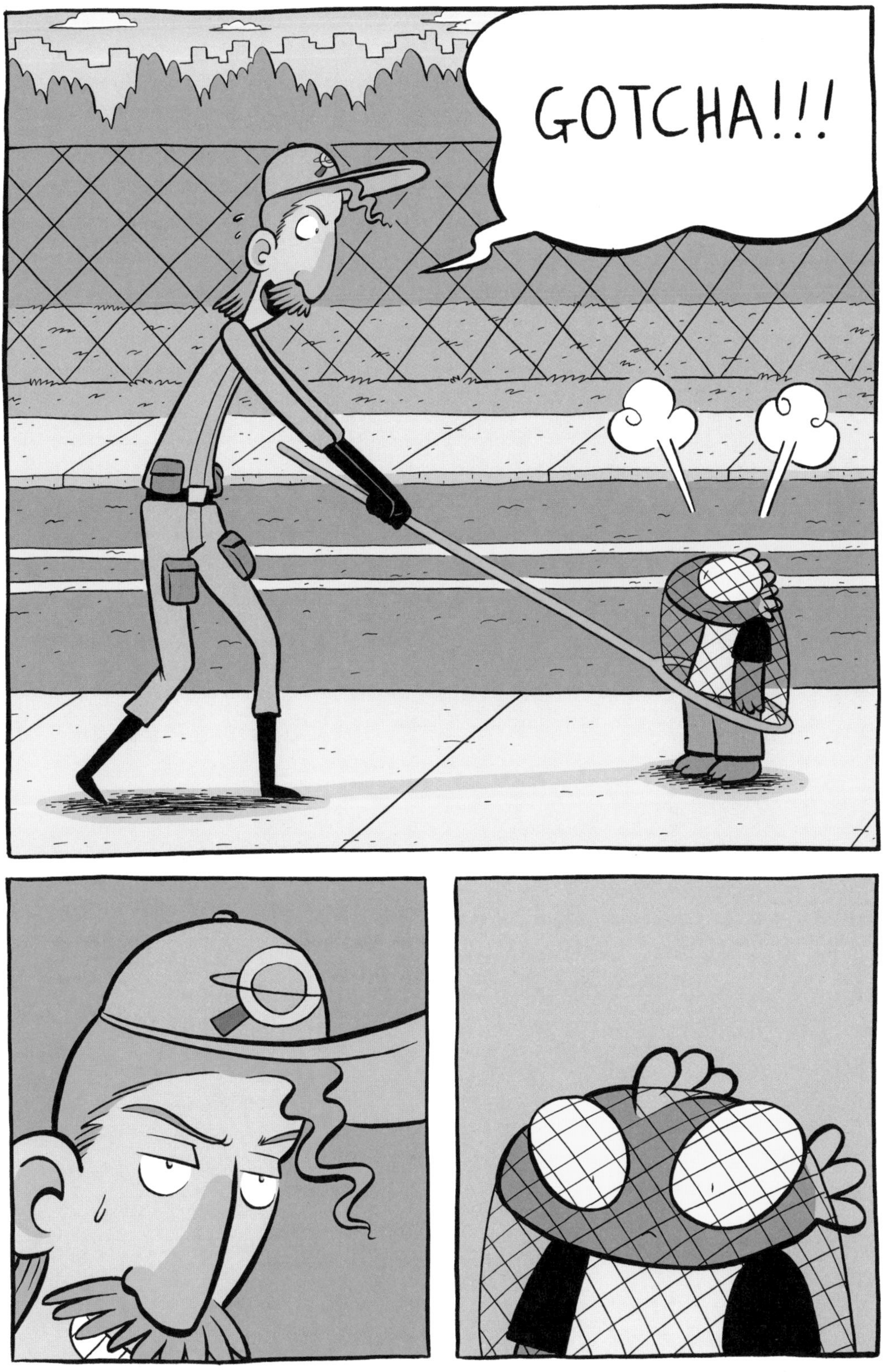
GOTCHA!!!

42

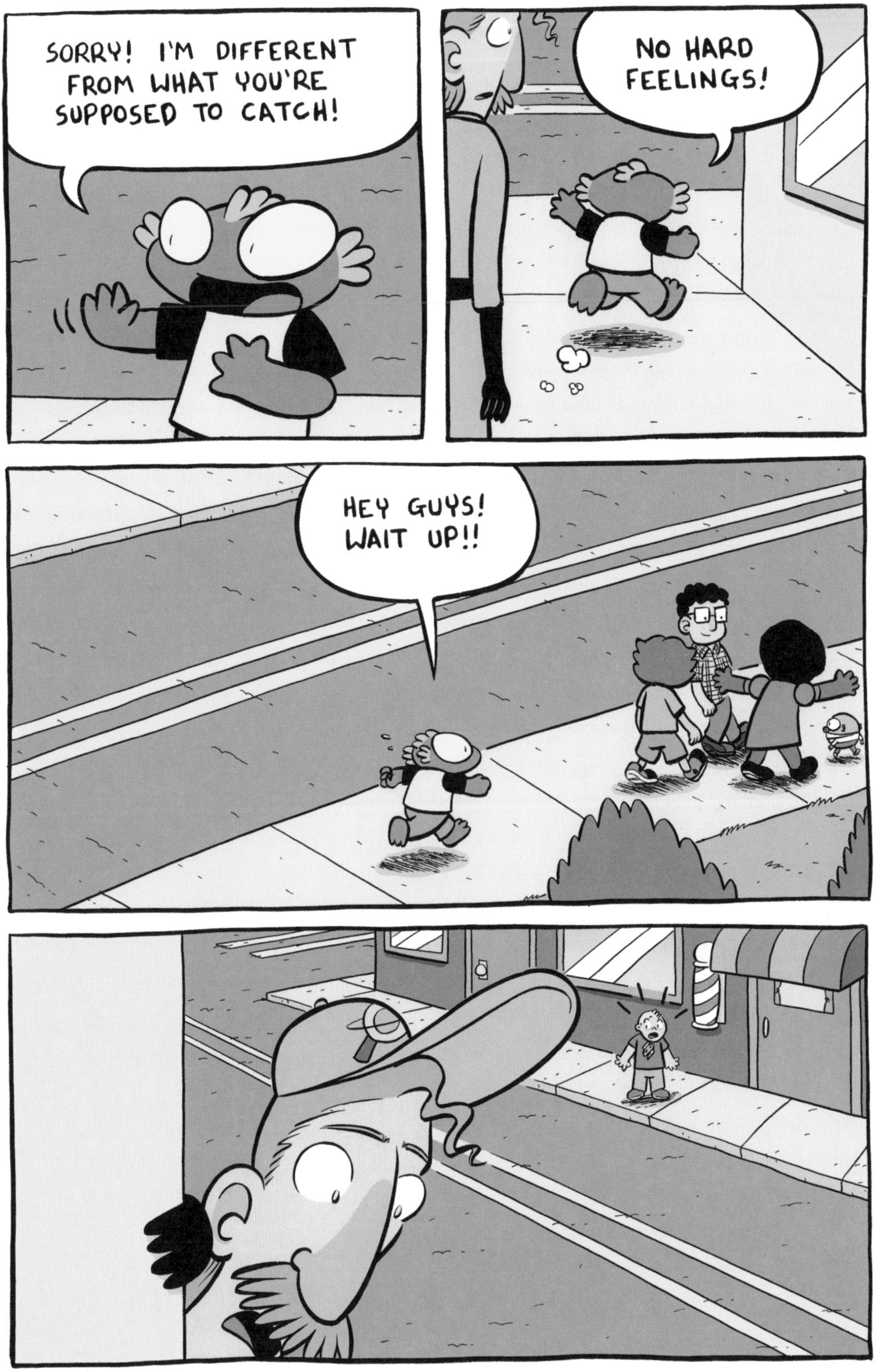
SORRY! I'M DIFFERENT FROM WHAT YOU'RE SUPPOSED TO CATCH!
NO HARD FEELINGS!
HEY GUYS! WAIT UP!!

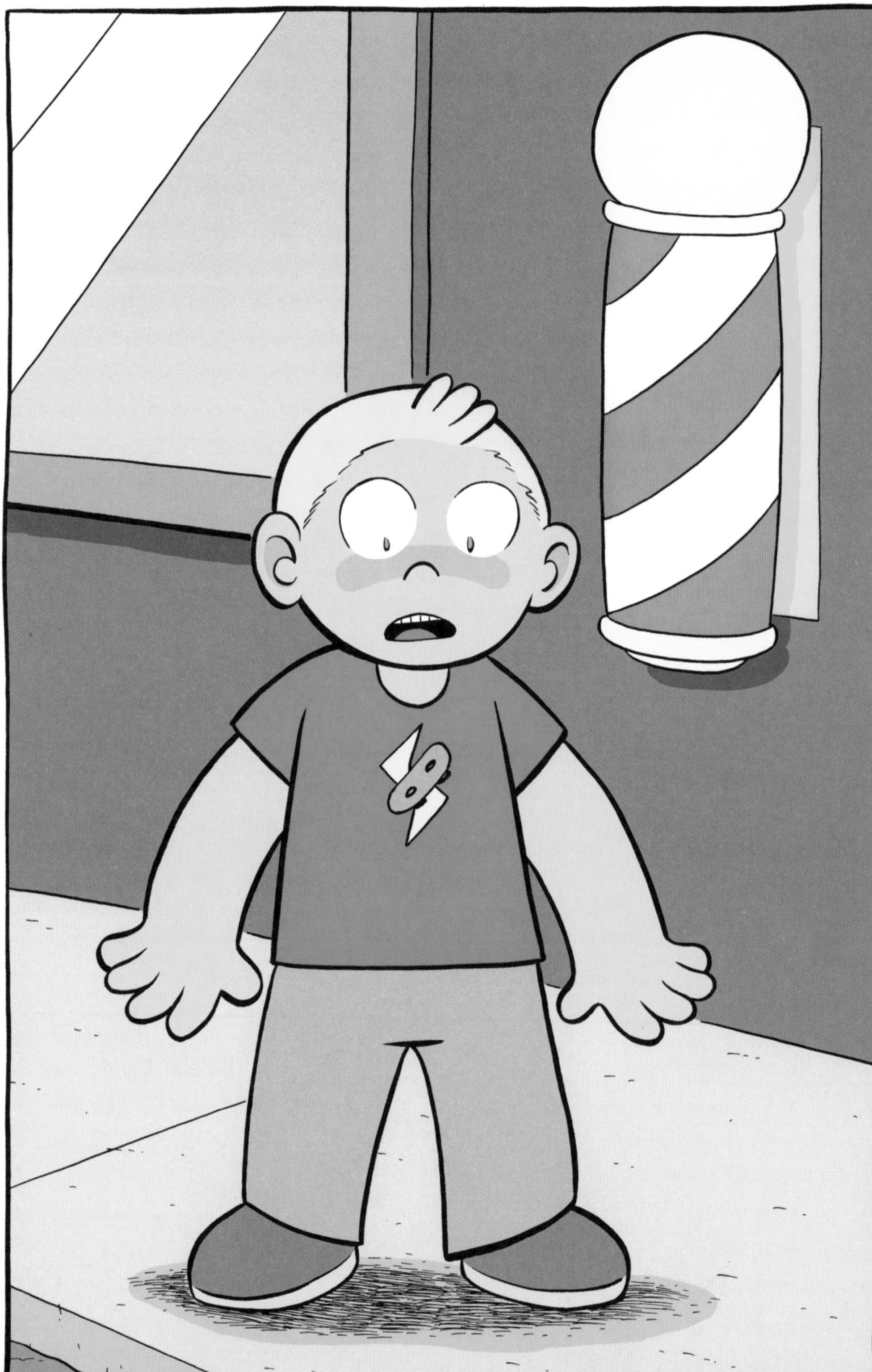

CHAPTER THREE

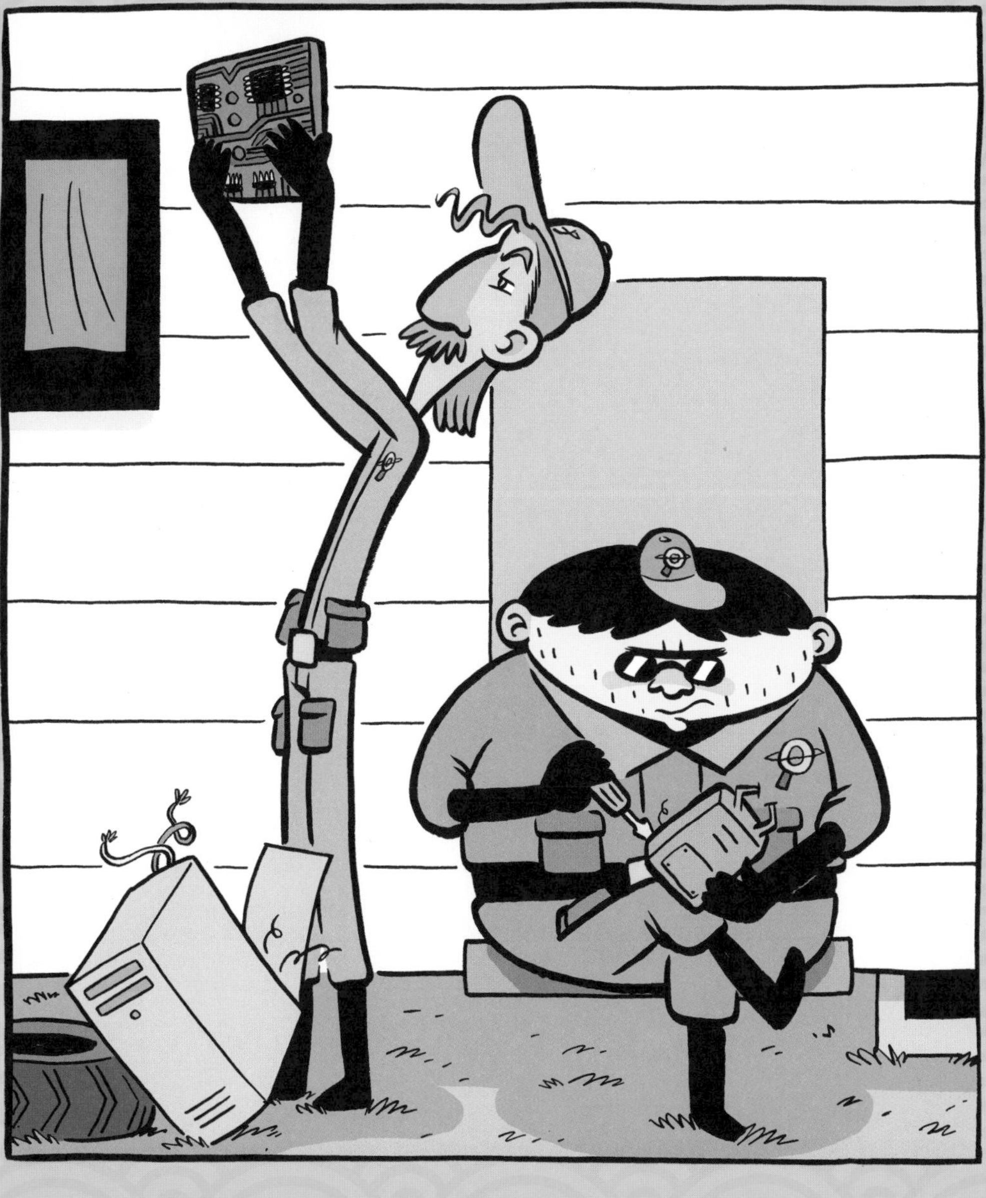

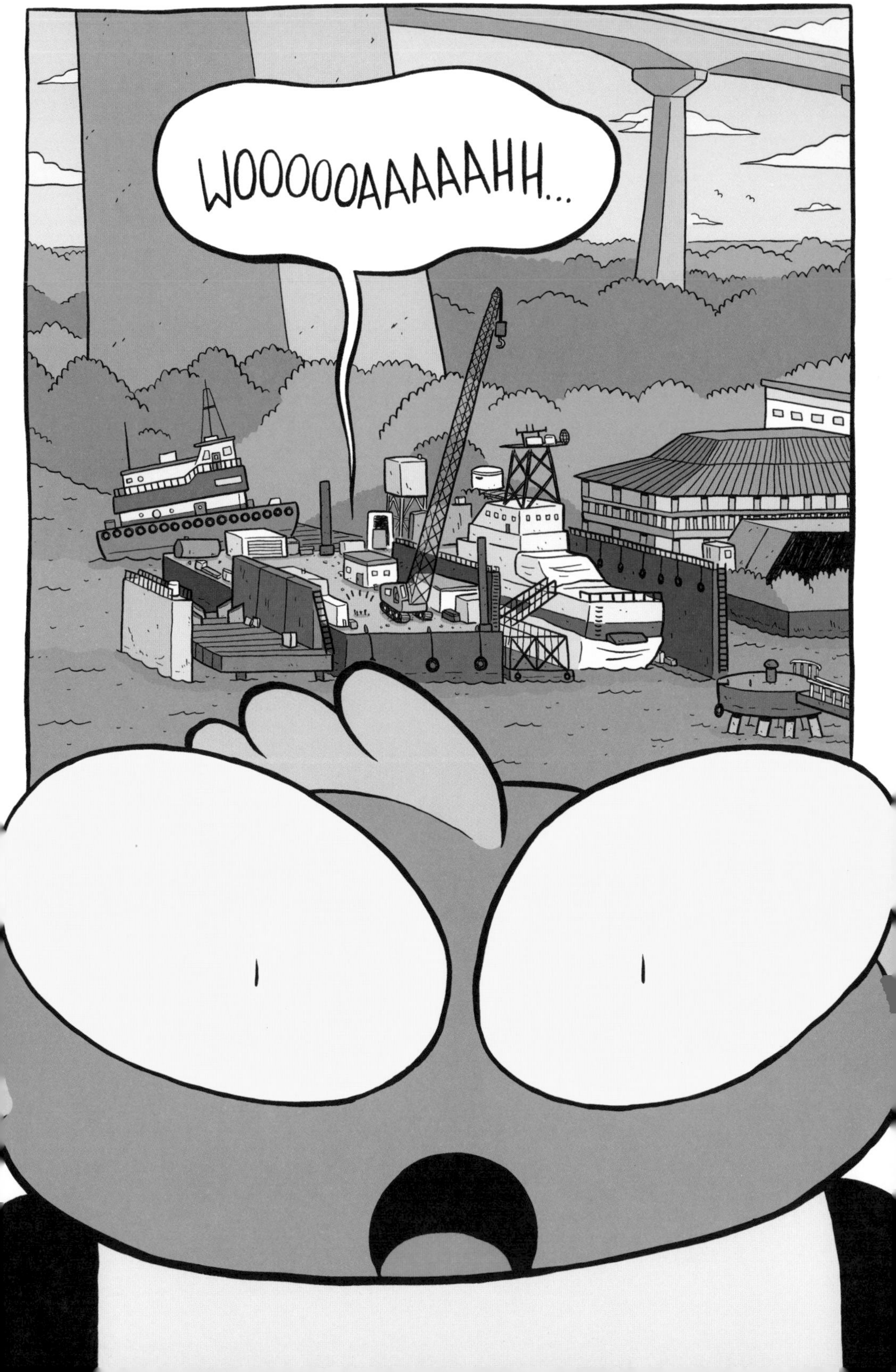
WOOOOOAAAAAHH...

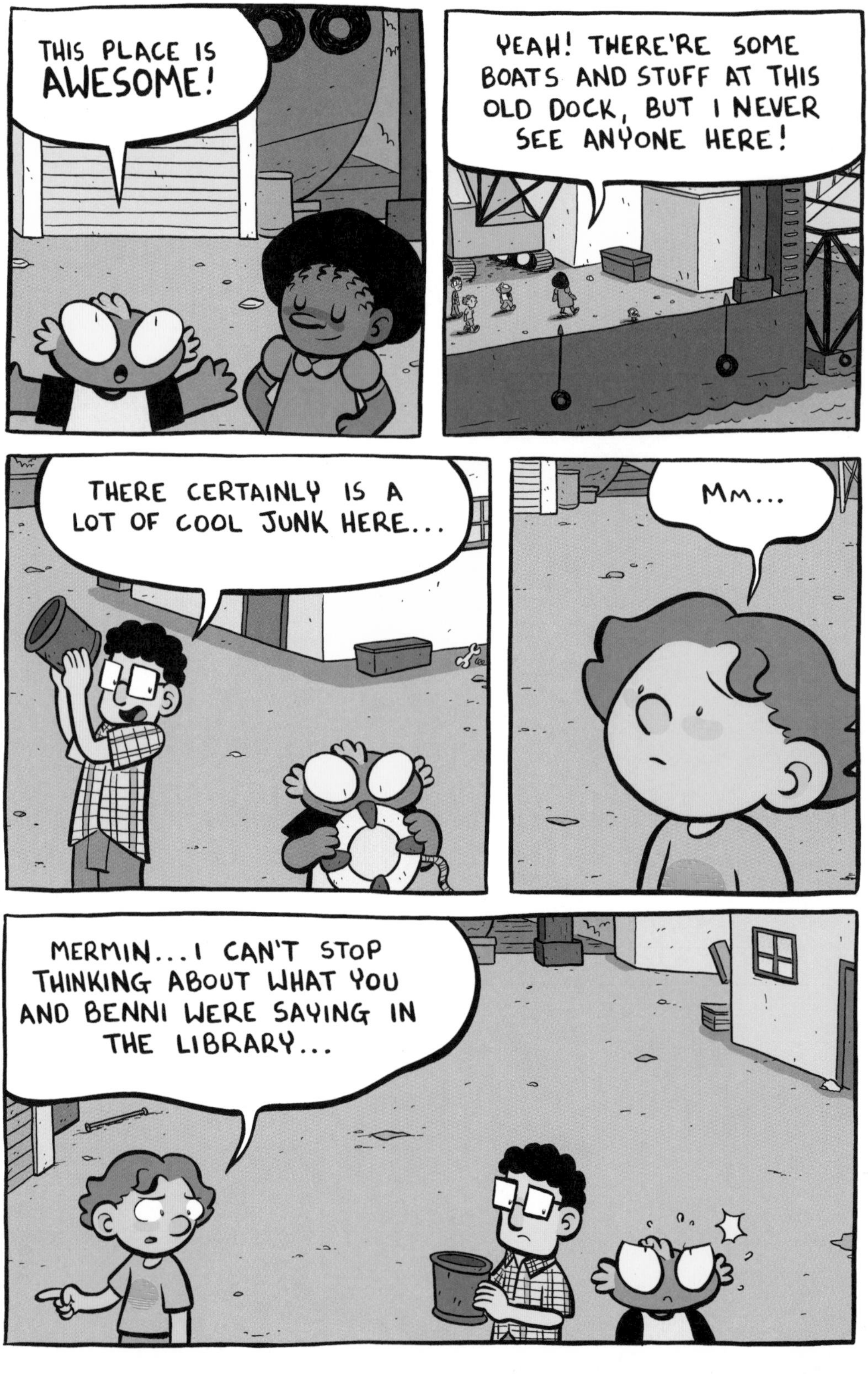
THIS PLACE IS AWESOME!
YEAH! THERE'RE SOME BOATS AND STUFF AT THIS OLD DOCK, BUT I NEVER SEE ANYONE HERE!
THERE CERTAINLY IS A LOT OF COOL JUNK HERE...
MM...
MERMIN...I CAN'T STOP THINKING ABOUT WHAT YOU AND BENNI WERE SAYING IN THE LIBRARY...

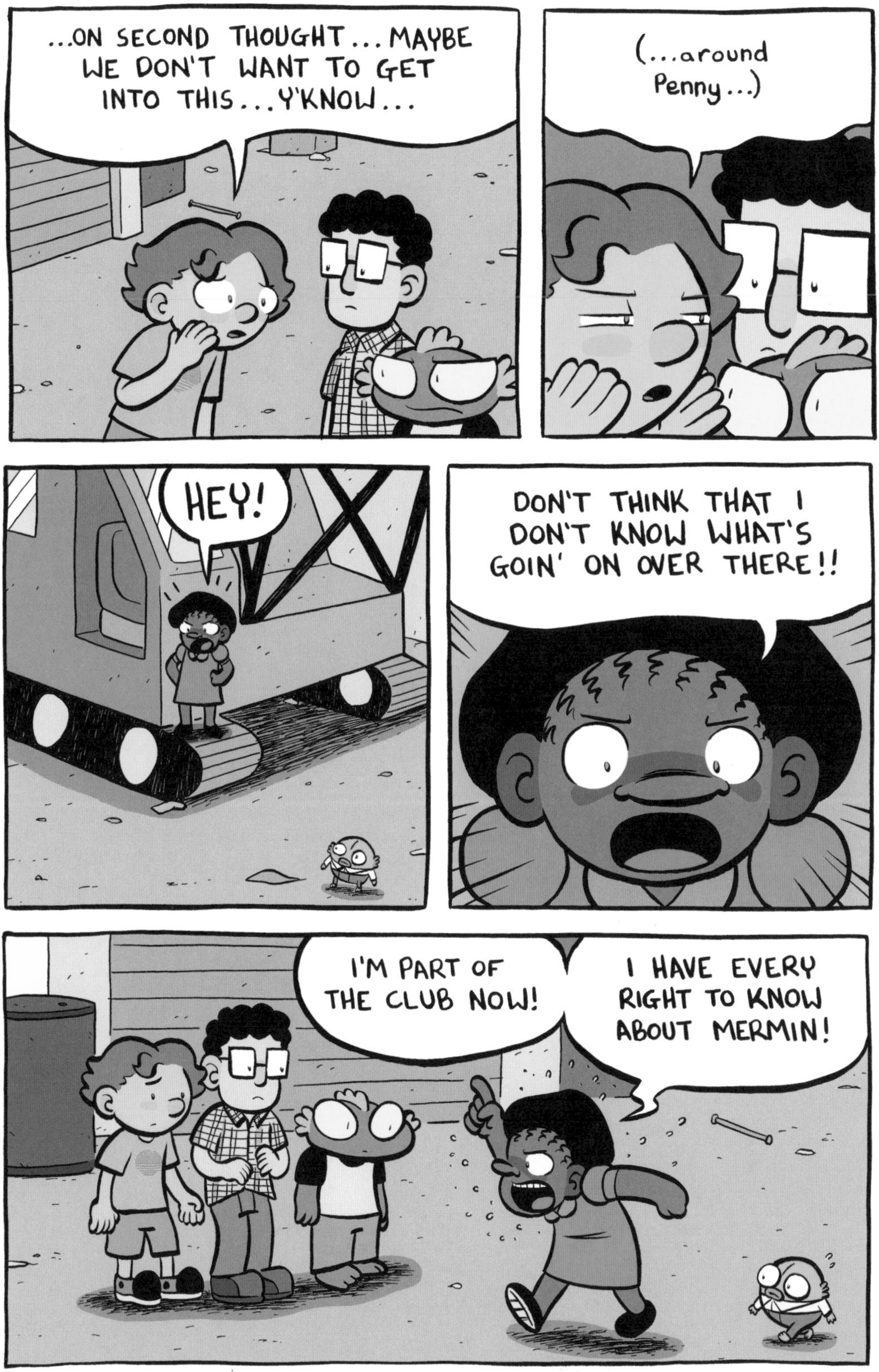
...ON SECOND THOUGHT... MAYBE WE DON'T WANT TO GET INTO THIS... Y'KNOW...
(...around Penny...)
HEY!
DON'T THINK THAT I DON'T KNOW WHAT'S GOIN' ON OVER THERE!!
I'M PART OF THE CLUB NOW!
I HAVE EVERY RIGHT TO KNOW ABOUT MERMIN!

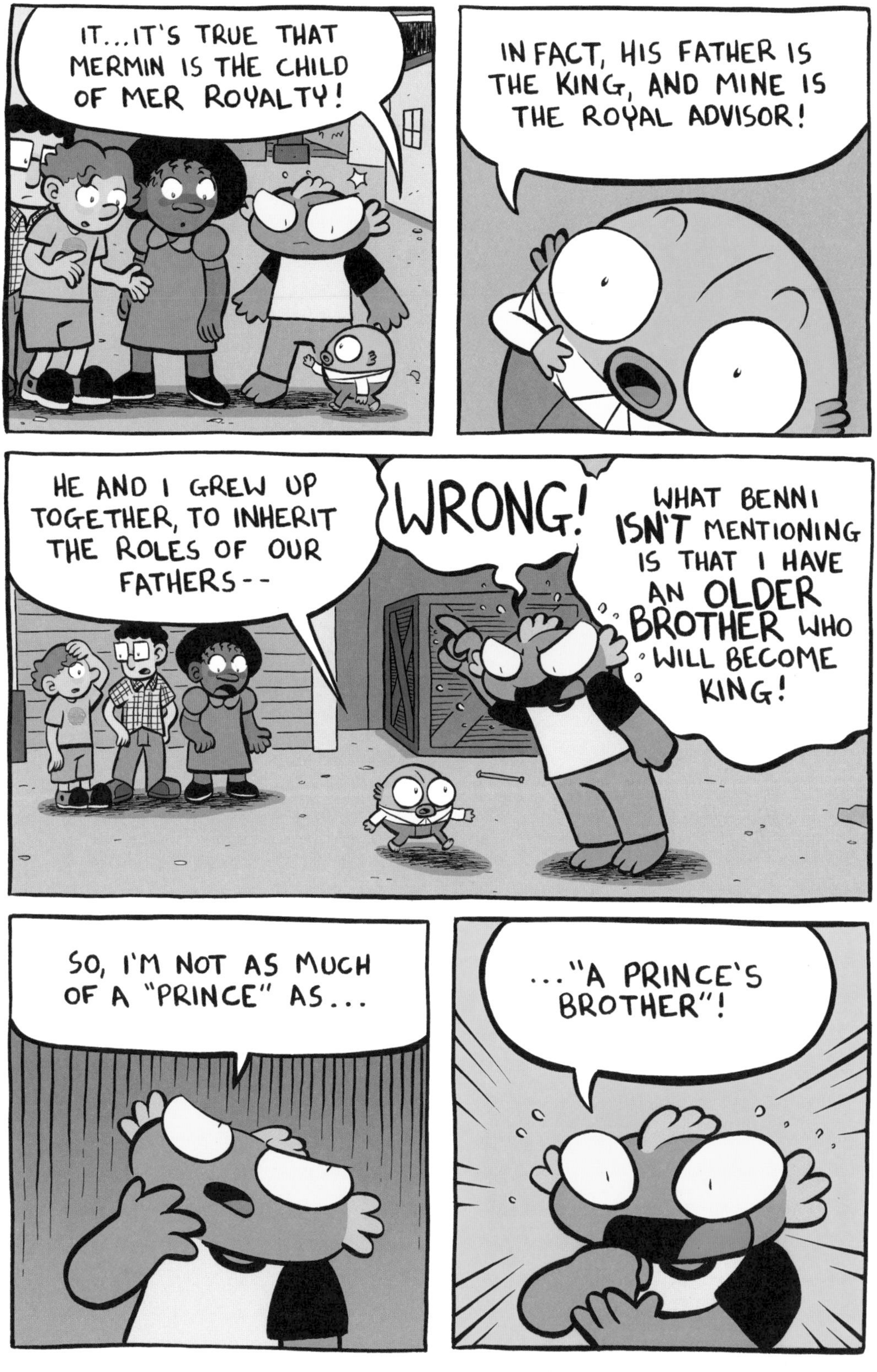
IT...IT'S TRUE THAT MERMIN IS THE CHILD OF MER ROYALTY!
IN FACT, HIS FATHER IS THE KING, AND MINE IS THE ROYAL ADVISOR!
HE AND I GREW UP TOGETHER, TO INHERIT THE ROLES OF OUR FATHERS--
WRONG!
WHAT BENNI ISN'T MENTIONING IS THAT I HAVE AN OLDER BROTHER WHO WILL BECOME KING!
SO, I'M NOT AS MUCH OF A "PRINCE" AS...
..."A PRINCE'S BROTHER"!

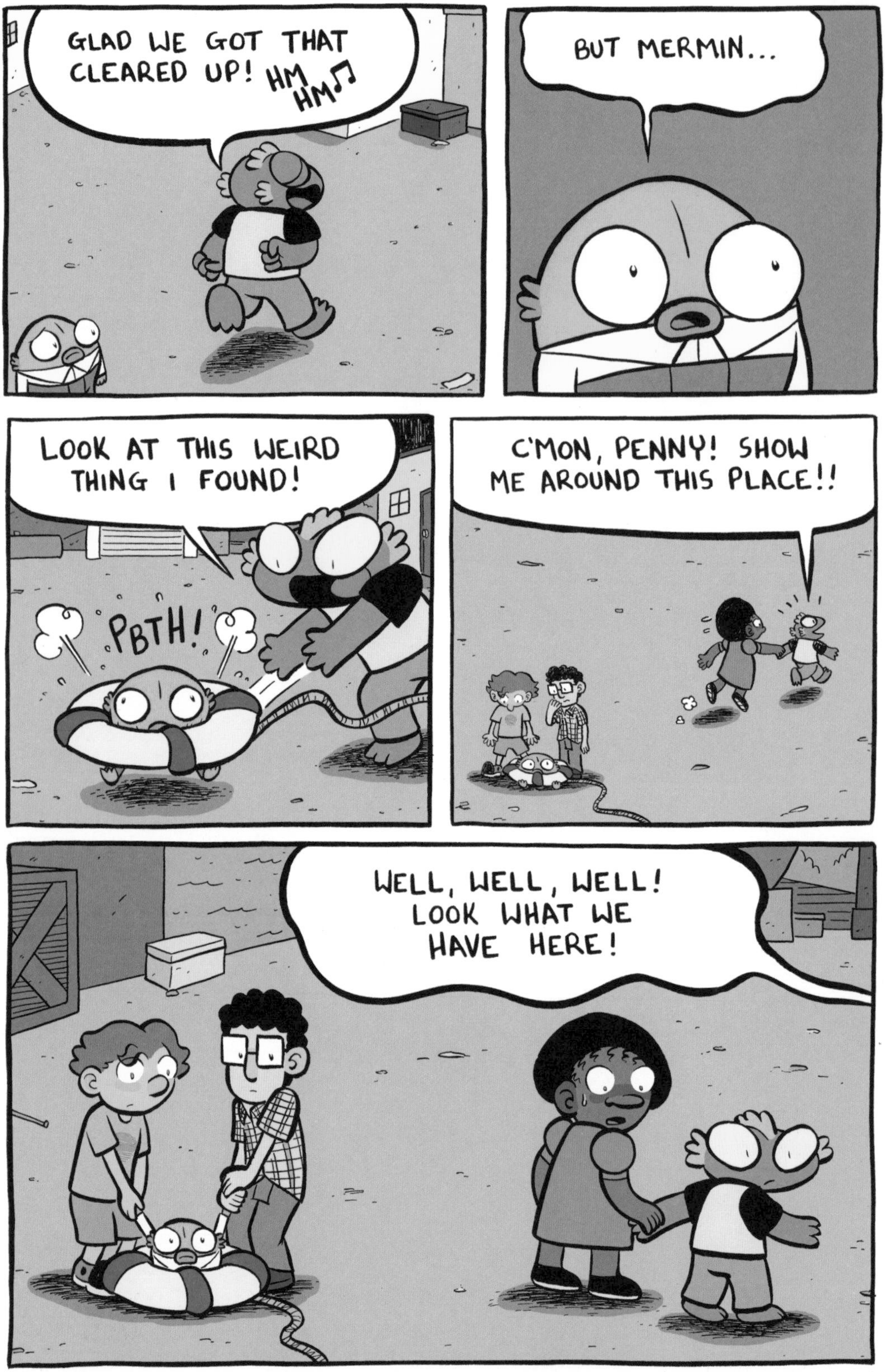
GLAD WE GOT THAT CLEARED UP! HM HM♫
BUT MERMIN...
LOOK AT THIS WEIRD THING I FOUND!
PBTH!
C'MON, PENNY! SHOW ME AROUND THIS PLACE!!
WELL, WELL, WELL! LOOK WHAT WE HAVE HERE!

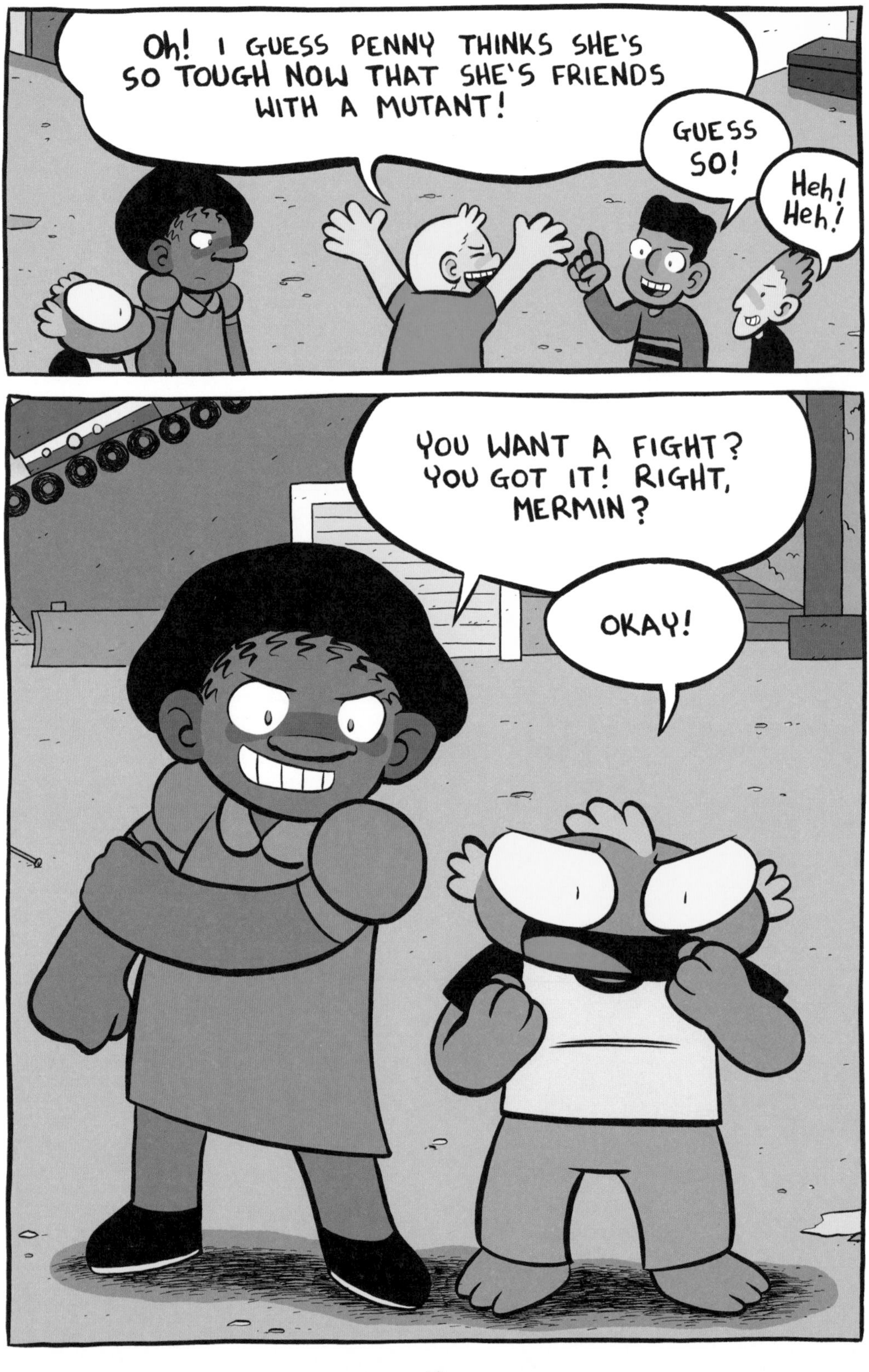
Oh! I GUESS PENNY THINKS SHE'S SO TOUGH NOW THAT SHE'S FRIENDS WITH A MUTANT!
GUESS SO!
Heh! Heh!
YOU WANT A FIGHT? YOU GOT IT! RIGHT, MERMIN?
OKAY!

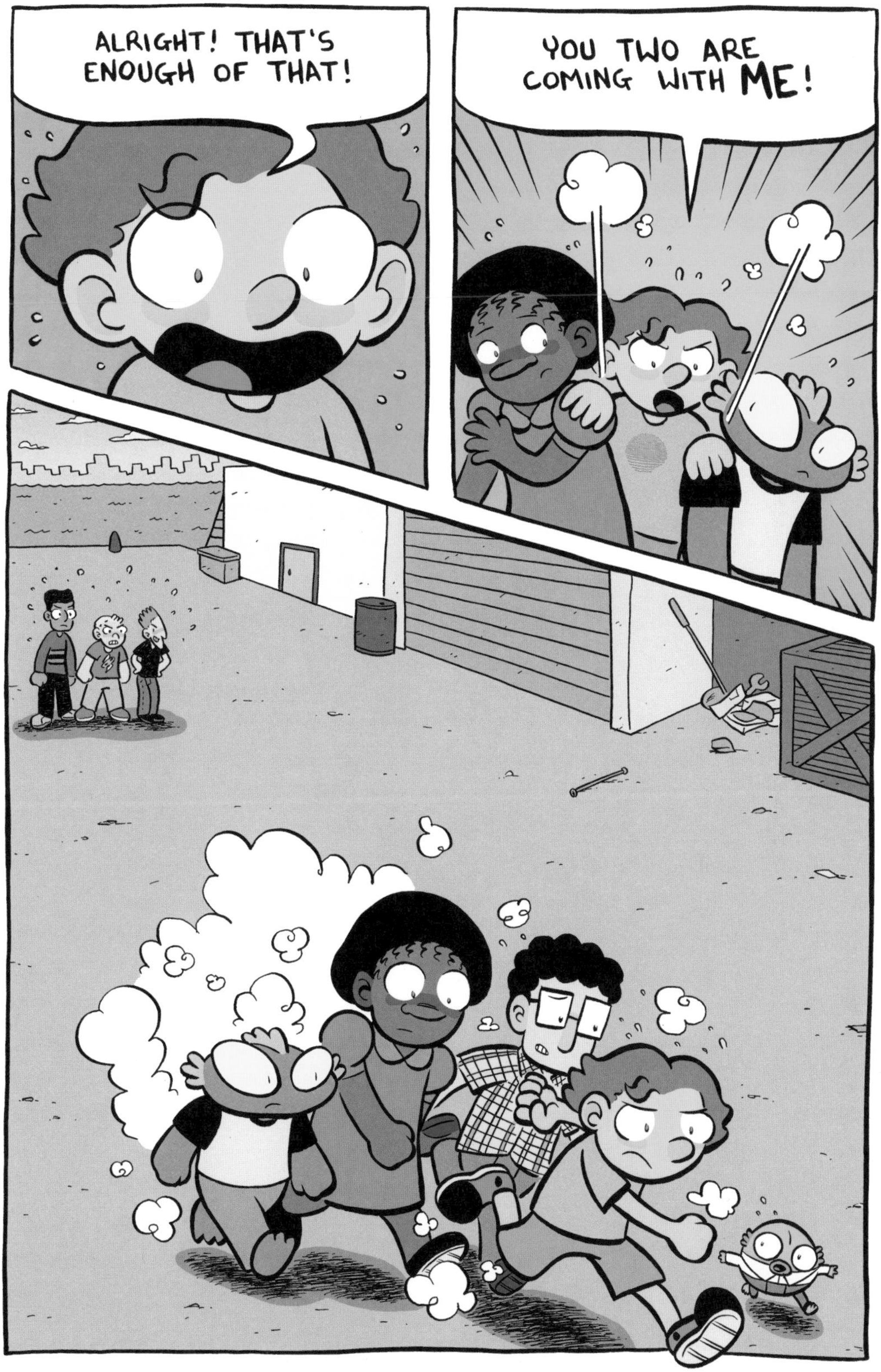
ALRIGHT! THAT'S ENOUGH OF THAT!
YOU TWO ARE COMING WITH ME!

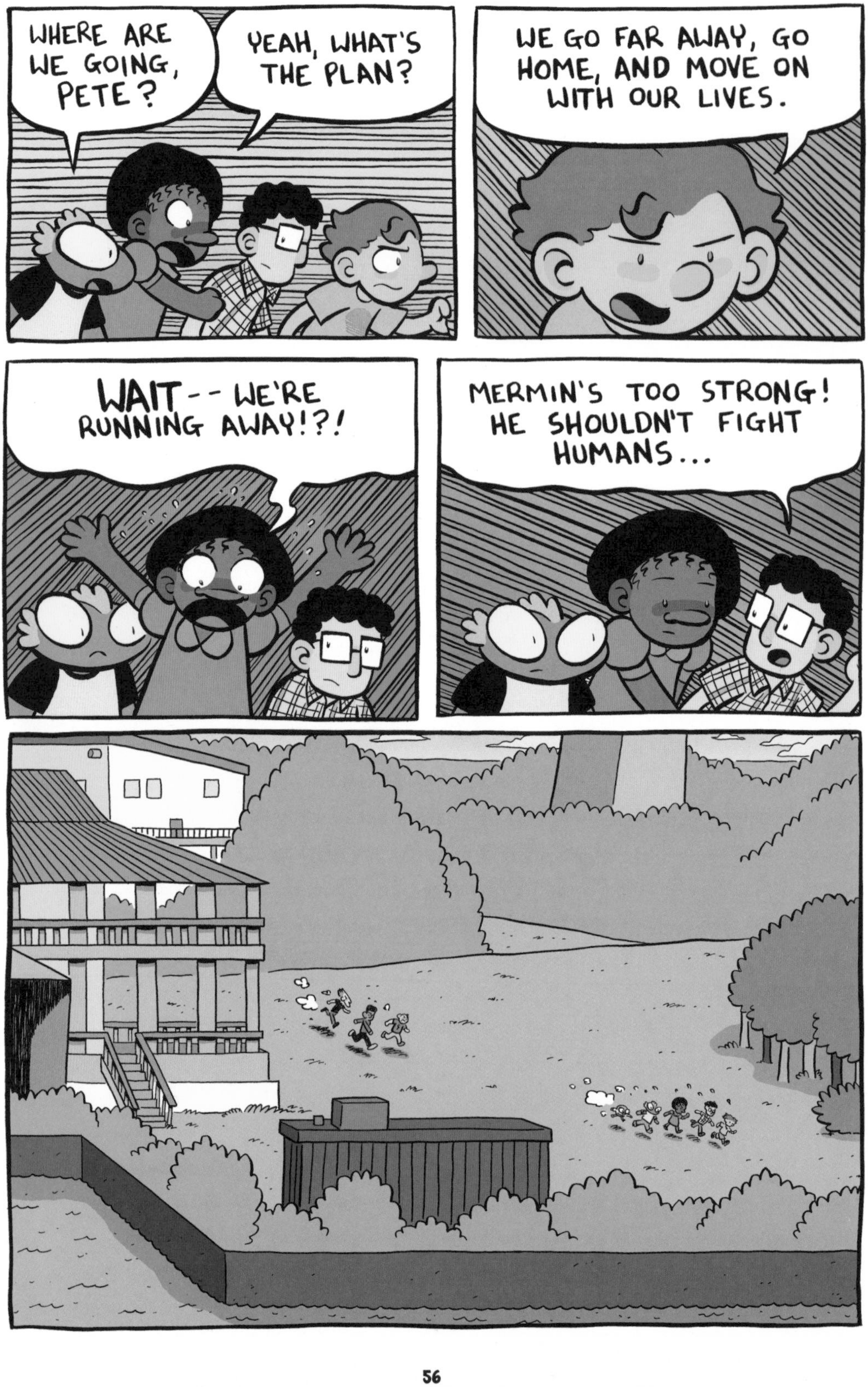
WHERE ARE WE GOING, PETE?
YEAH, WHAT'S THE PLAN?
WE GO FAR AWAY, GO HOME, AND MOVE ON WITH OUR LIVES.
WAIT-- WE'RE RUNNING AWAY!?!
MERMIN'S TOO STRONG! HE SHOULDN'T FIGHT HUMANS...

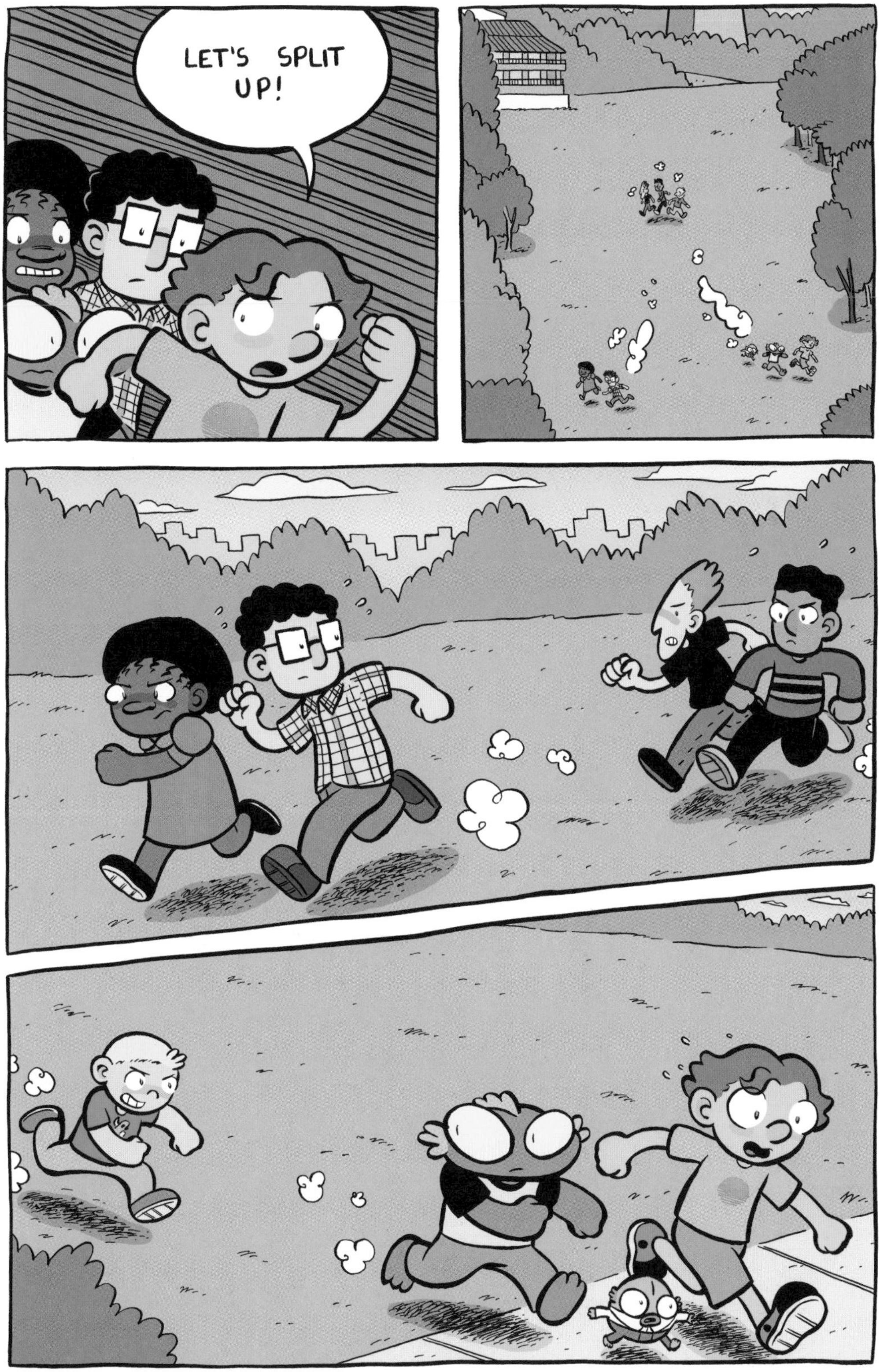
LET'S SPLIT UP!

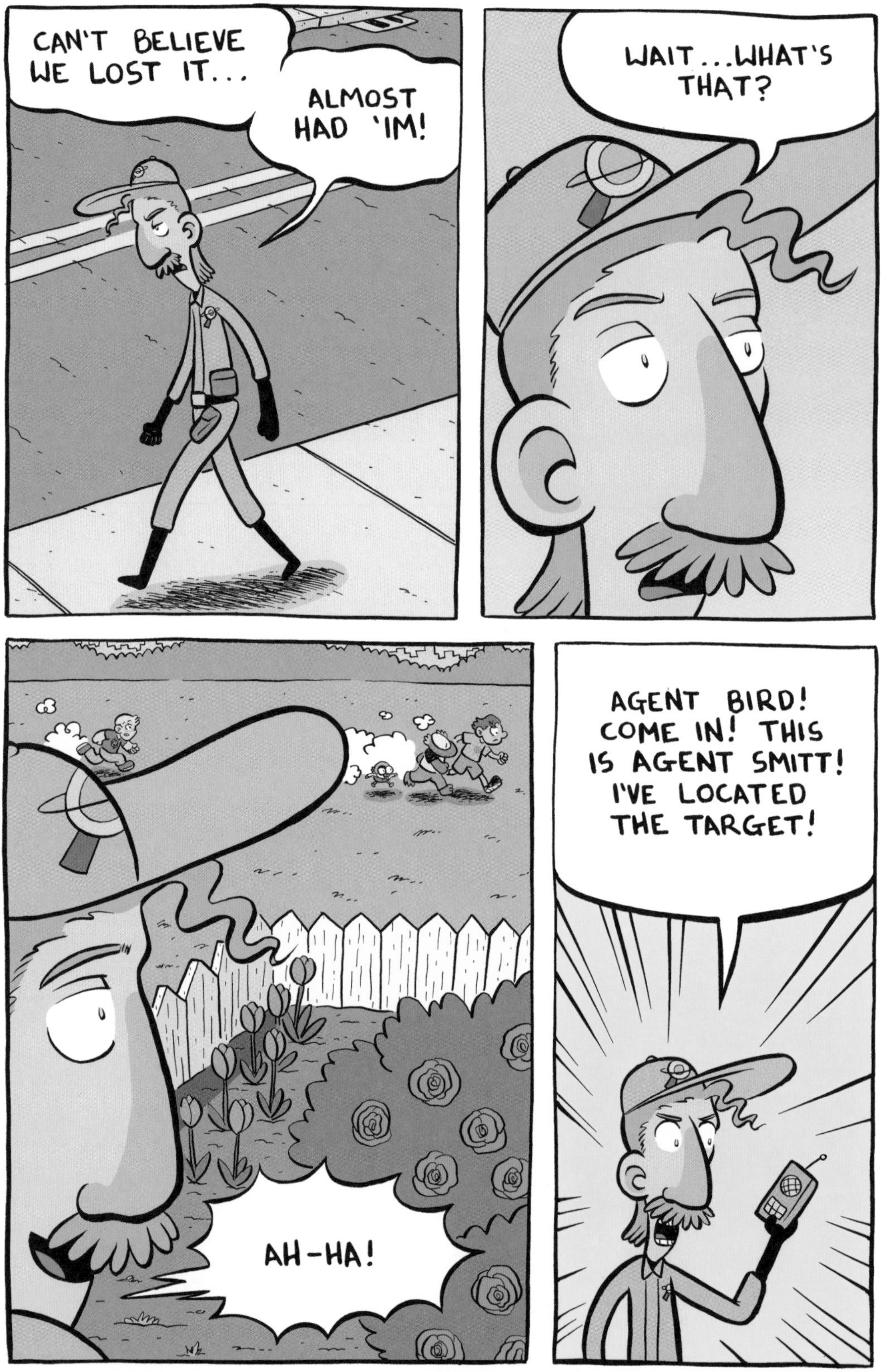
CAN'T BELIEVE WE LOST IT...
ALMOST HAD 'IM!
WAIT...WHAT'S THAT?
AH-HA!
AGENT BIRD! COME IN! THIS IS AGENT SMITT! I'VE LOCATED THE TARGET!

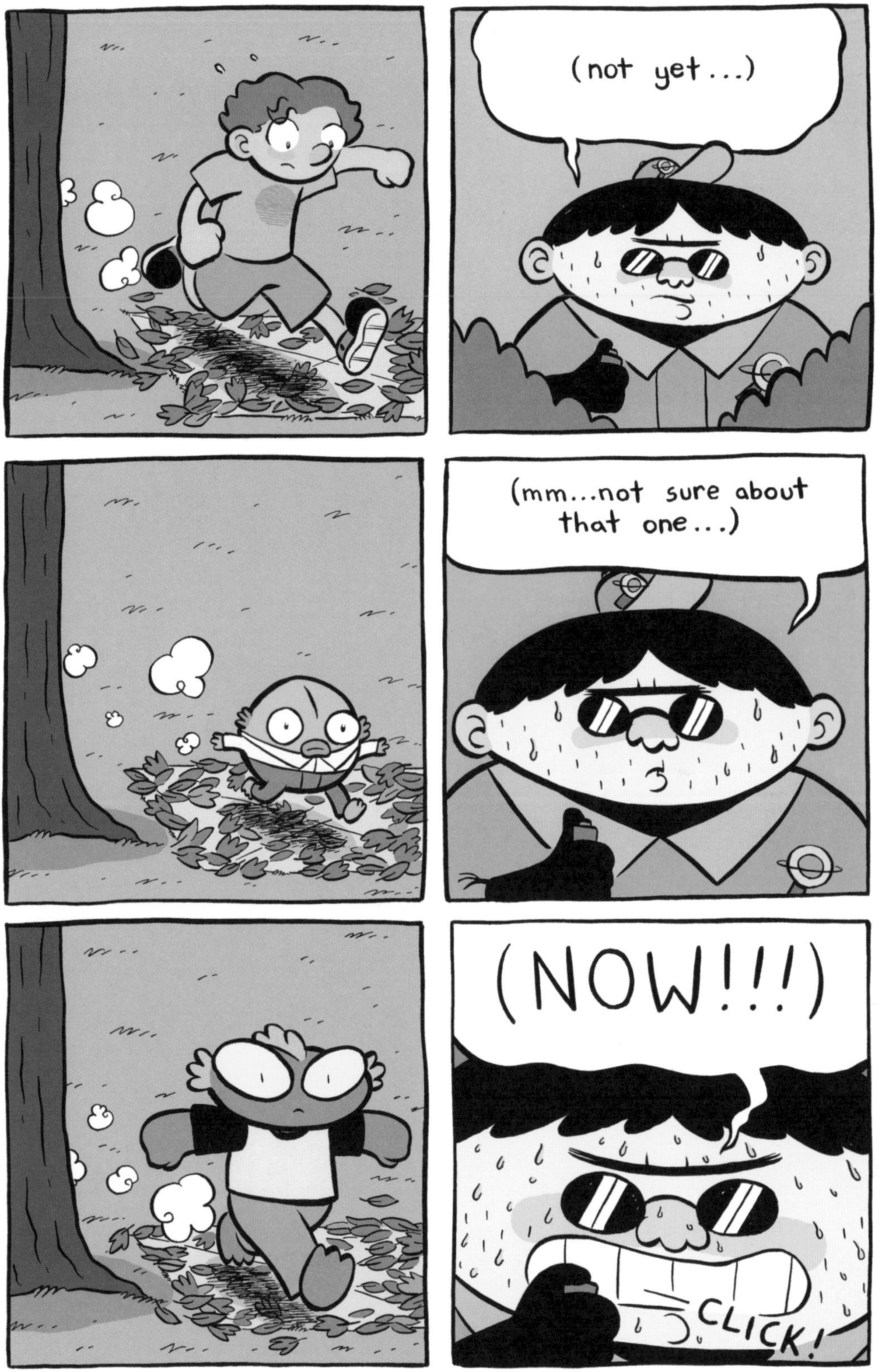
(not yet...)
(mm...not sure about that one...)
(NOW!!!)
CLICK!

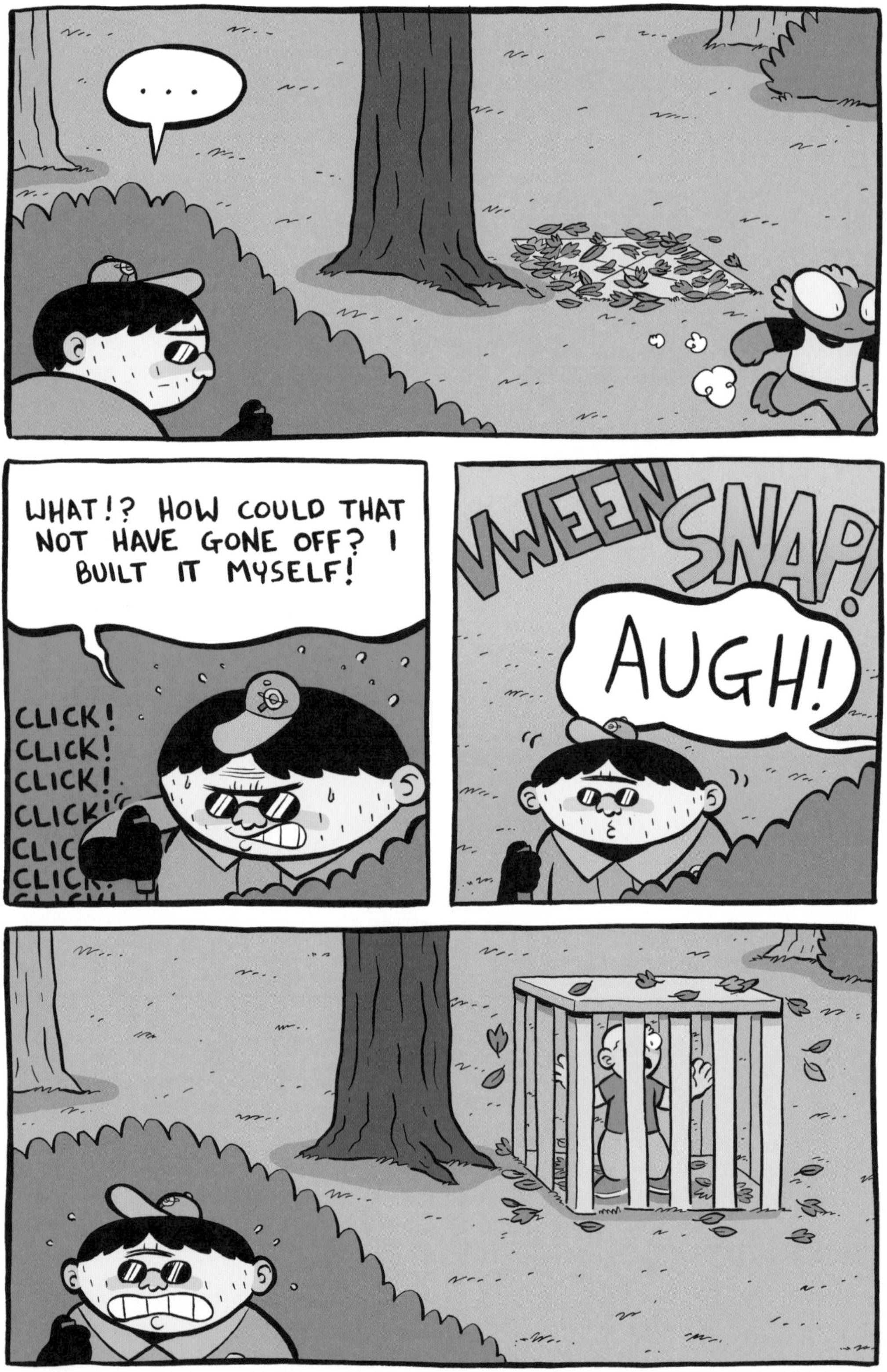
...
WHAT!? HOW COULD THAT NOT HAVE GONE OFF? I BUILT IT MYSELF!
CLICK! CLICK! CLICK! CLICK! CLIC CLICK
VWEEN SNAP!
AUGH!

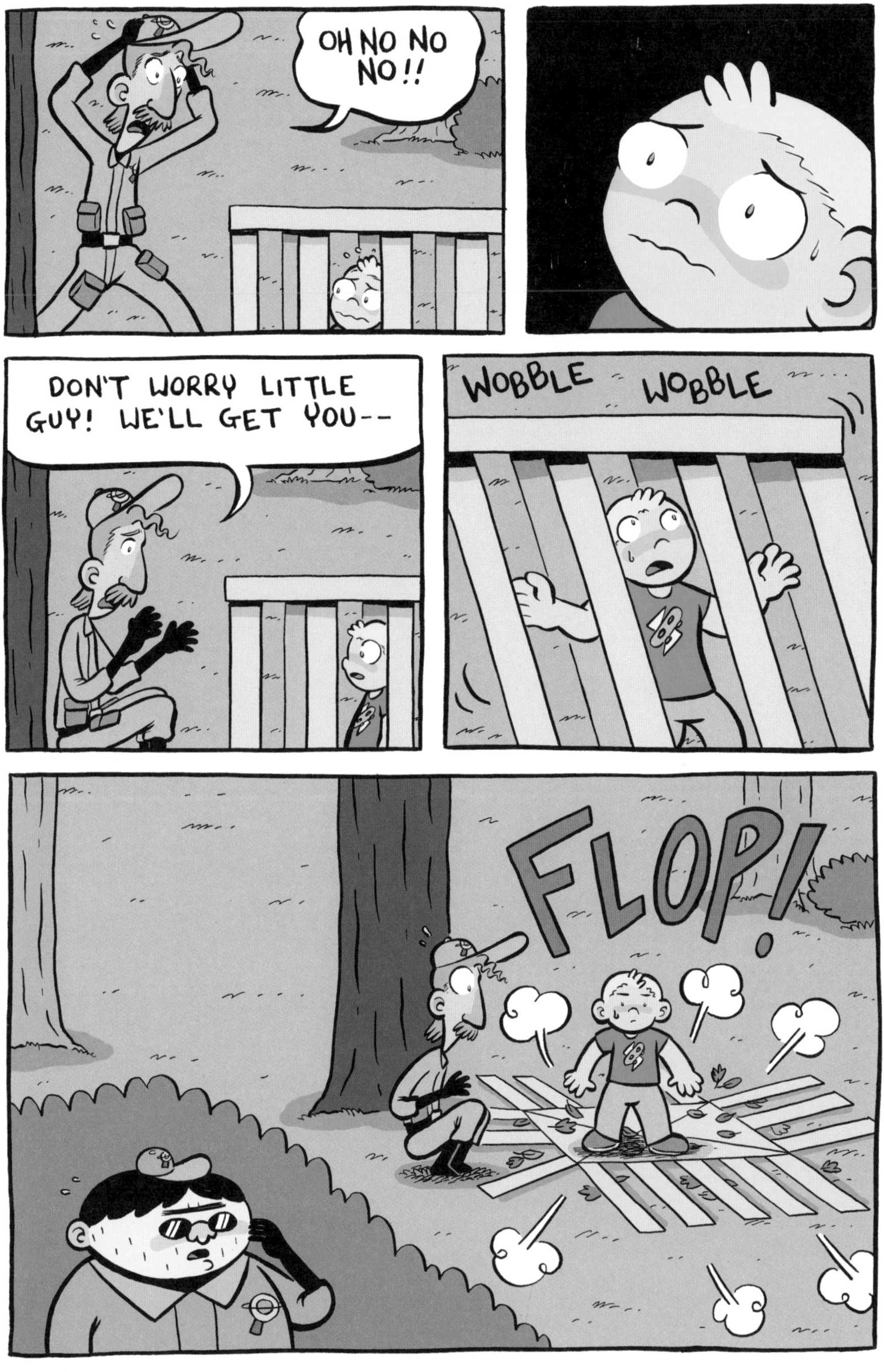
OH NO NO NO!!
DON'T WORRY LITTLE GUY! WE'LL GET YOU--
WOBBLE WOBBLE
FLOP!

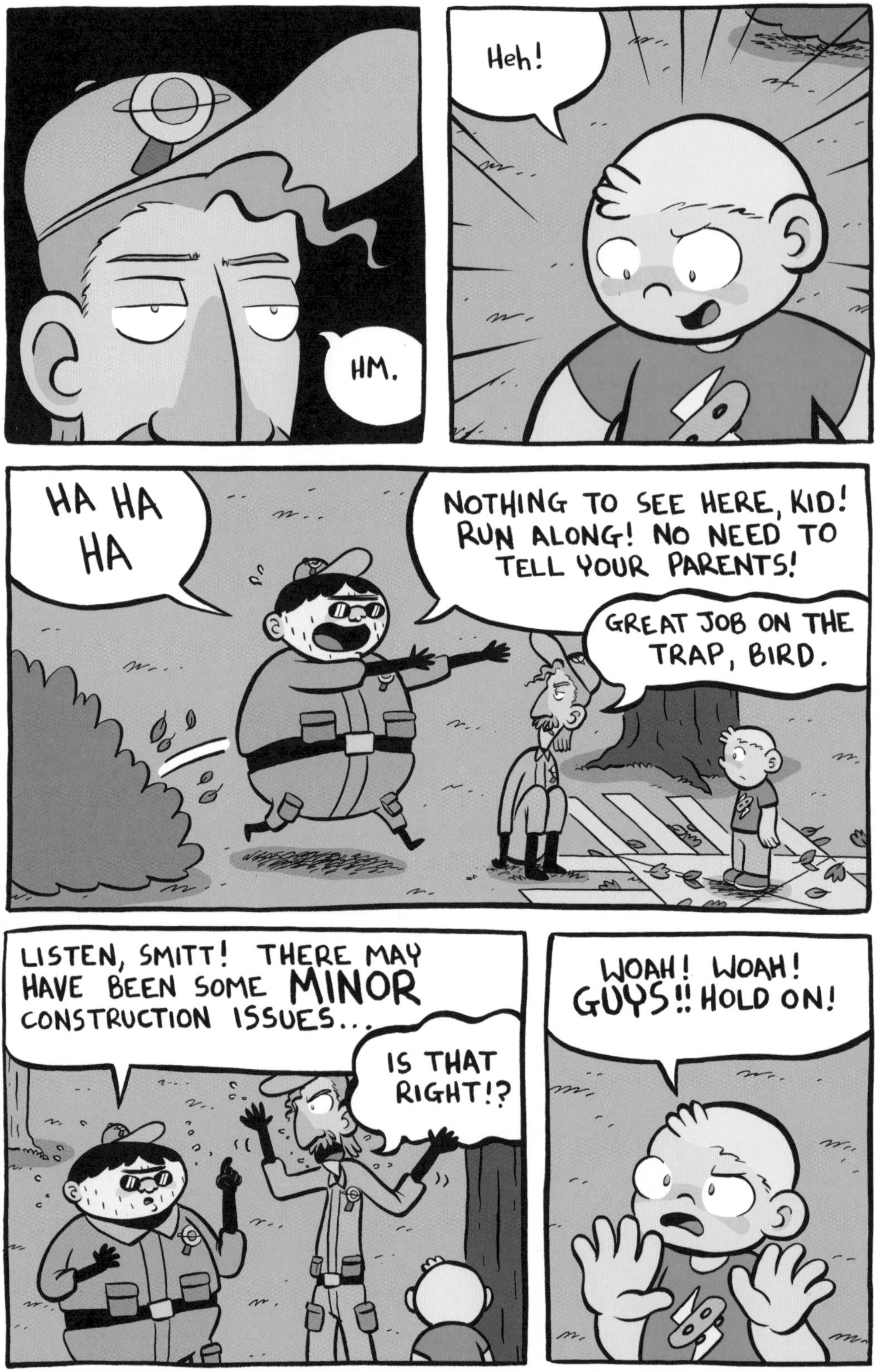
HM.
Heh!
HA HA HA
NOTHING TO SEE HERE, KID! RUN ALONG! NO NEED TO TELL YOUR PARENTS!
GREAT JOB ON THE TRAP, BIRD.
LISTEN, SMITT! THERE MAY HAVE BEEN SOME MINOR CONSTRUCTION ISSUES...
IS THAT RIGHT!?
WOAH! WOAH! GUYS!! HOLD ON!

CHAPTER FOUR

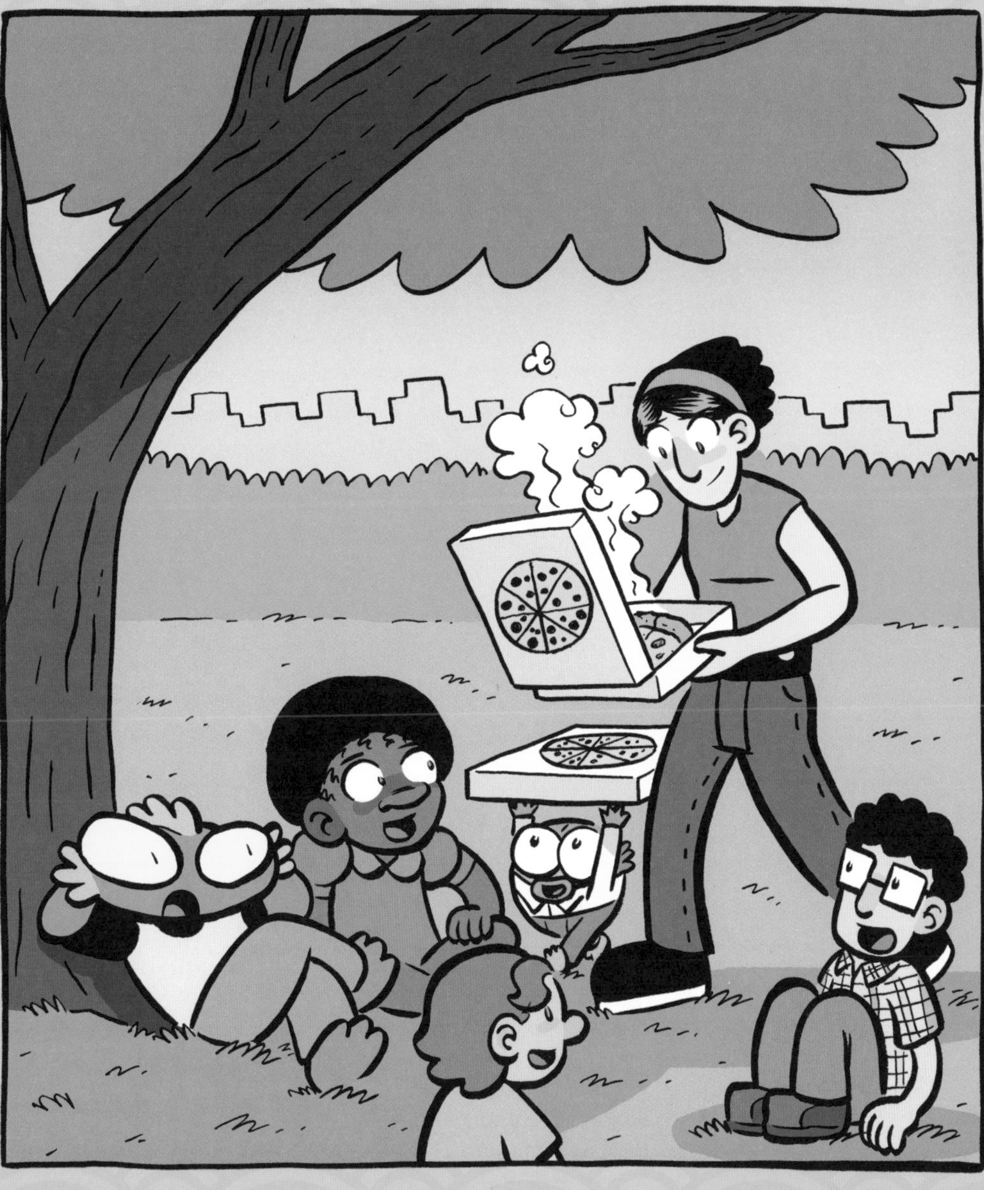

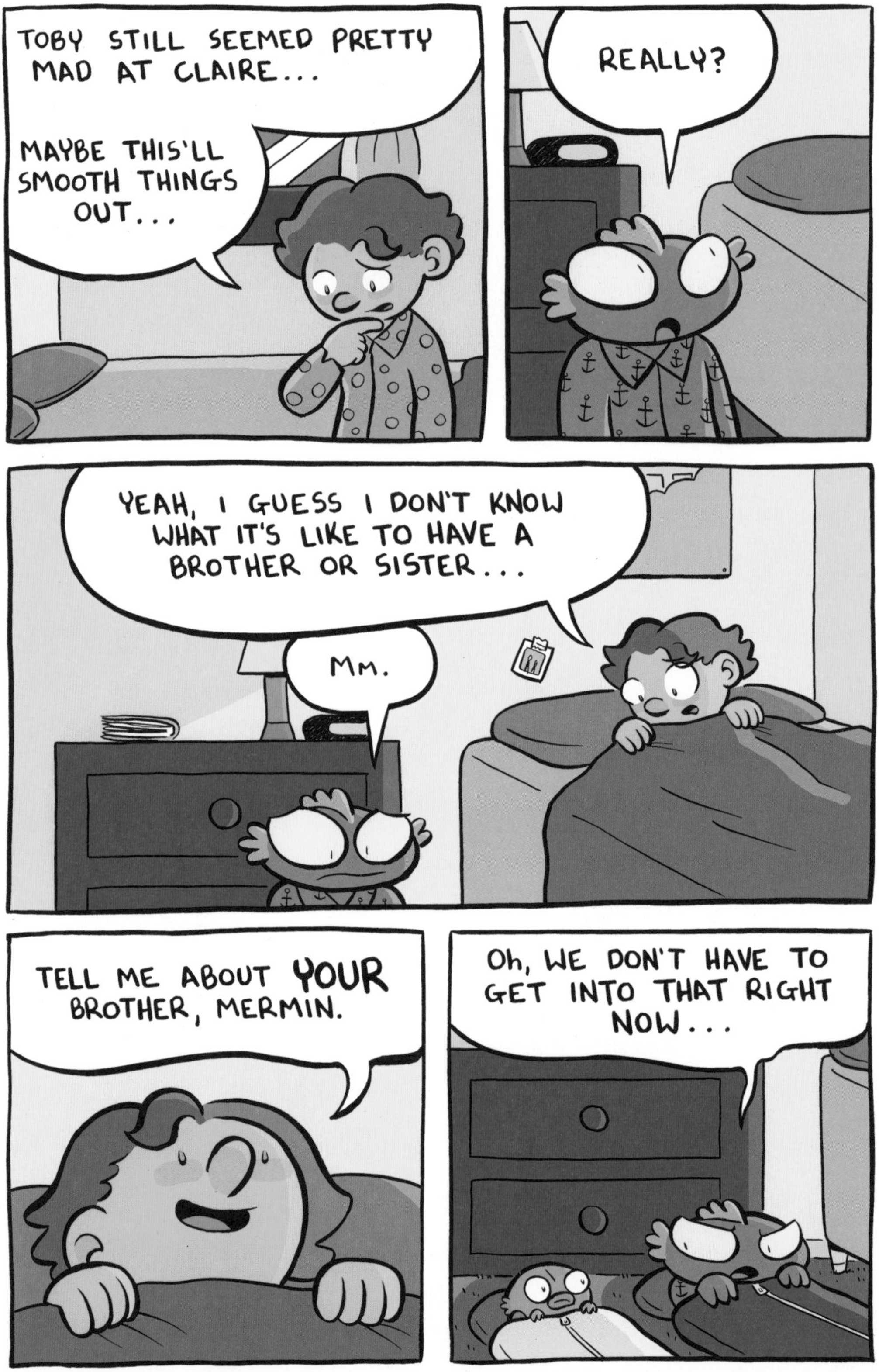
TOBY STILL SEEMED PRETTY MAD AT CLAIRE...
MAYBE THIS'LL SMOOTH THINGS OUT...
REALLY?
YEAH, I GUESS I DON'T KNOW WHAT IT'S LIKE TO HAVE A BROTHER OR SISTER...
MM.
TELL ME ABOUT YOUR BROTHER, MERMIN.
Oh, WE DON'T HAVE TO GET INTO THAT RIGHT NOW...

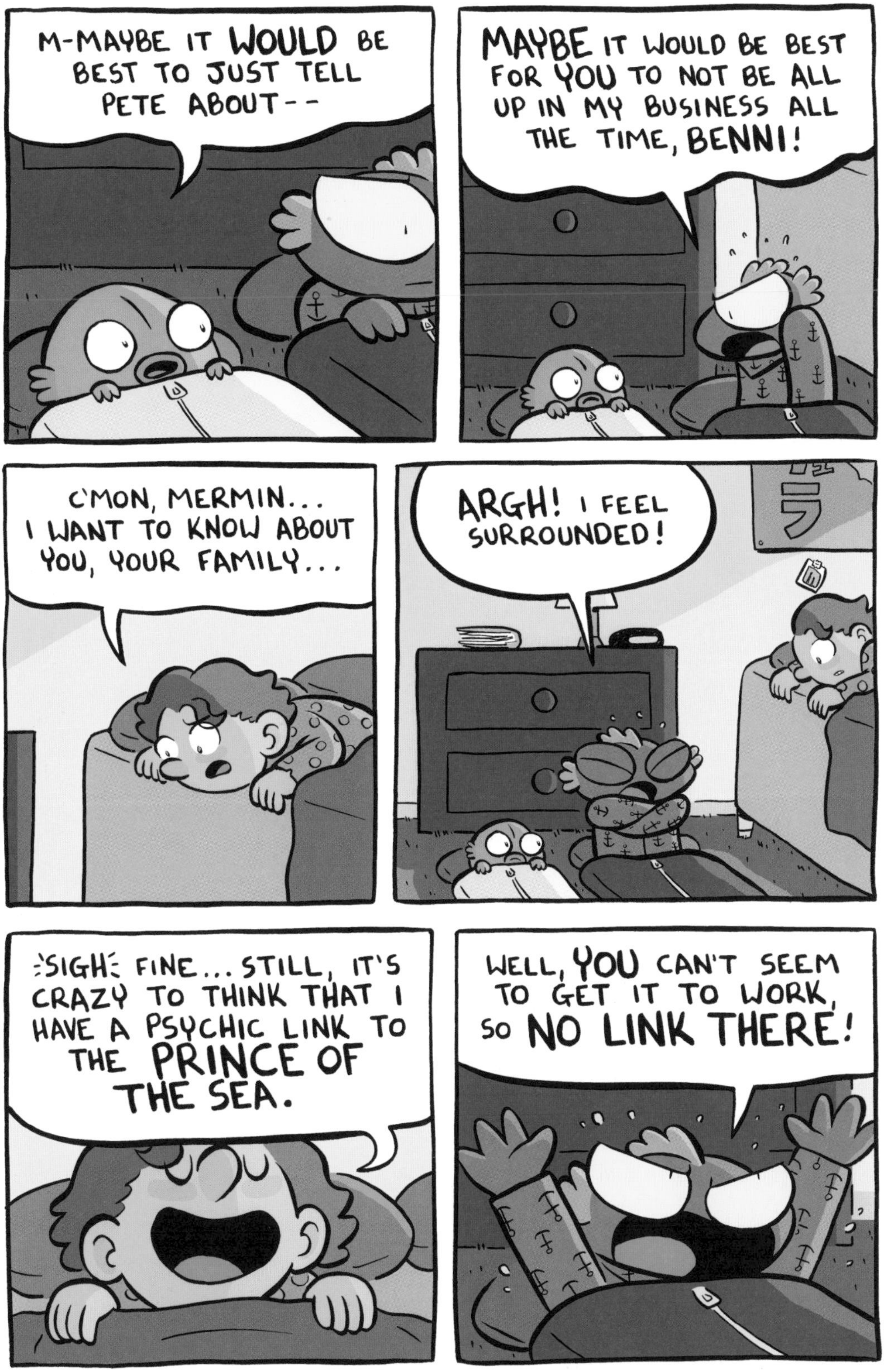
M-MAYBE IT WOULD BE BEST TO JUST TELL PETE ABOUT--
MAYBE IT WOULD BE BEST FOR YOU TO NOT BE ALL UP IN MY BUSINESS ALL THE TIME, BENNI!
C'MON, MERMIN... I WANT TO KNOW ABOUT YOU, YOUR FAMILY...
ARGH! I FEEL SURROUNDED!
:SIGH: FINE... STILL, IT'S CRAZY TO THINK THAT I HAVE A PSYCHIC LINK TO THE PRINCE OF THE SEA.
WELL, YOU CAN'T SEEM TO GET IT TO WORK, SO NO LINK THERE!

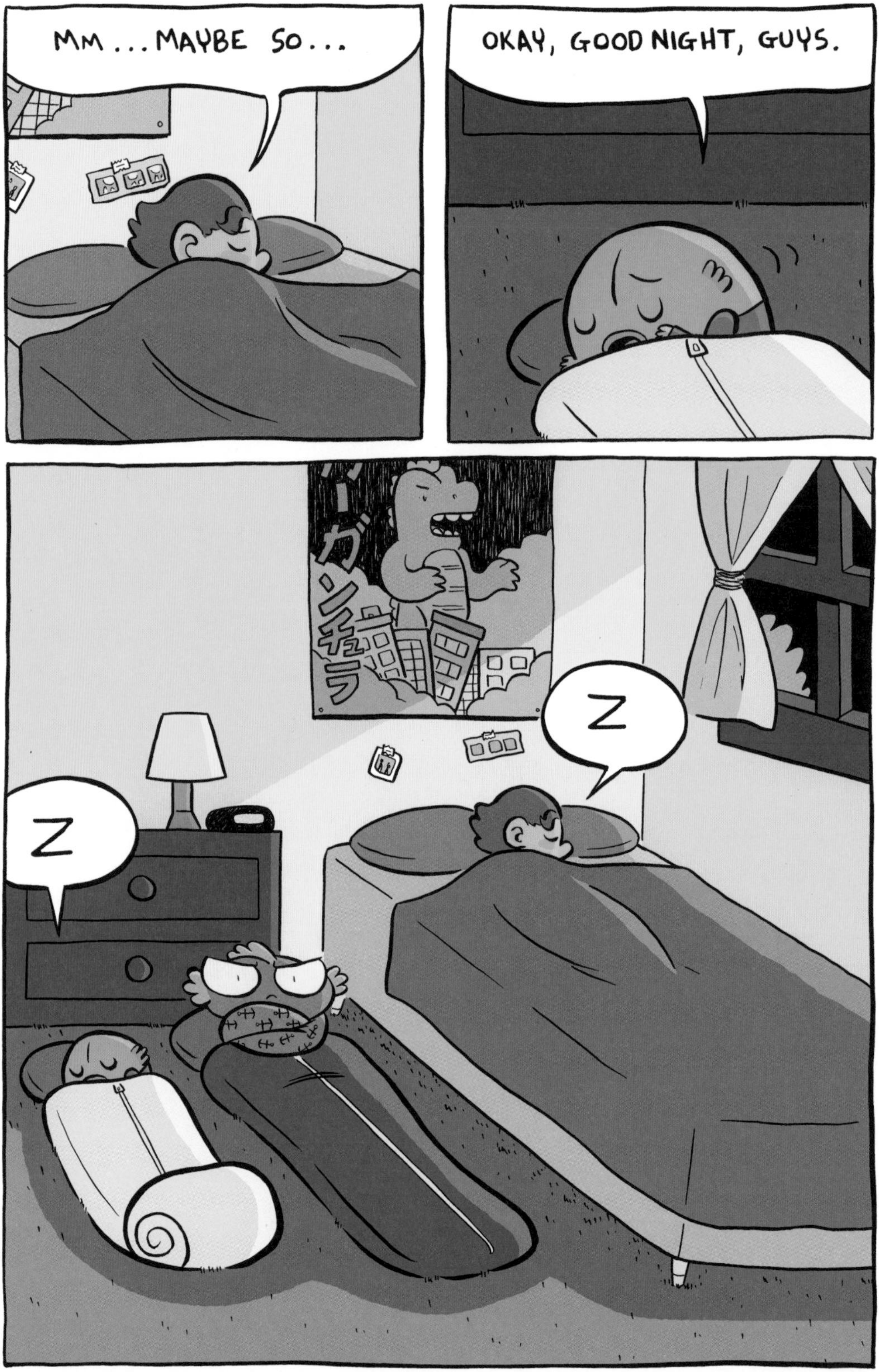
MM . . . MAYBE SO . . .
OKAY, GOOD NIGHT, GUYS.
Z
Z

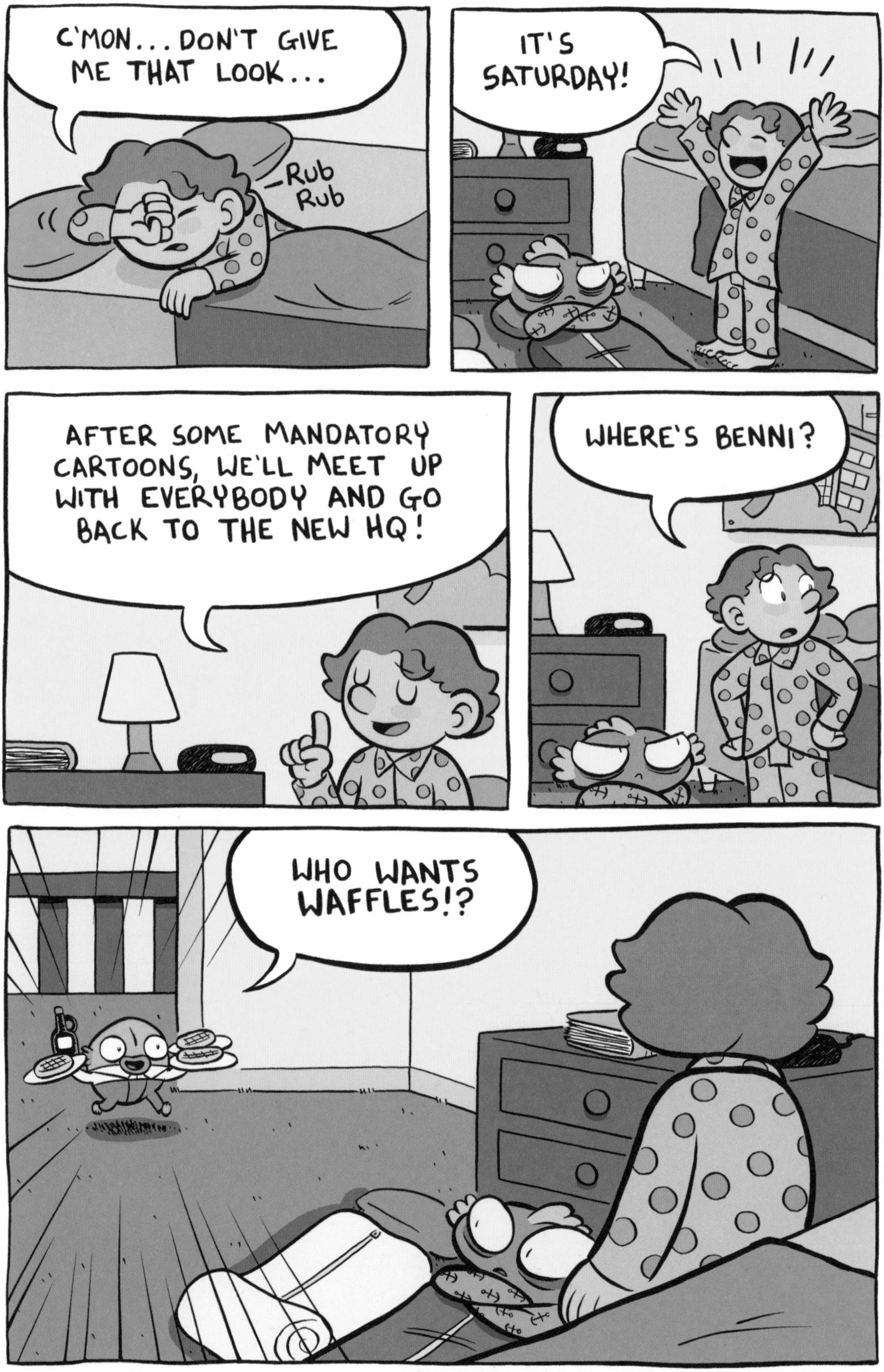
C'MON... DON'T GIVE ME THAT LOOK...
RUB RUB
IT'S SATURDAY!
AFTER SOME MANDATORY CARTOONS, WE'LL MEET UP WITH EVERYBODY AND GO BACK TO THE NEW HQ!
WHERE'S BENNI?
WHO WANTS WAFFLES!?

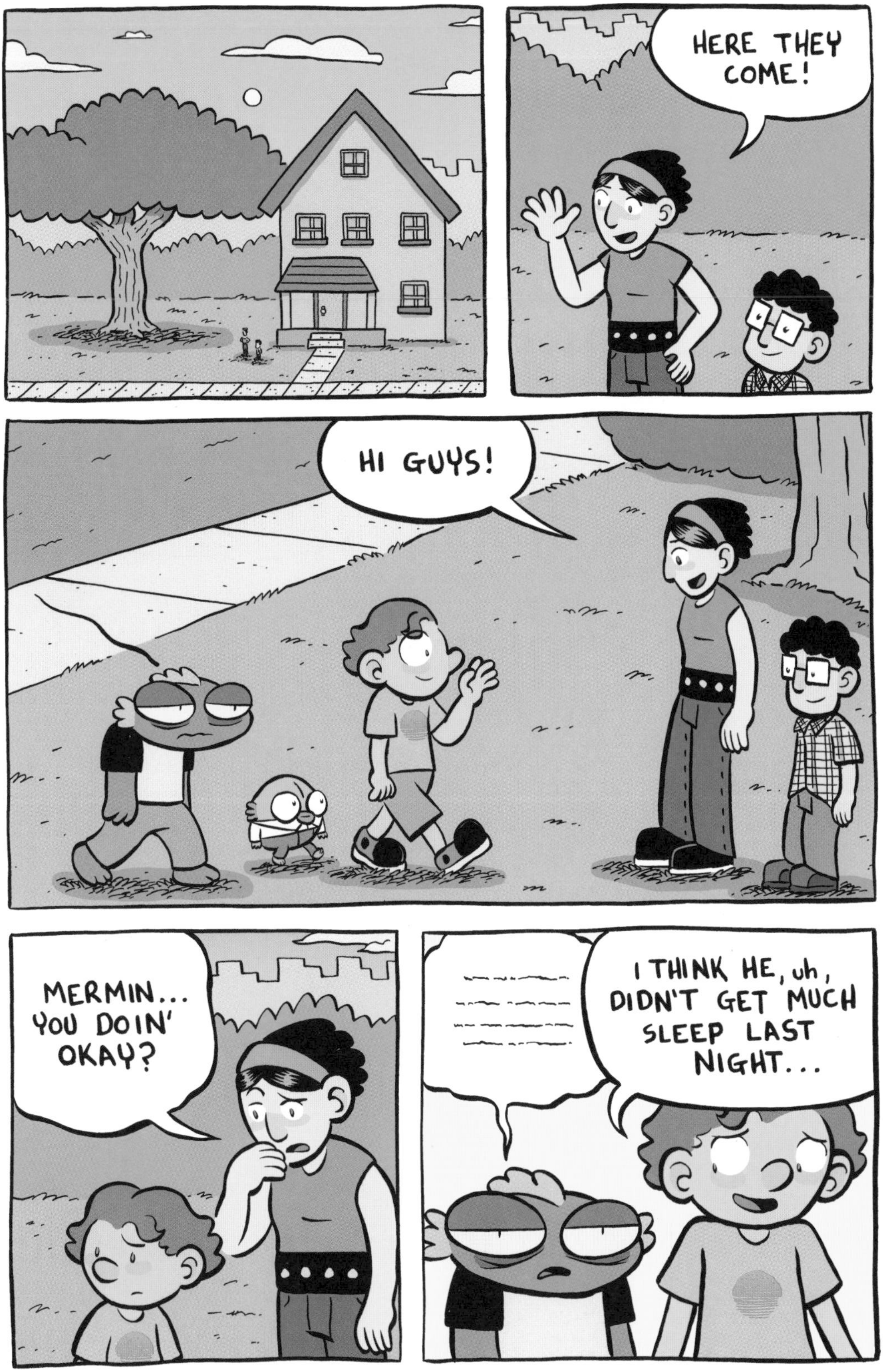
HERE THEY COME!
HI GUYS!
MERMIN... YOU DOIN' OKAY?
I THINK HE, uh, DIDN'T GET MUCH SLEEP LAST NIGHT...

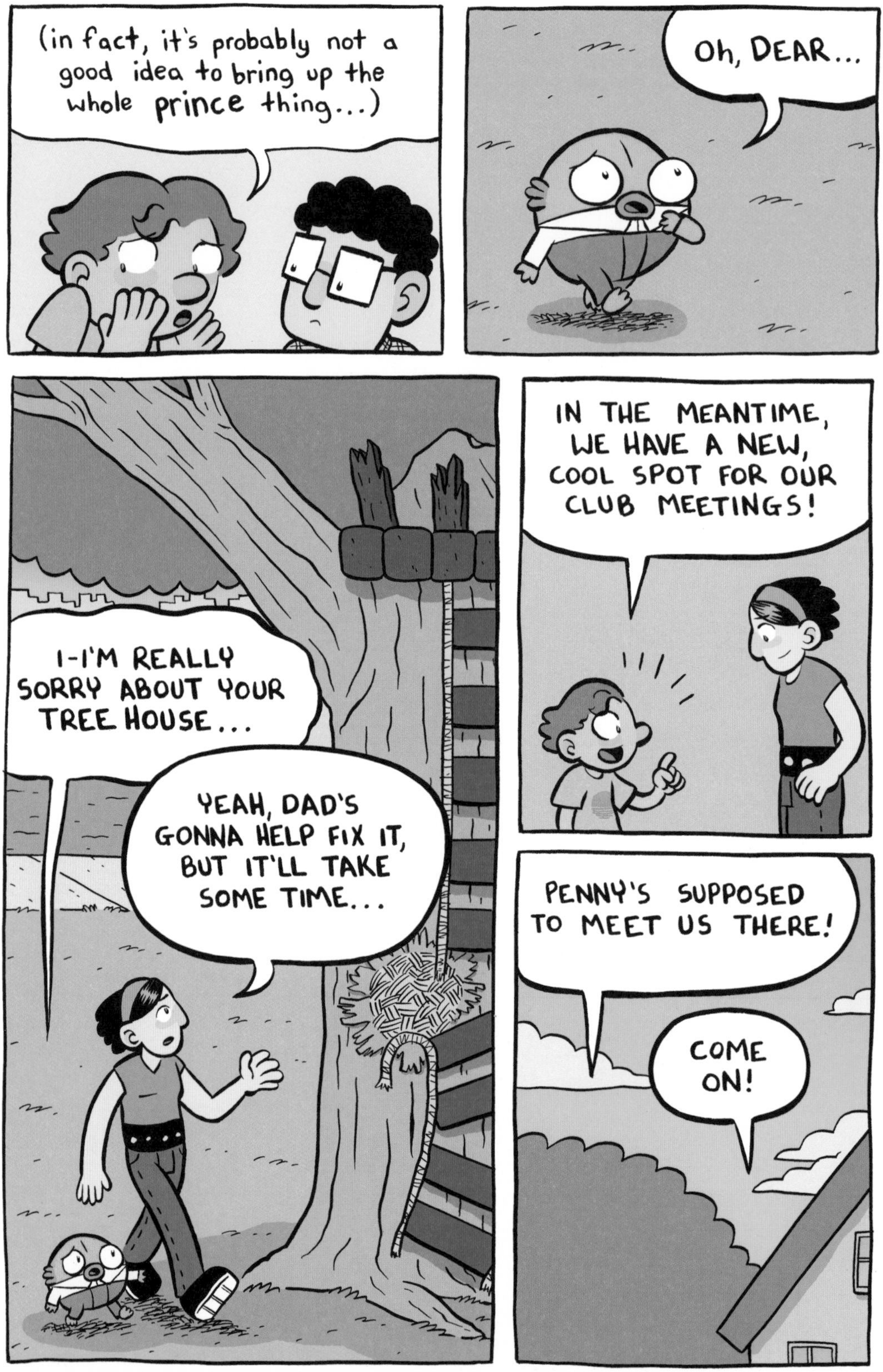
(in fact, it's probably not a good idea to bring up the whole prince thing...)
Oh, DEAR...
I-I'M REALLY SORRY ABOUT YOUR TREE HOUSE...
YEAH, DAD'S GONNA HELP FIX IT, BUT IT'LL TAKE SOME TIME...
IN THE MEANTIME, WE HAVE A NEW, COOL SPOT FOR OUR CLUB MEETINGS!
PENNY'S SUPPOSED TO MEET US THERE!
COME ON!

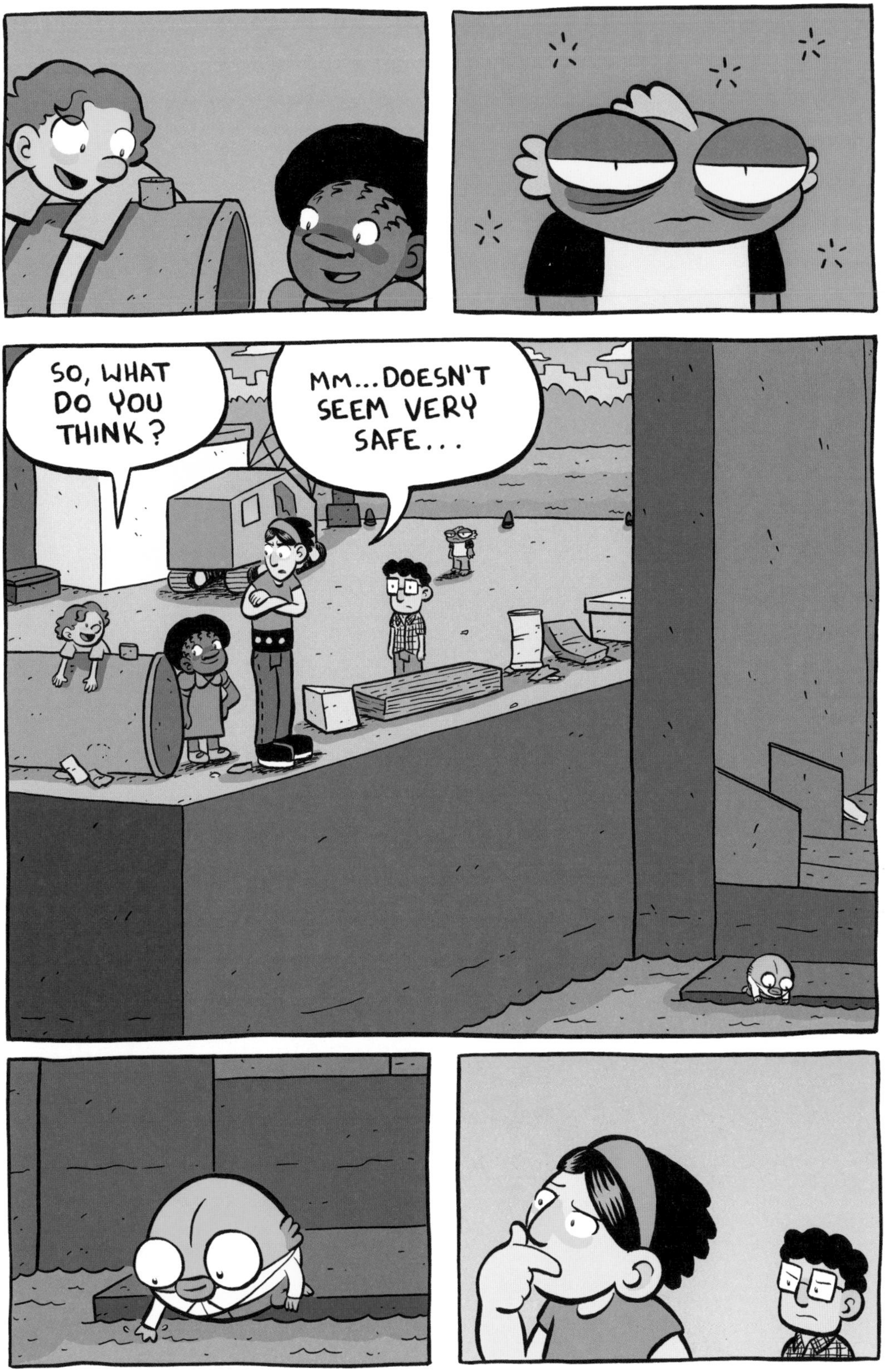
SO, WHAT DO YOU THINK?
MM... DOESN'T SEEM VERY SAFE...

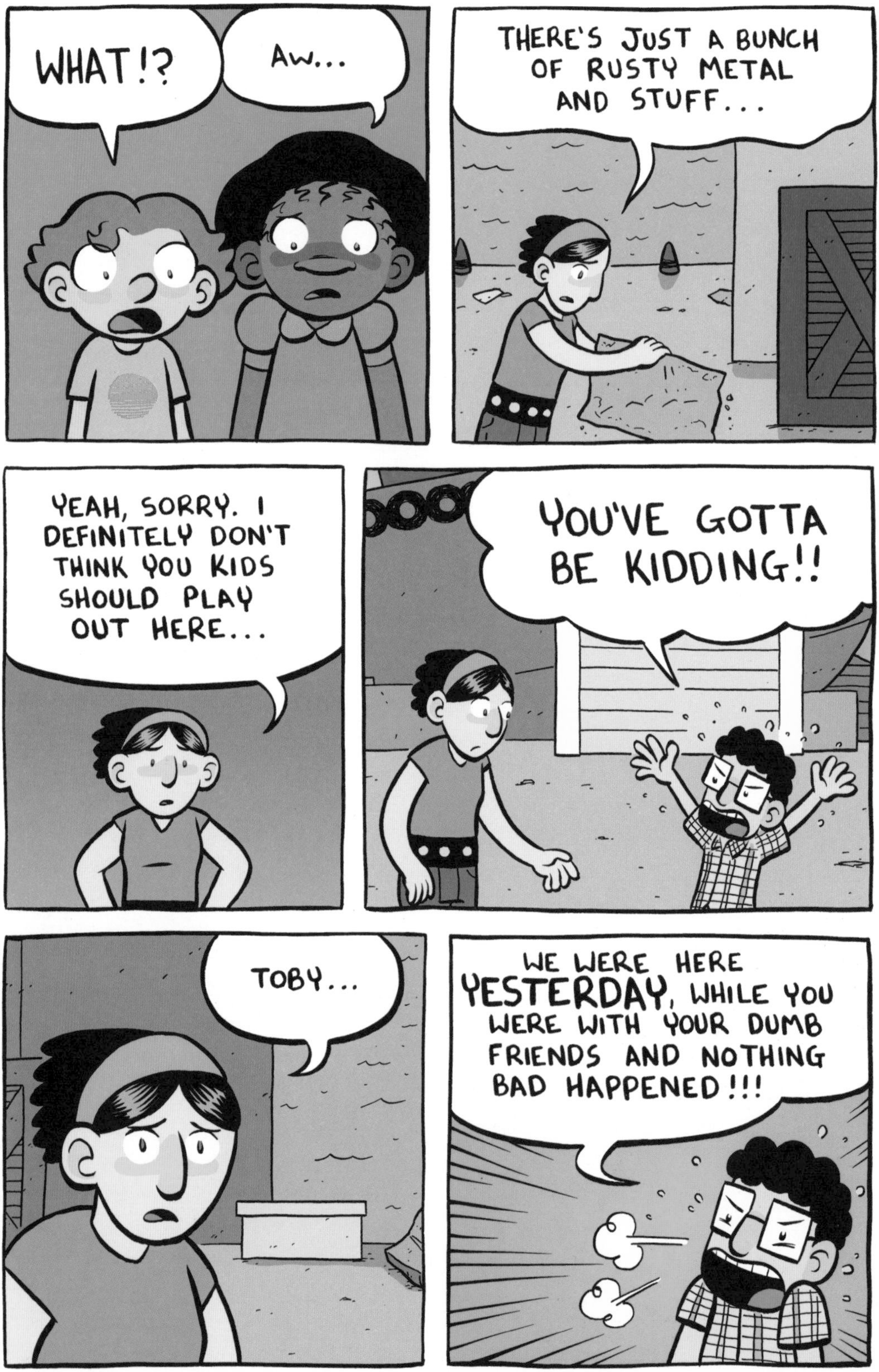
WHAT!?
AW...
THERE'S JUST A BUNCH OF RUSTY METAL AND STUFF...
YEAH, SORRY. I DEFINITELY DON'T THINK YOU KIDS SHOULD PLAY OUT HERE...
YOU'VE GOTTA BE KIDDING!!
TOBY...
WE WERE HERE YESTERDAY, WHILE YOU WERE WITH YOUR DUMB FRIENDS AND NOTHING BAD HAPPENED!!!

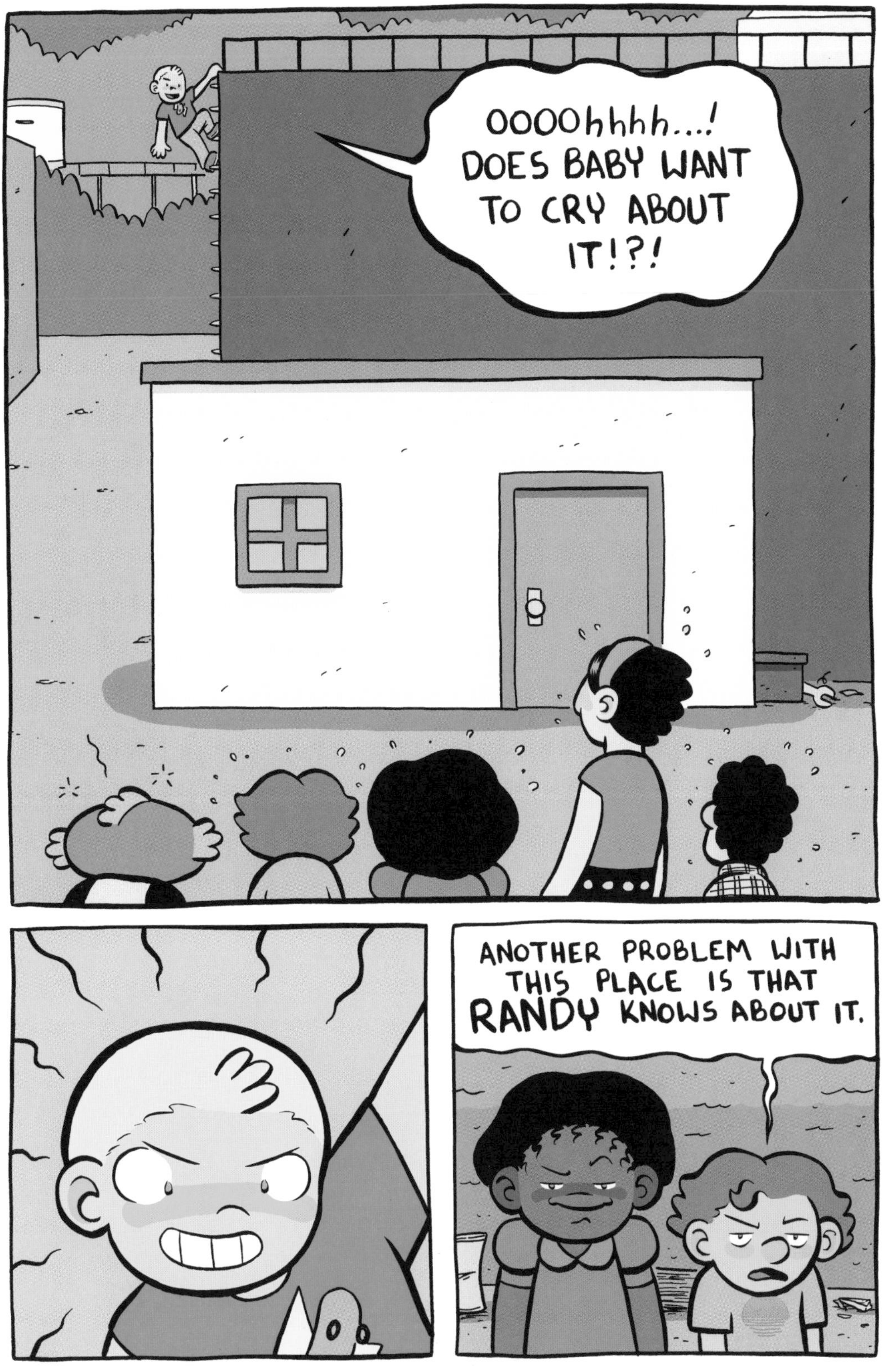
OOOOhhhh...!
DOES BABY WANT TO CRY ABOUT IT!?!
ANOTHER PROBLEM WITH THIS PLACE IS THAT RANDY KNOWS ABOUT IT.

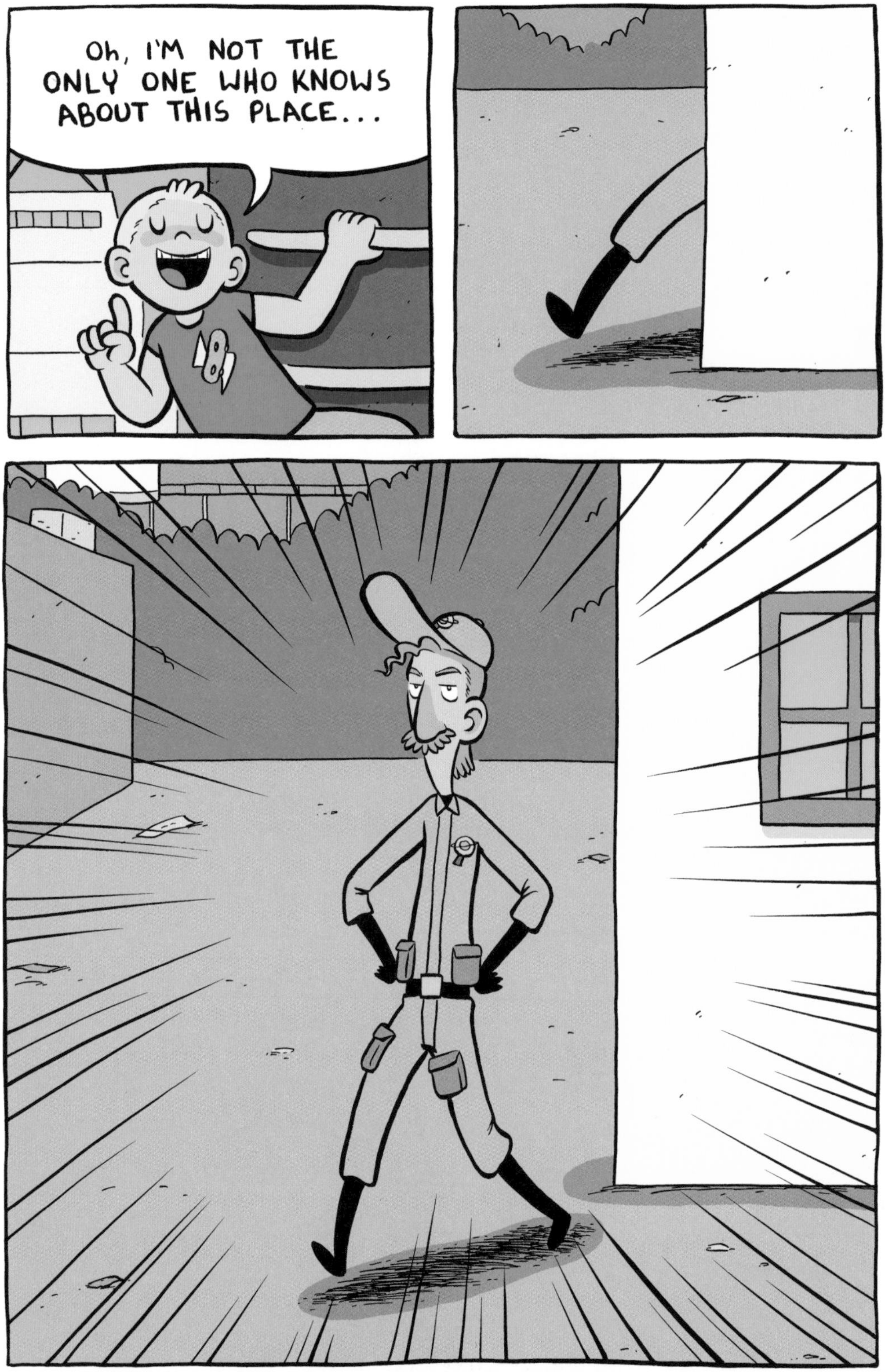
Oh, I'M NOT THE ONLY ONE WHO KNOWS ABOUT THIS PLACE...

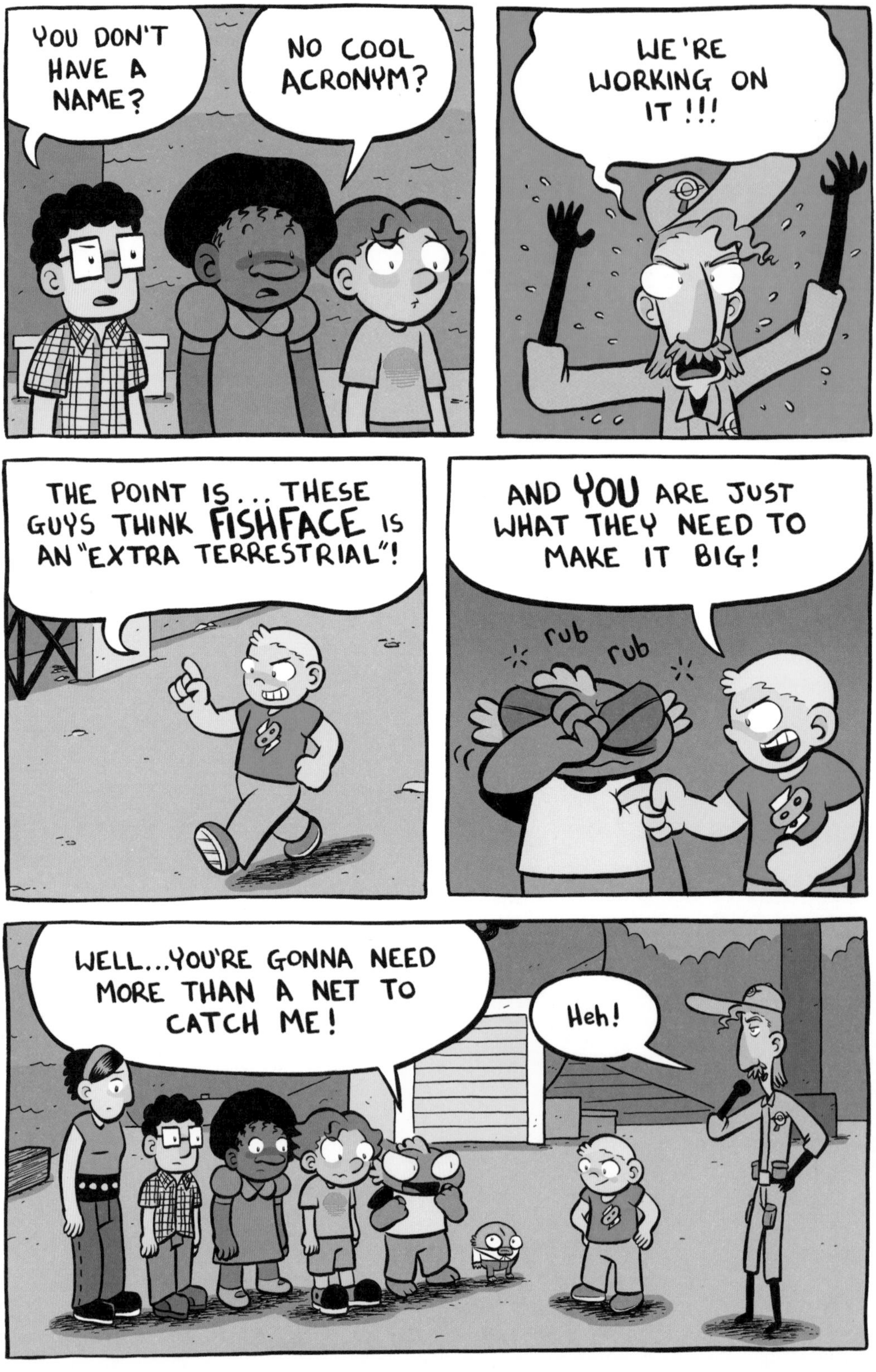
YOU DON'T HAVE A NAME?
NO COOL ACRONYM?
WE'RE WORKING ON IT!!!
THE POINT IS... THESE GUYS THINK FISHFACE IS AN "EXTRA TERRESTRIAL"!
AND YOU ARE JUST WHAT THEY NEED TO MAKE IT BIG!
rub
rub
WELL...YOU'RE GONNA NEED MORE THAN A NET TO CATCH ME!
Heh!

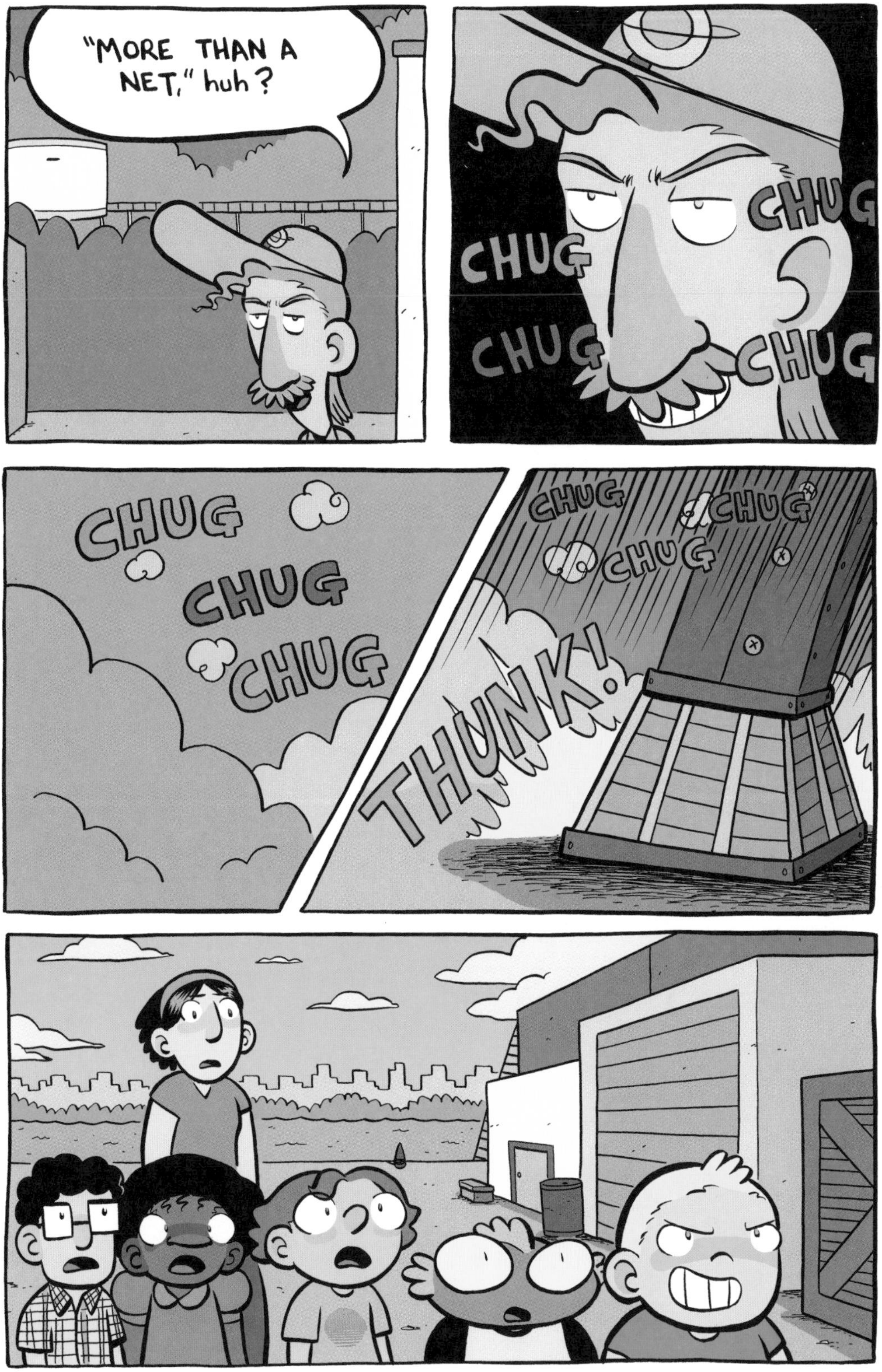
"MORE THAN A NET," huh?
CHUG
CHUG
CHUG
CHUG
CHUG
CHUG
CHUG
CHUG
CHUG
CHUG
CHUG
THUNK!

CHAPTER FIVE

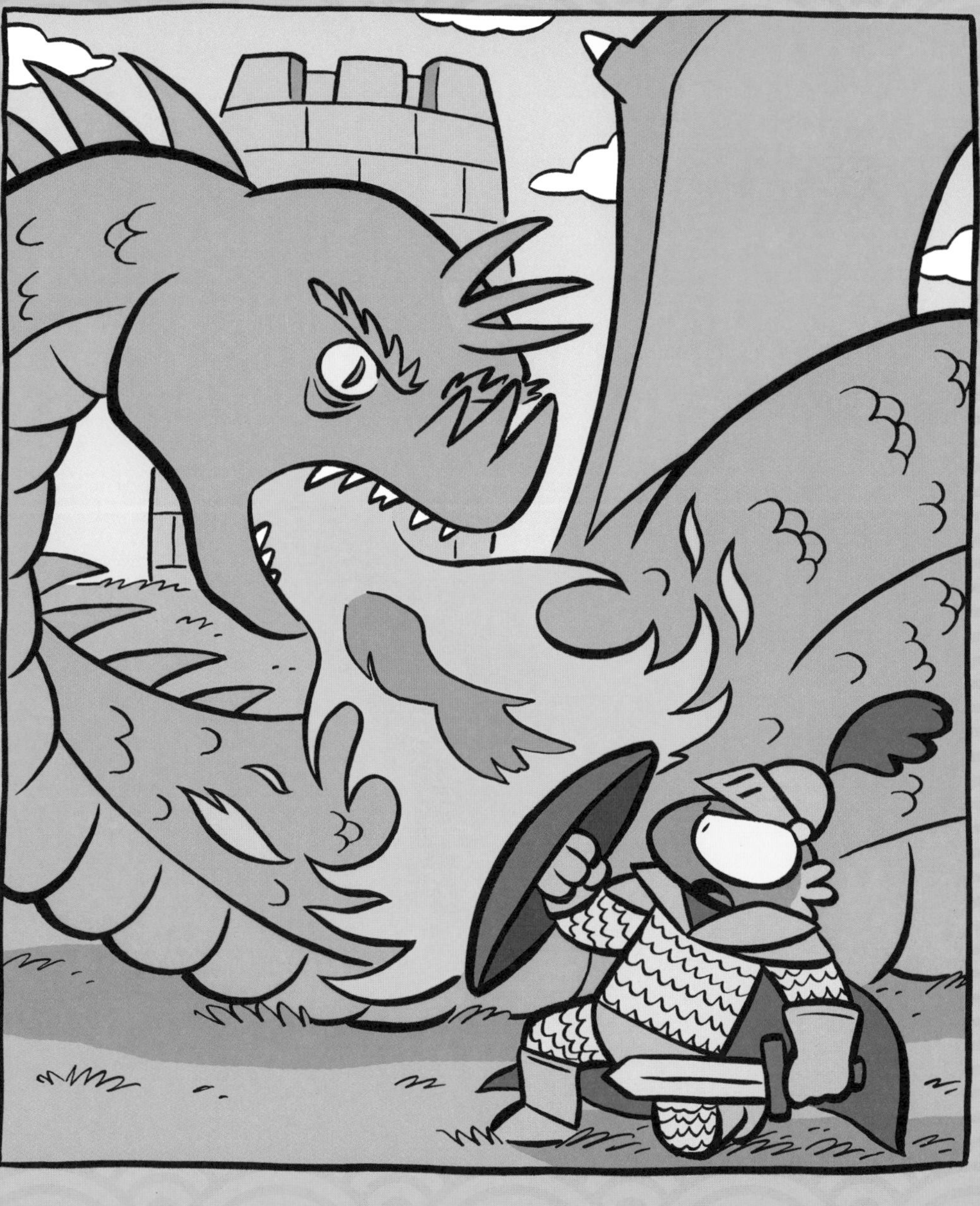

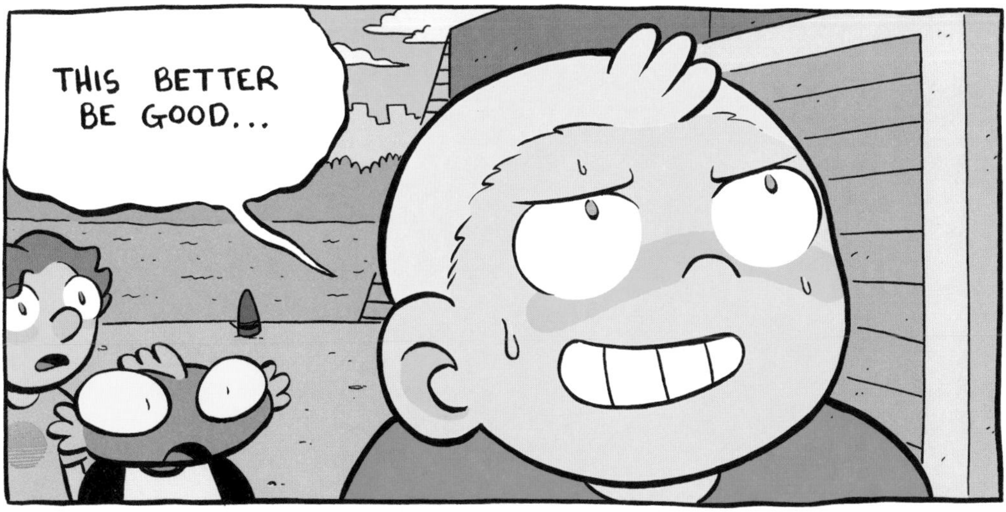
THIS BETTER BE GOOD...

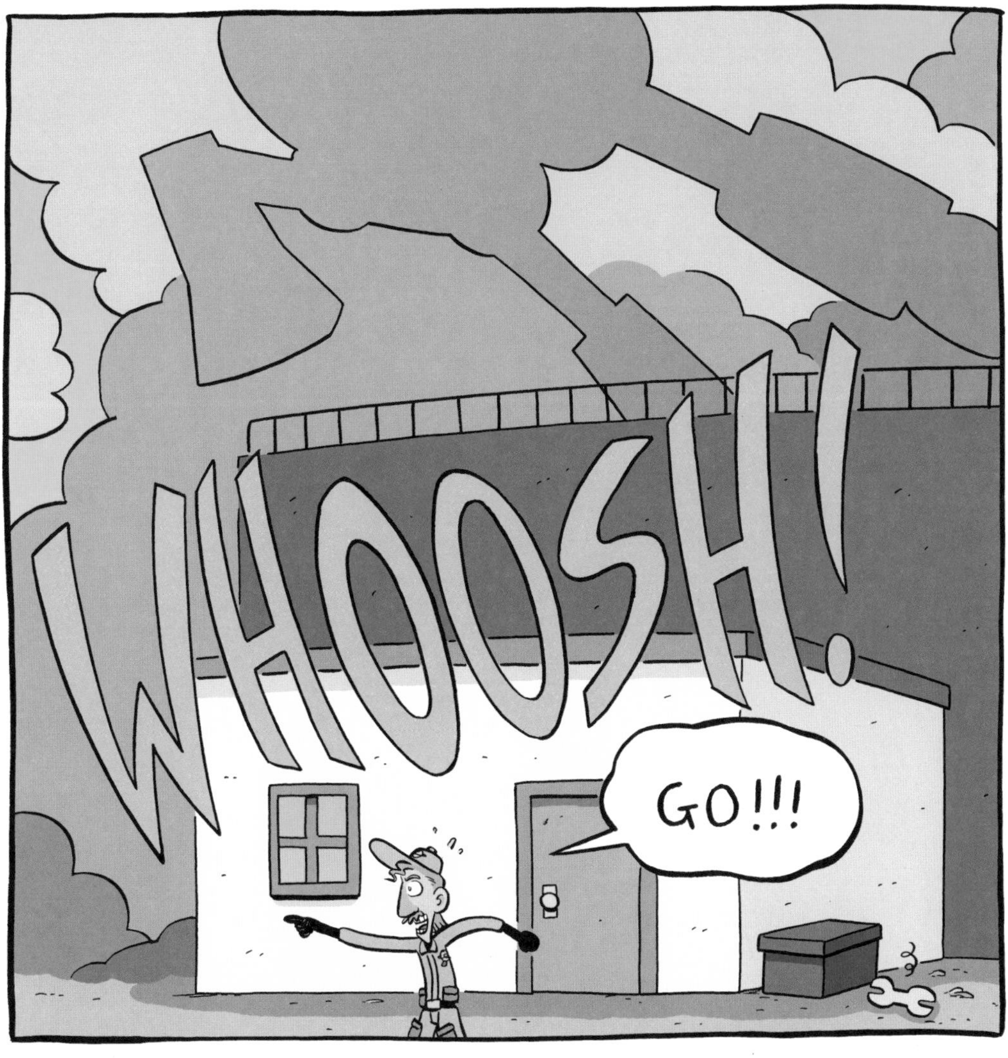
WHOOSH!
GO!!!

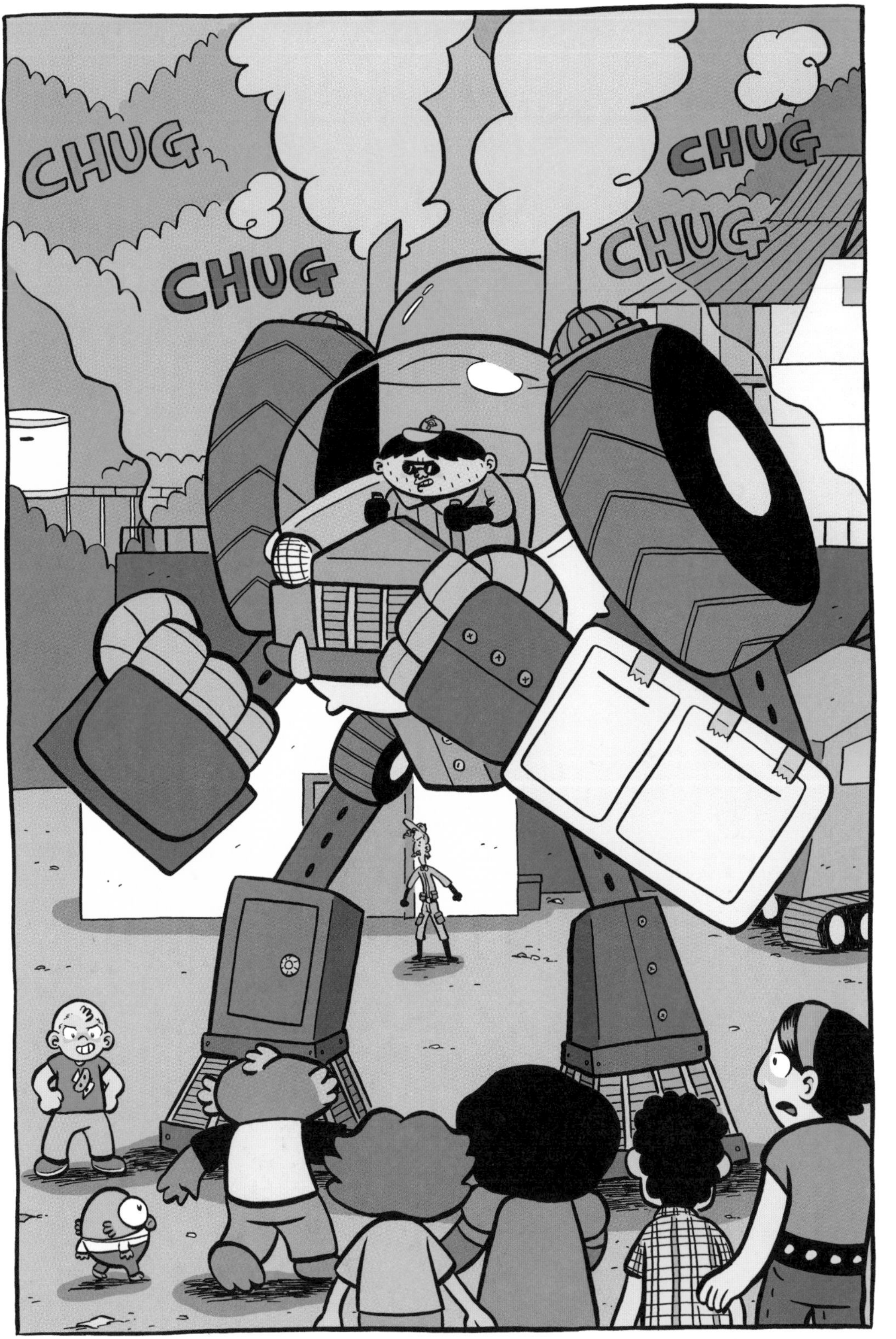
CHUG
CHUG
CHUG
CHUG

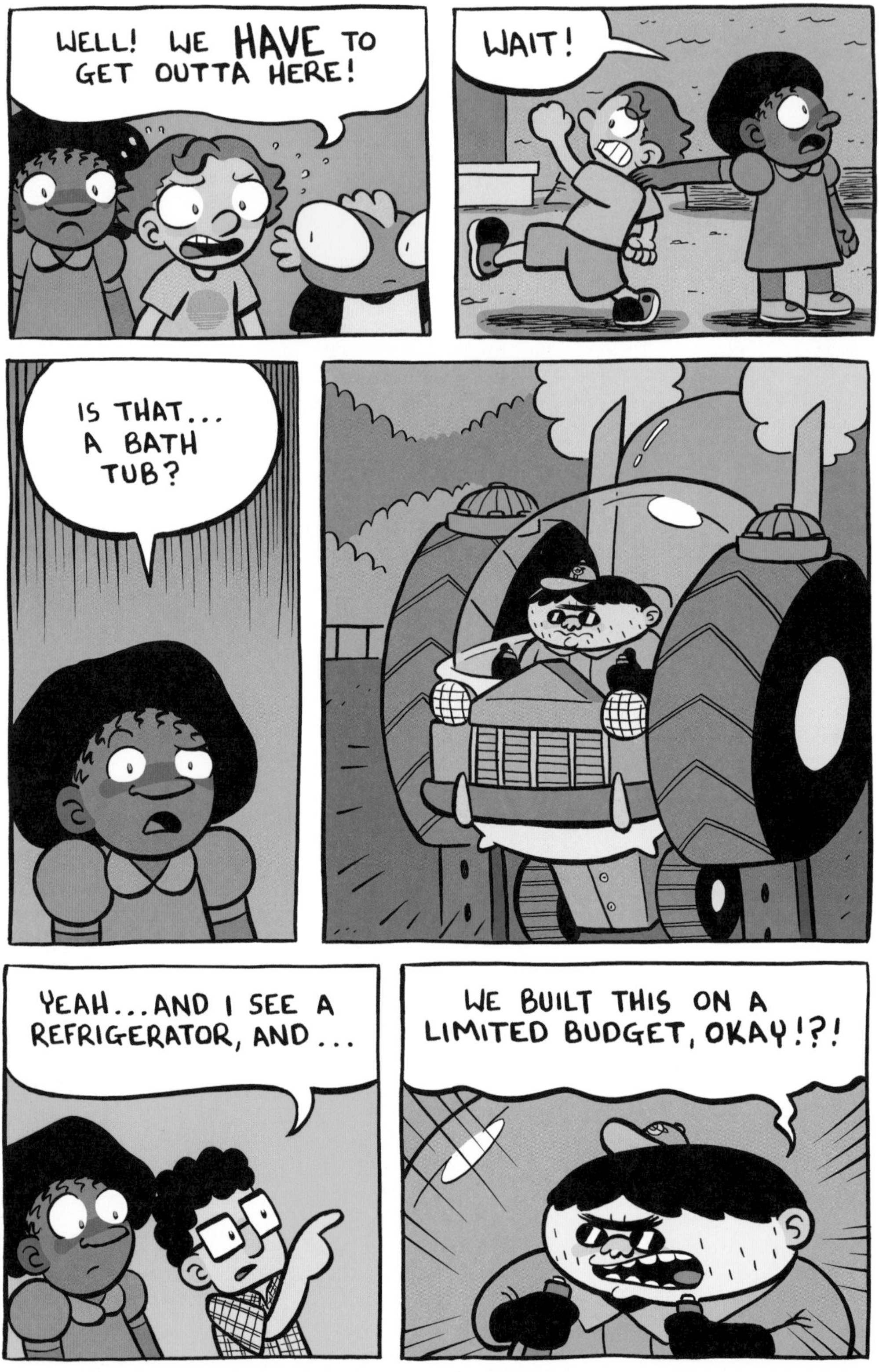
WELL! WE HAVE TO GET OUTTA HERE!
WAIT!
IS THAT... A BATH TUB?
YEAH...AND I SEE A REFRIGERATOR, AND...
WE BUILT THIS ON A LIMITED BUDGET, OKAY!?!

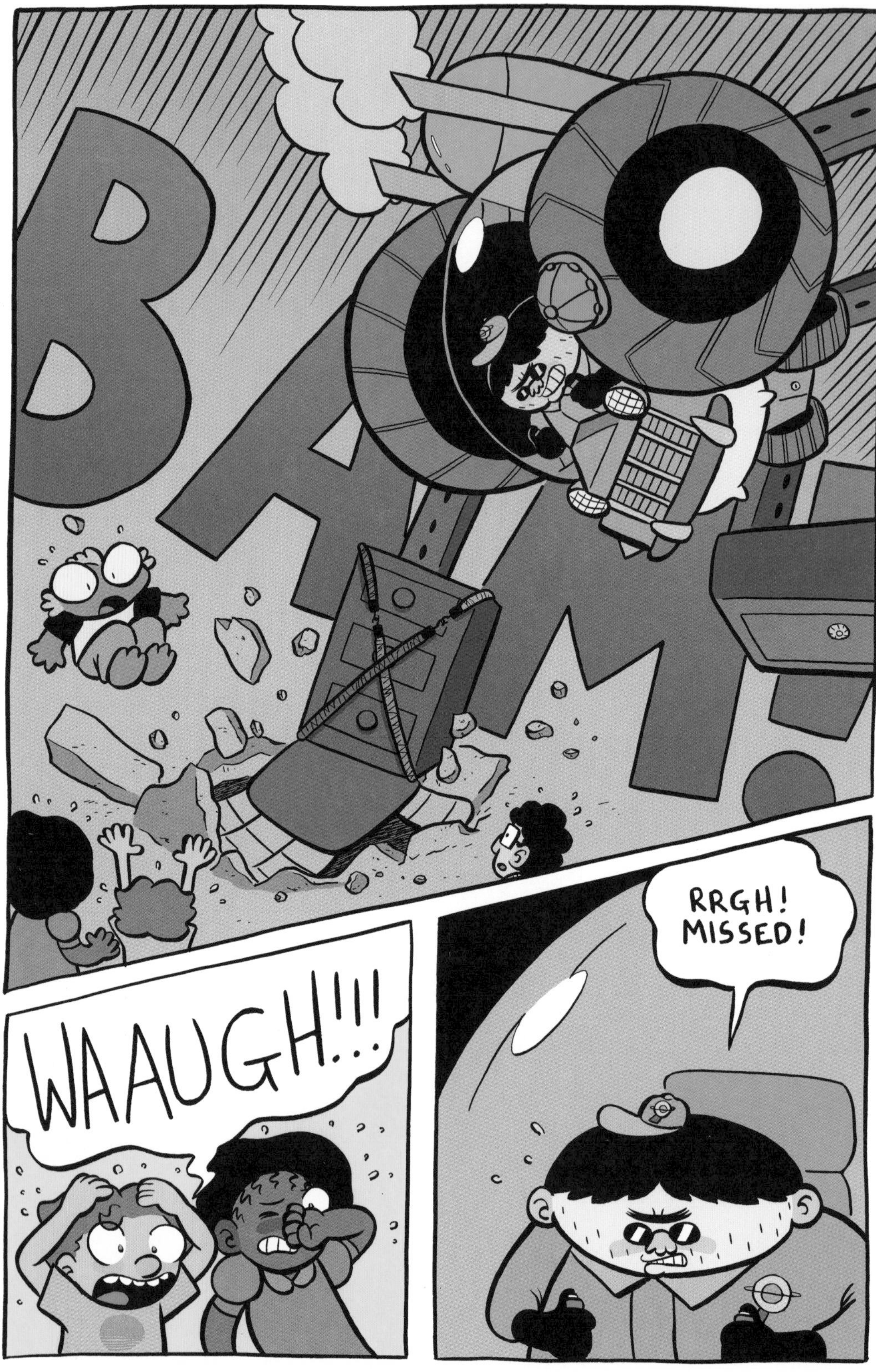
BAM!
WAAUGH!!!...
RRGH! MISSED!

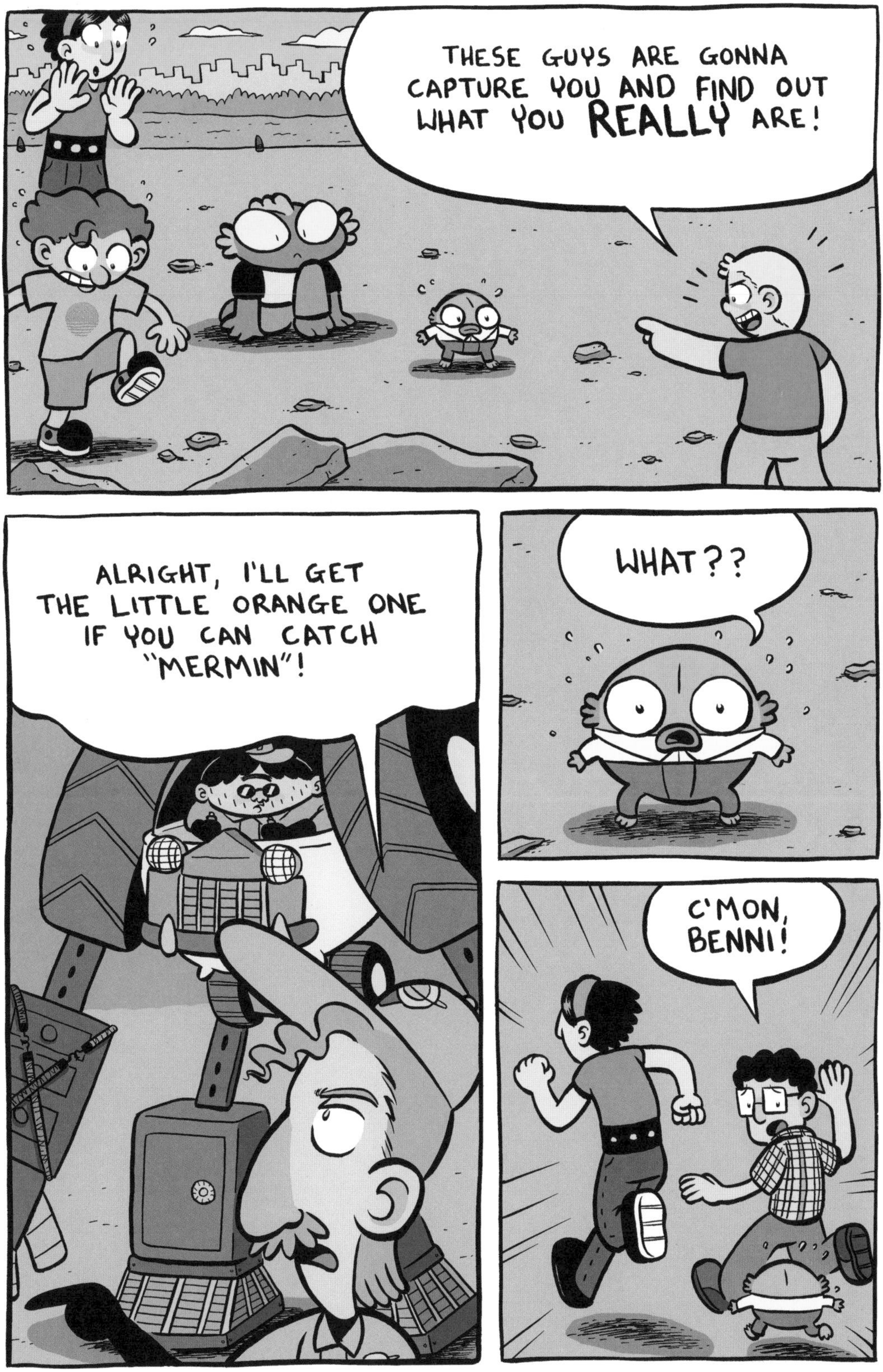
THESE GUYS ARE GONNA CAPTURE YOU AND FIND OUT WHAT YOU REALLY ARE!
ALRIGHT, I'LL GET THE LITTLE ORANGE ONE IF YOU CAN CATCH "MERMIN"!
WHAT??
C'MON, BENNI!

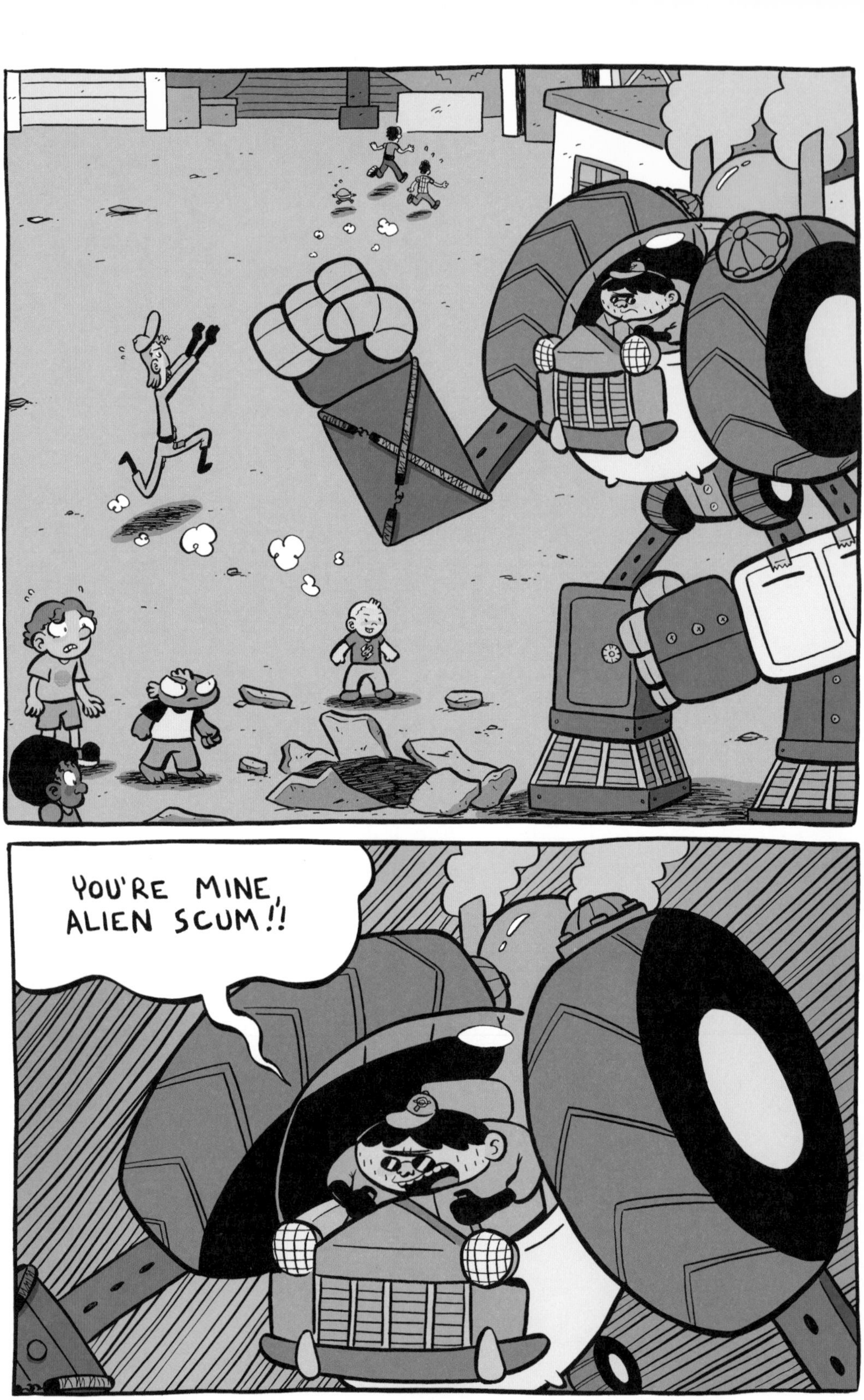
YOU'RE MINE, ALIEN SCUM!!

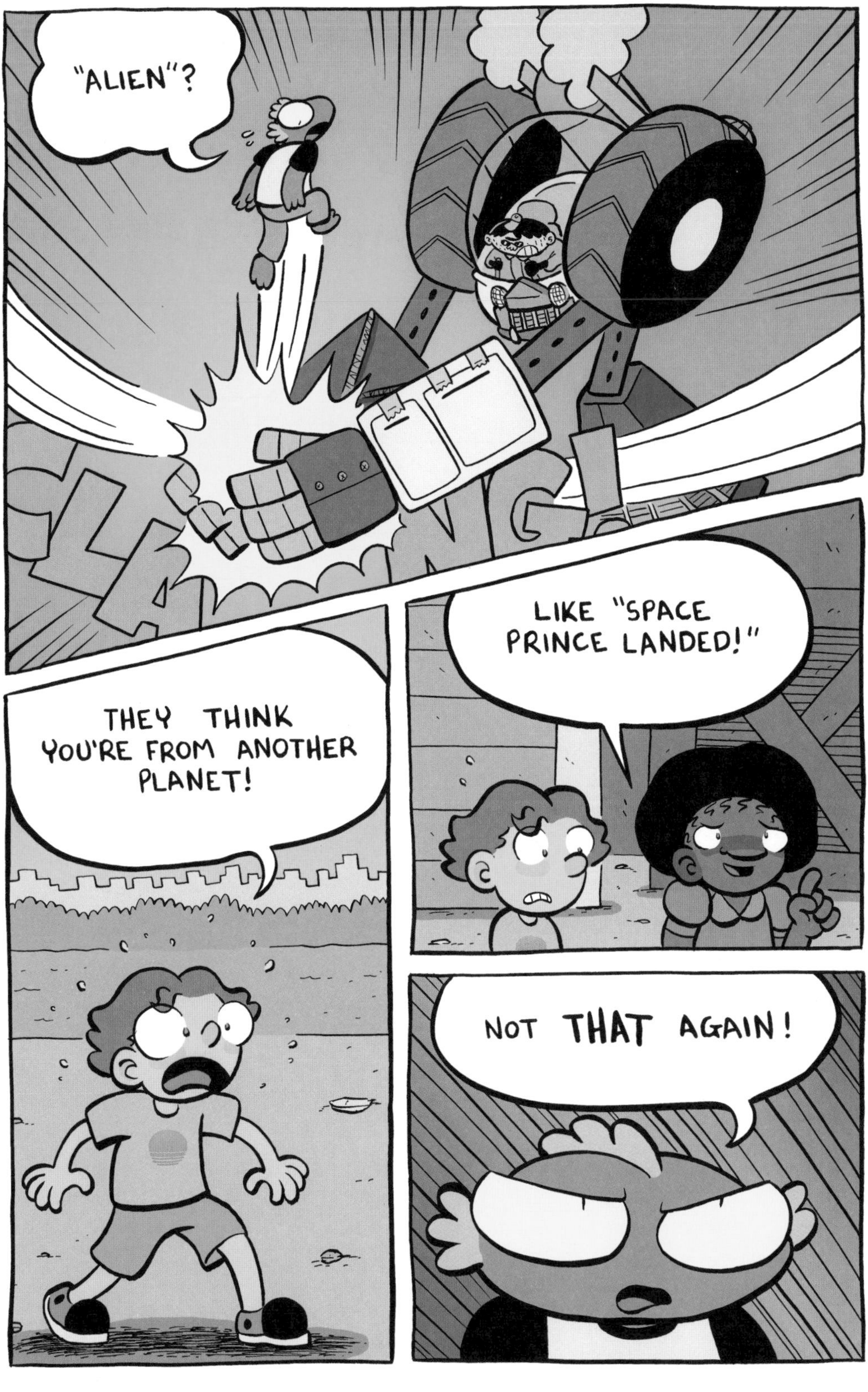
"ALIEN"?
THEY THINK YOU'RE FROM ANOTHER PLANET!
LIKE "SPACE PRINCE LANDED!"
NOT **THAT** AGAIN!

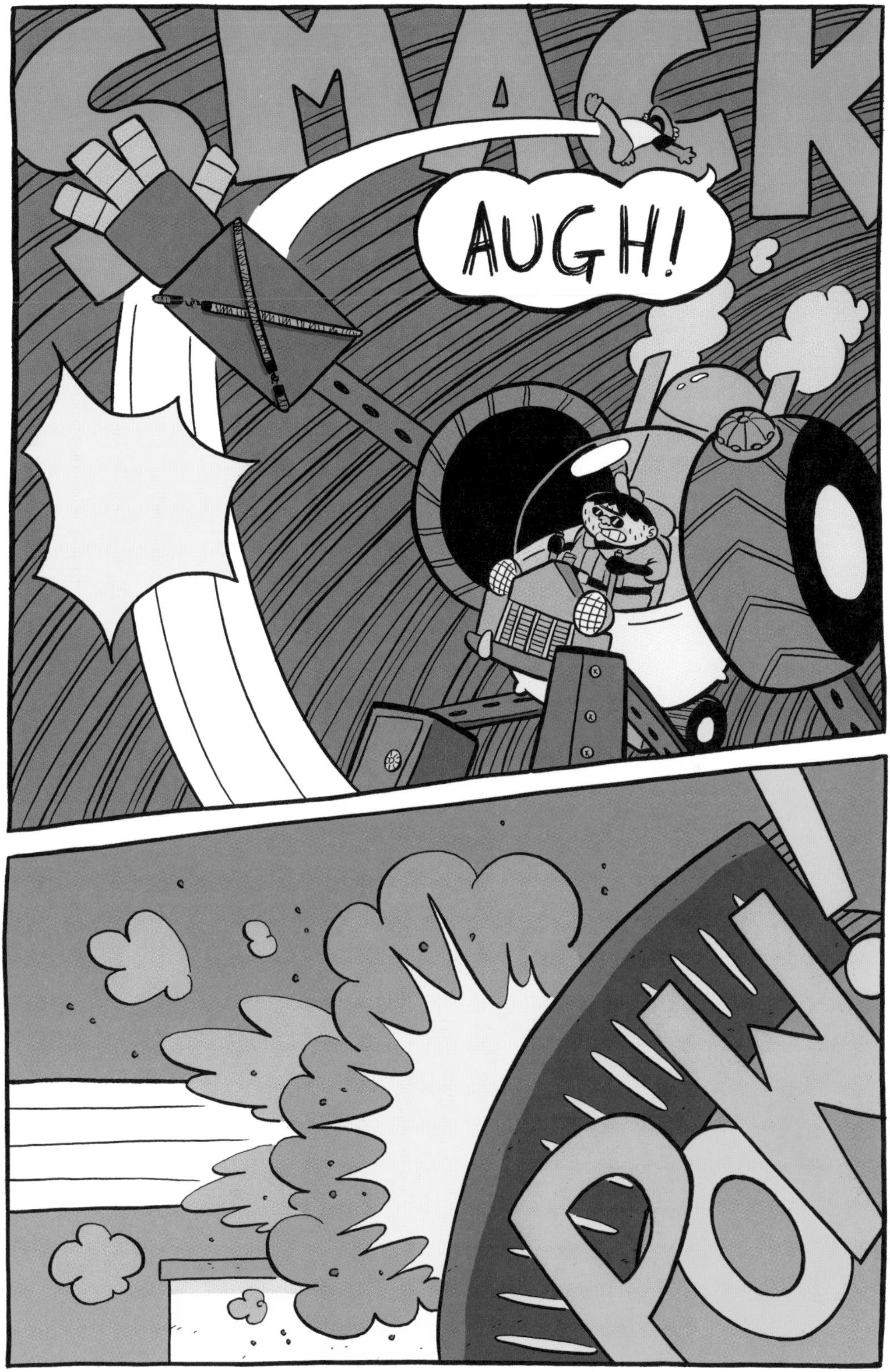
SMACK
AUGH!
POW!

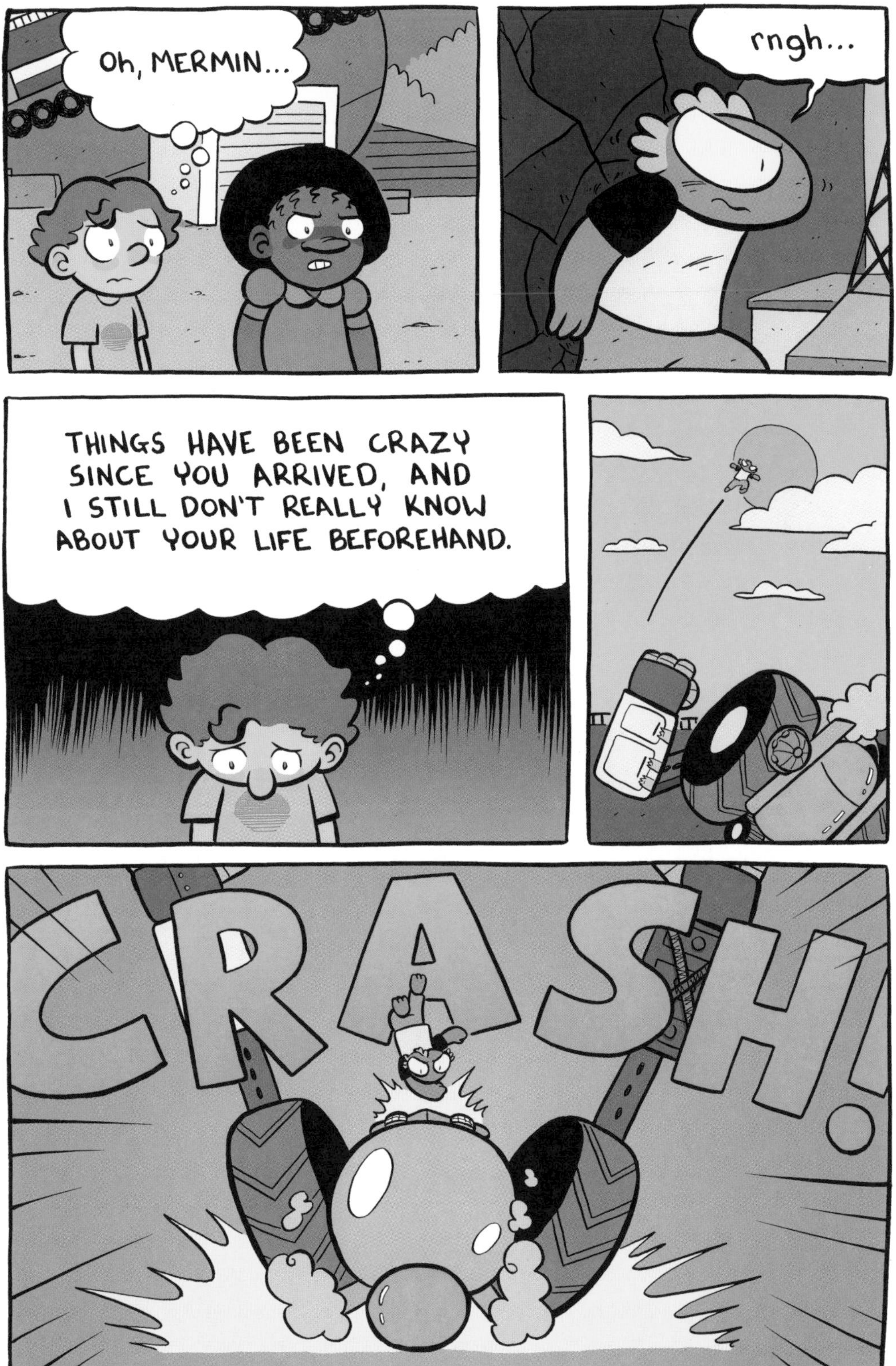
Oh, MERMIN...
rngh...
THINGS HAVE BEEN CRAZY SINCE YOU ARRIVED, AND I STILL DON'T REALLY KNOW ABOUT YOUR LIFE BEFOREHAND.
CRASH!

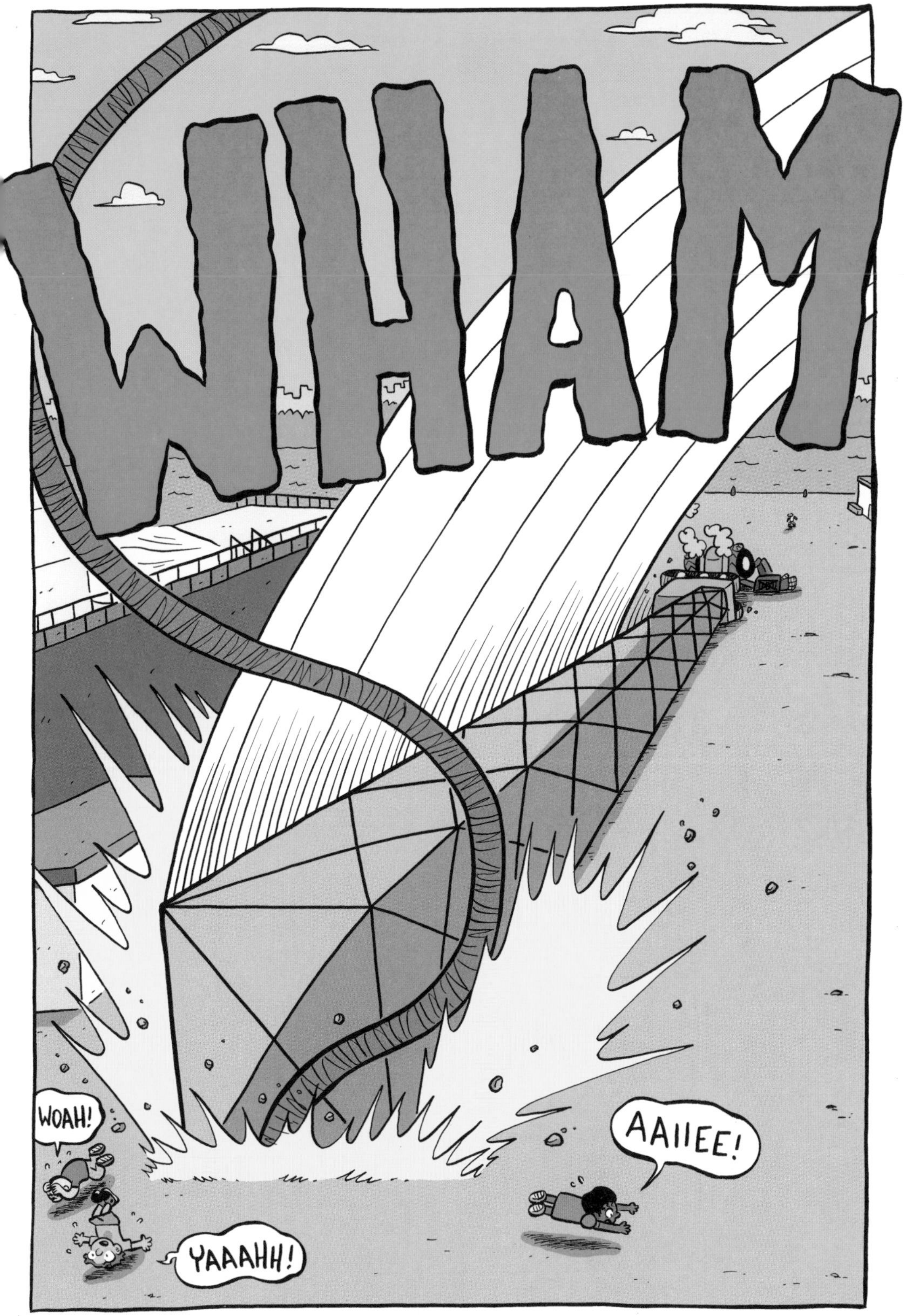
WHAM
WOAH!
AAIIEE!
YAAAHH!

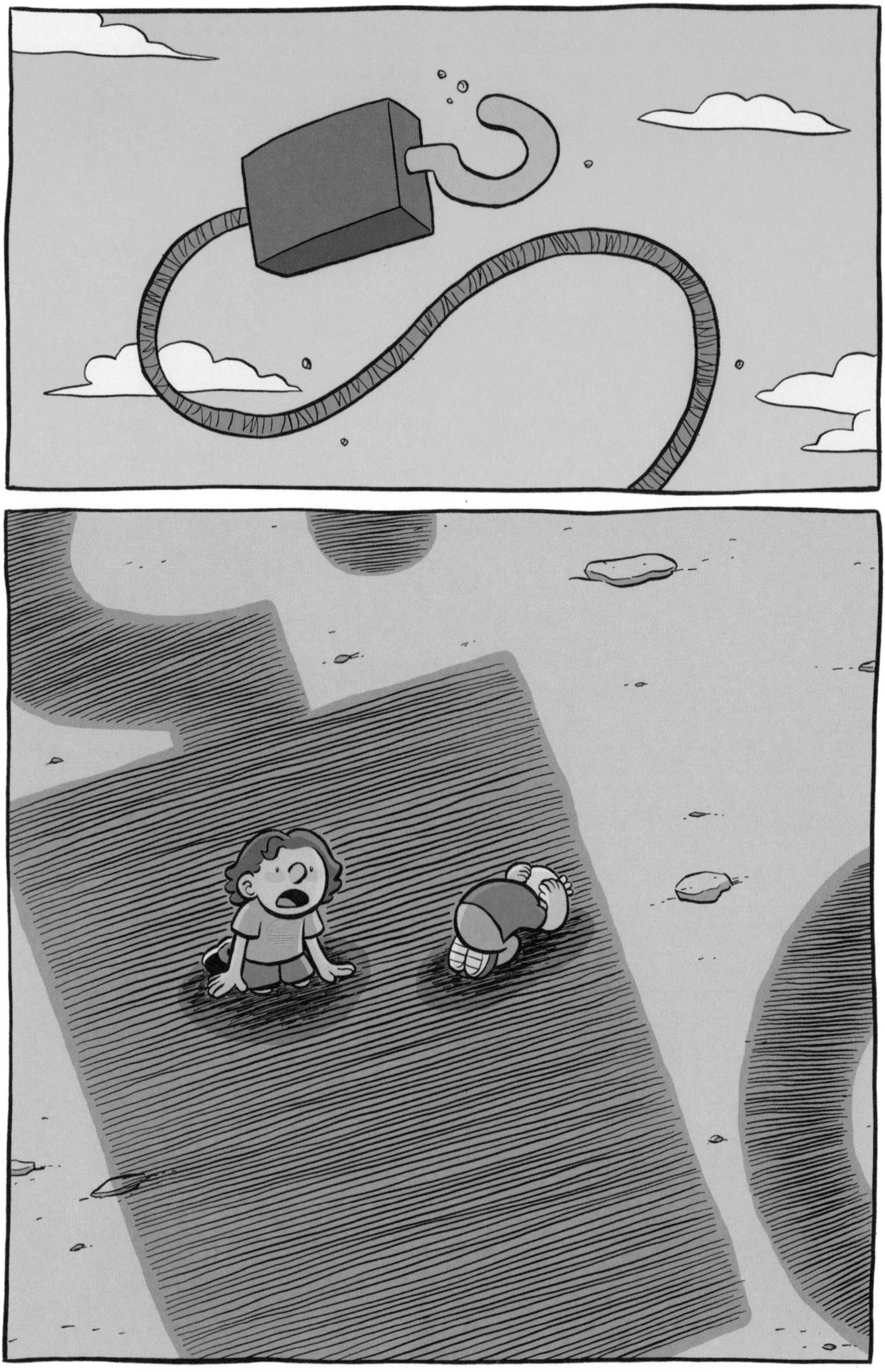

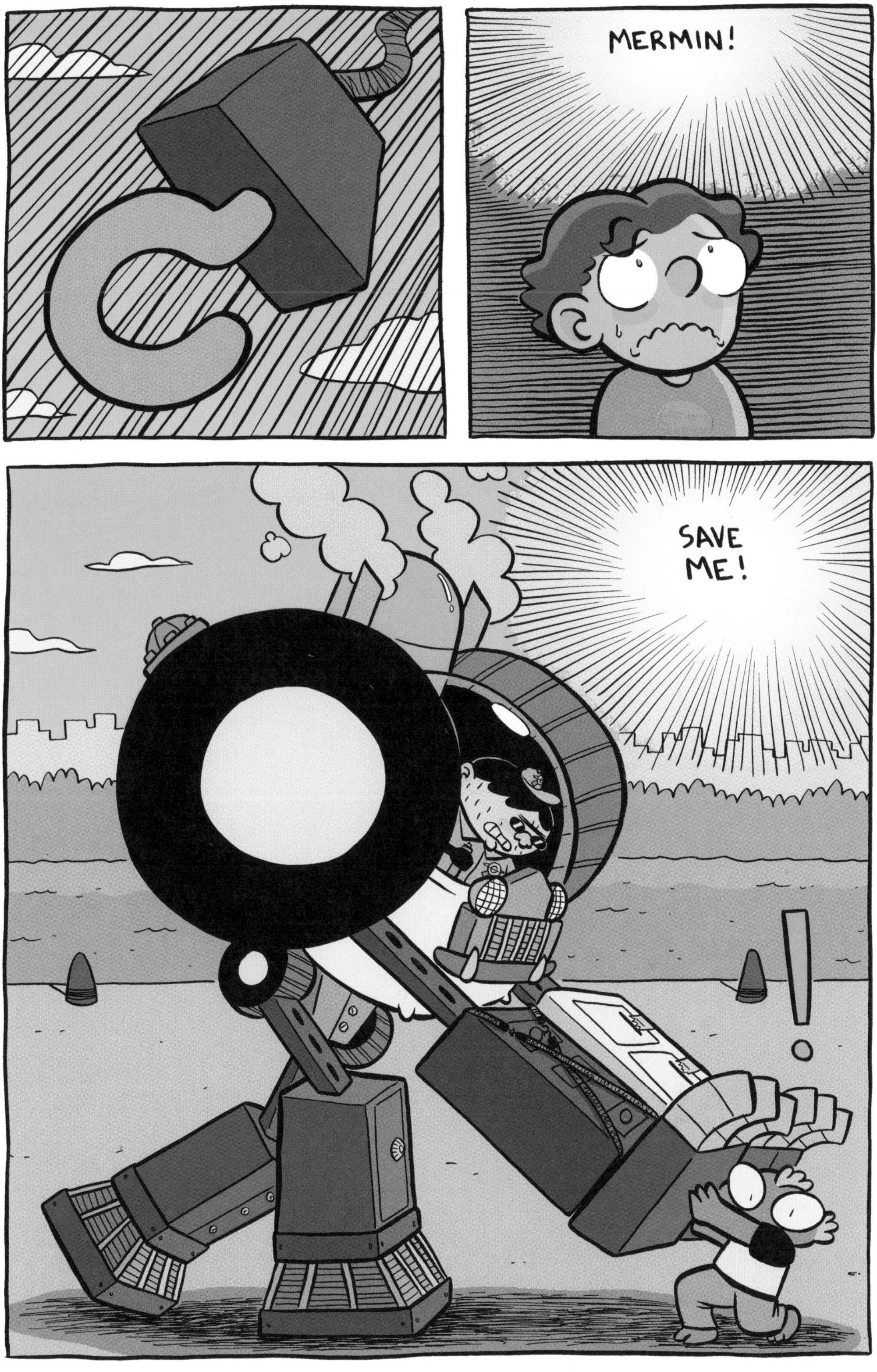
MERMIN!
SAVE ME!
!

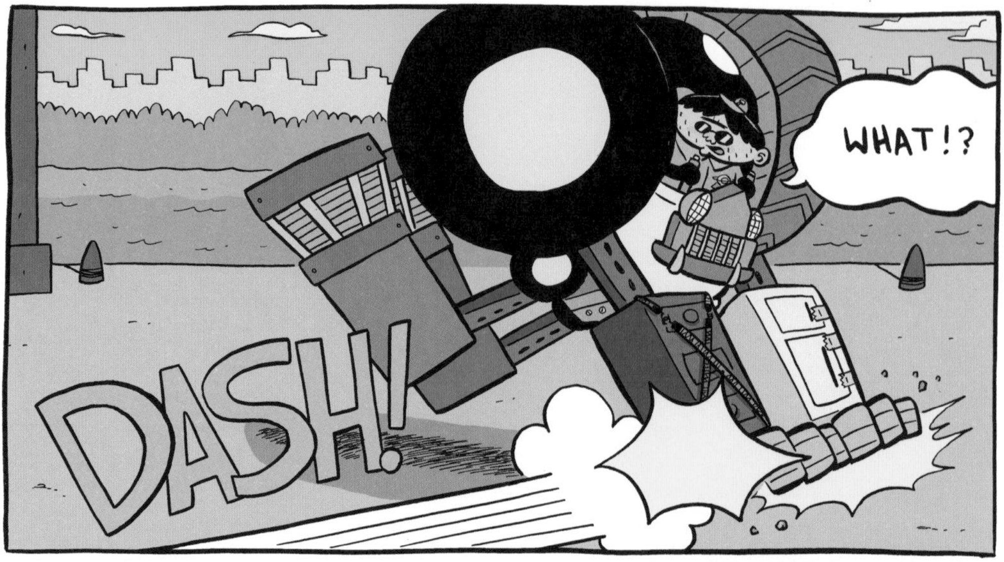
WHAT!?
DASH!

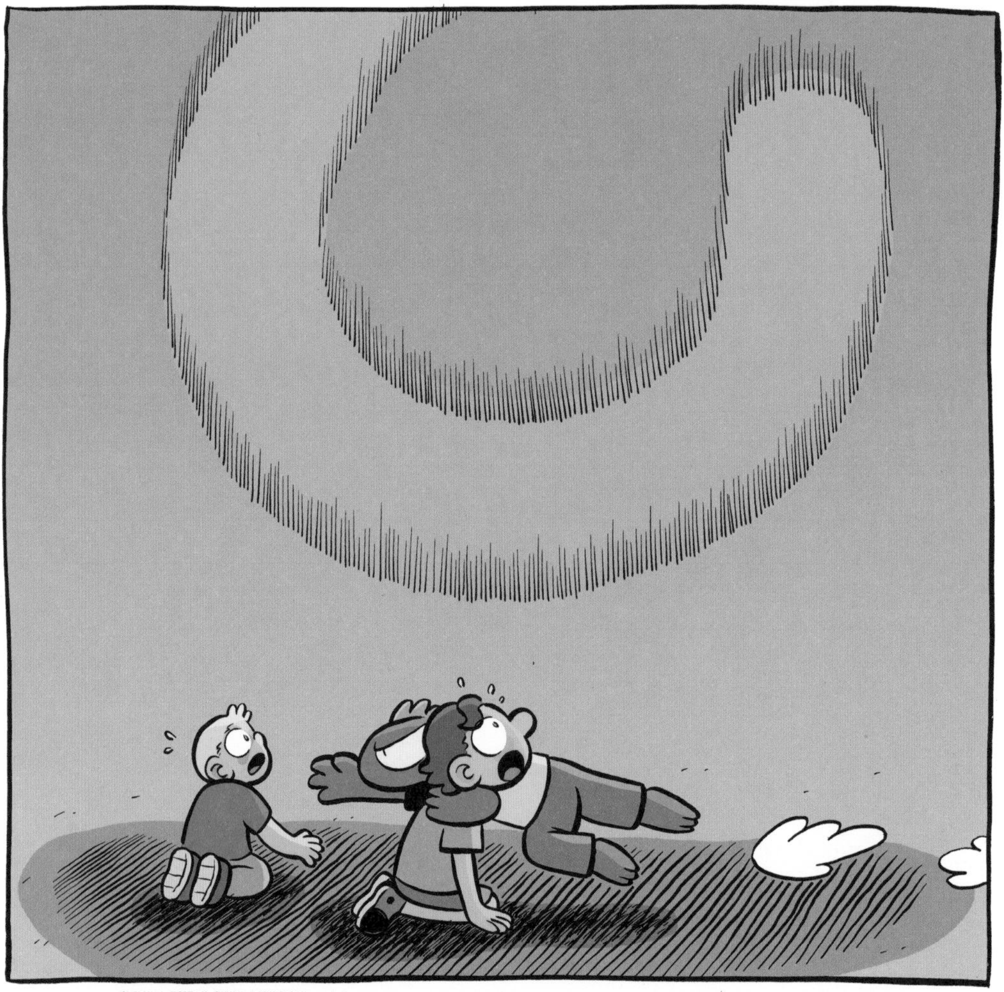

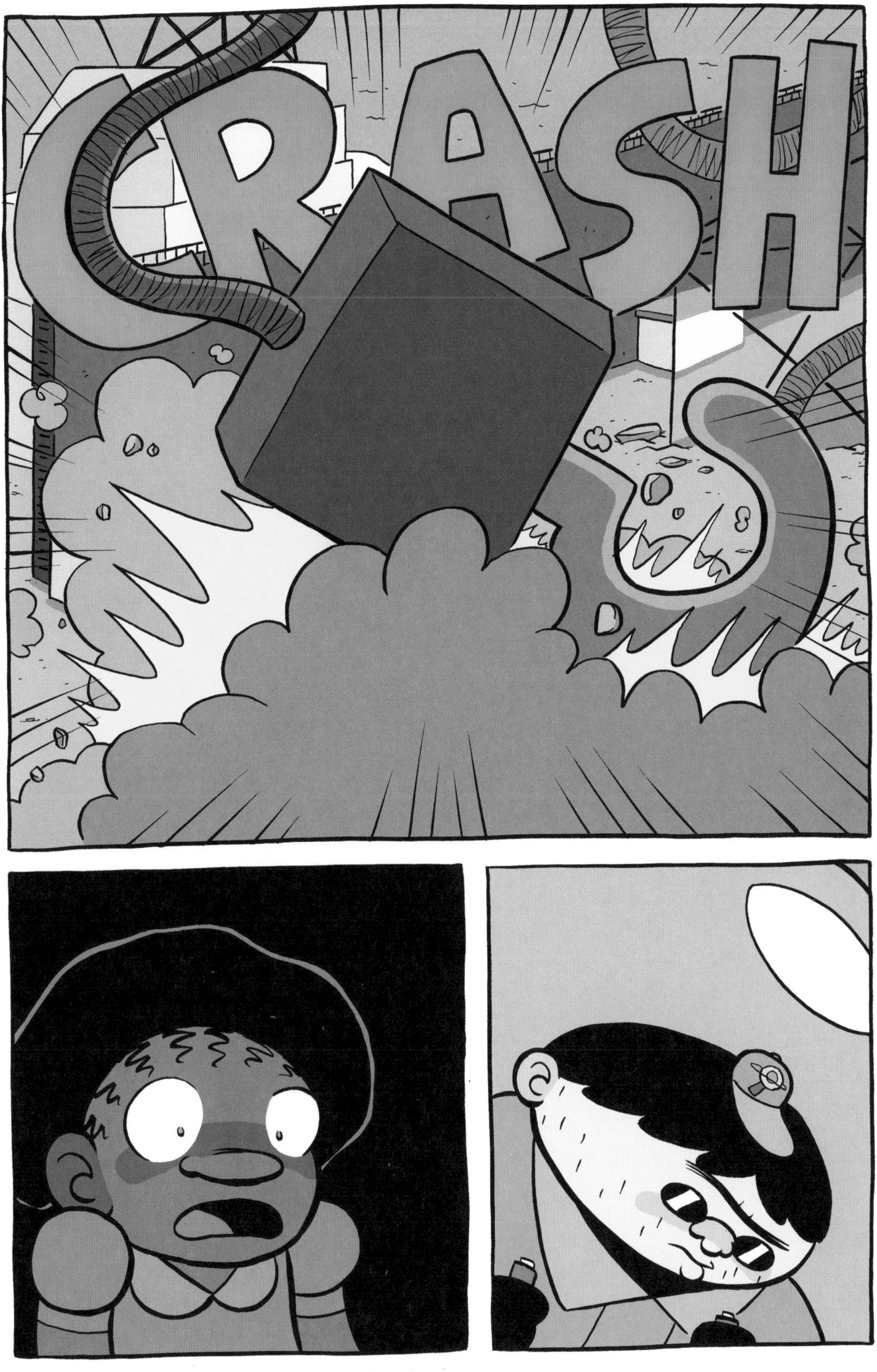
CRASH

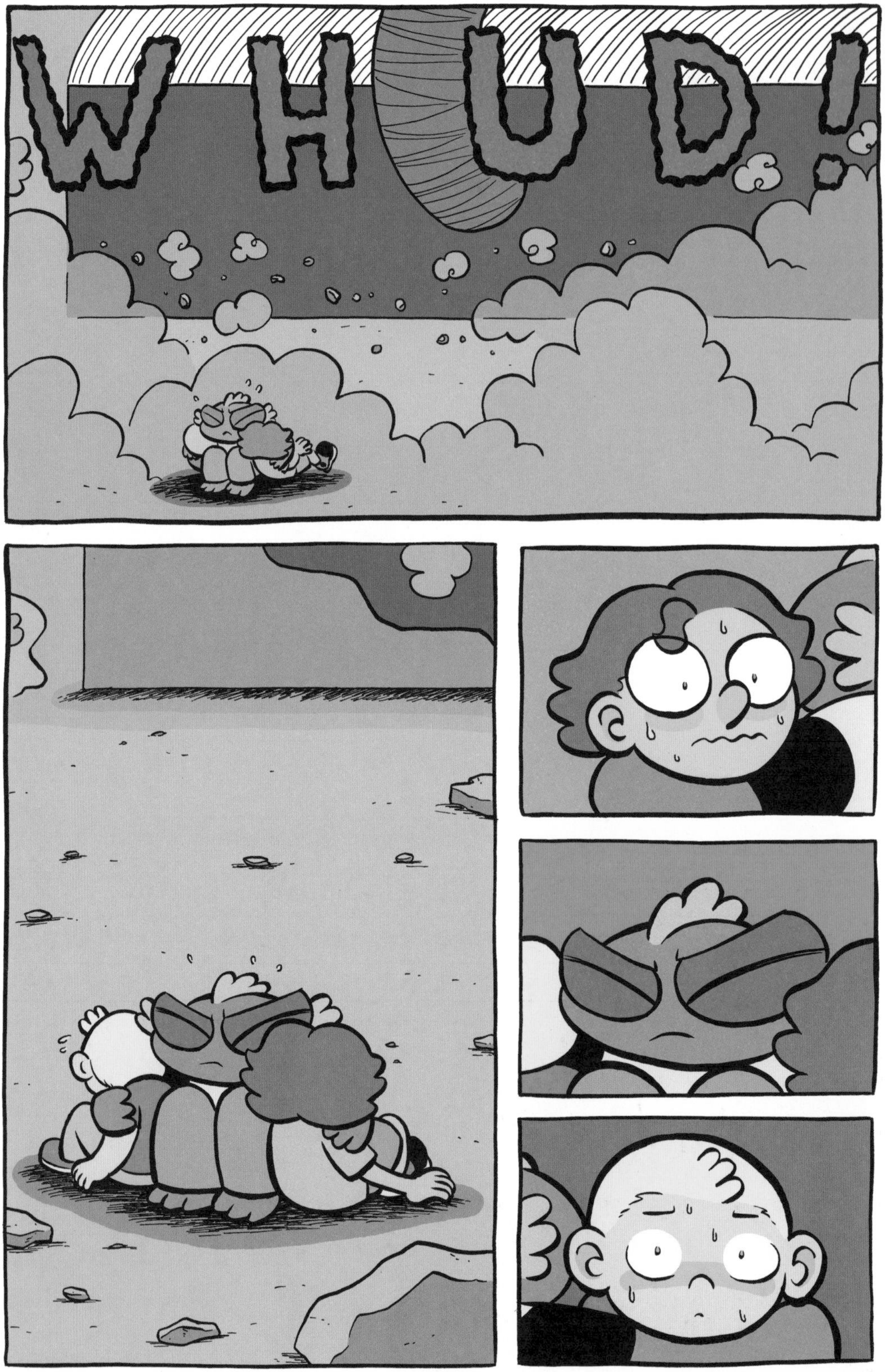
WHUD!

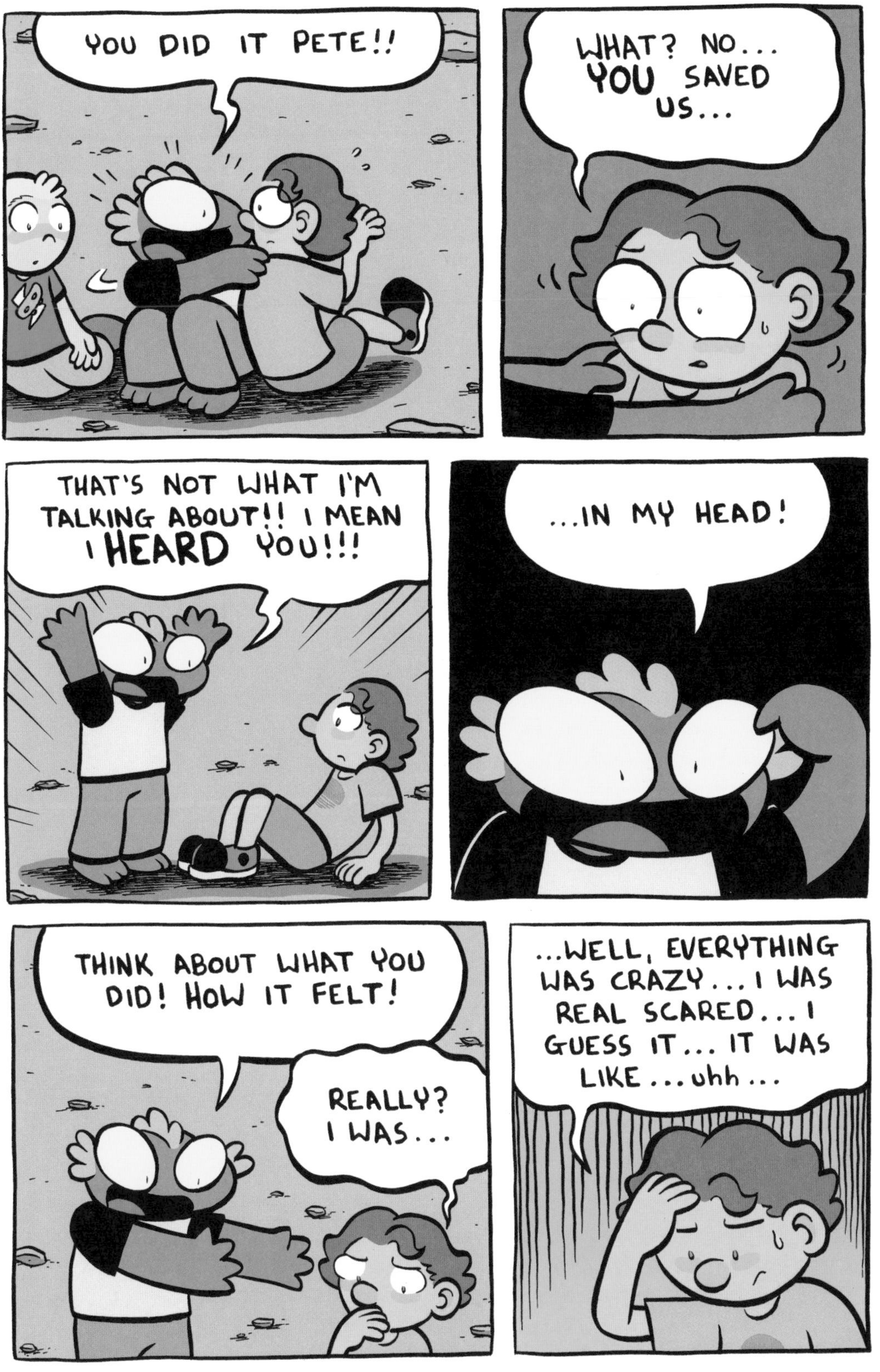
YOU DID IT PETE!!
WHAT? NO... YOU SAVED US...
THAT'S NOT WHAT I'M TALKING ABOUT!! I MEAN I HEARD YOU!!!
...IN MY HEAD!
THINK ABOUT WHAT YOU DID! HOW IT FELT!
REALLY? I WAS...
...WELL, EVERYTHING WAS CRAZY... I WAS REAL SCARED... I GUESS IT... IT WAS LIKE... uhh...

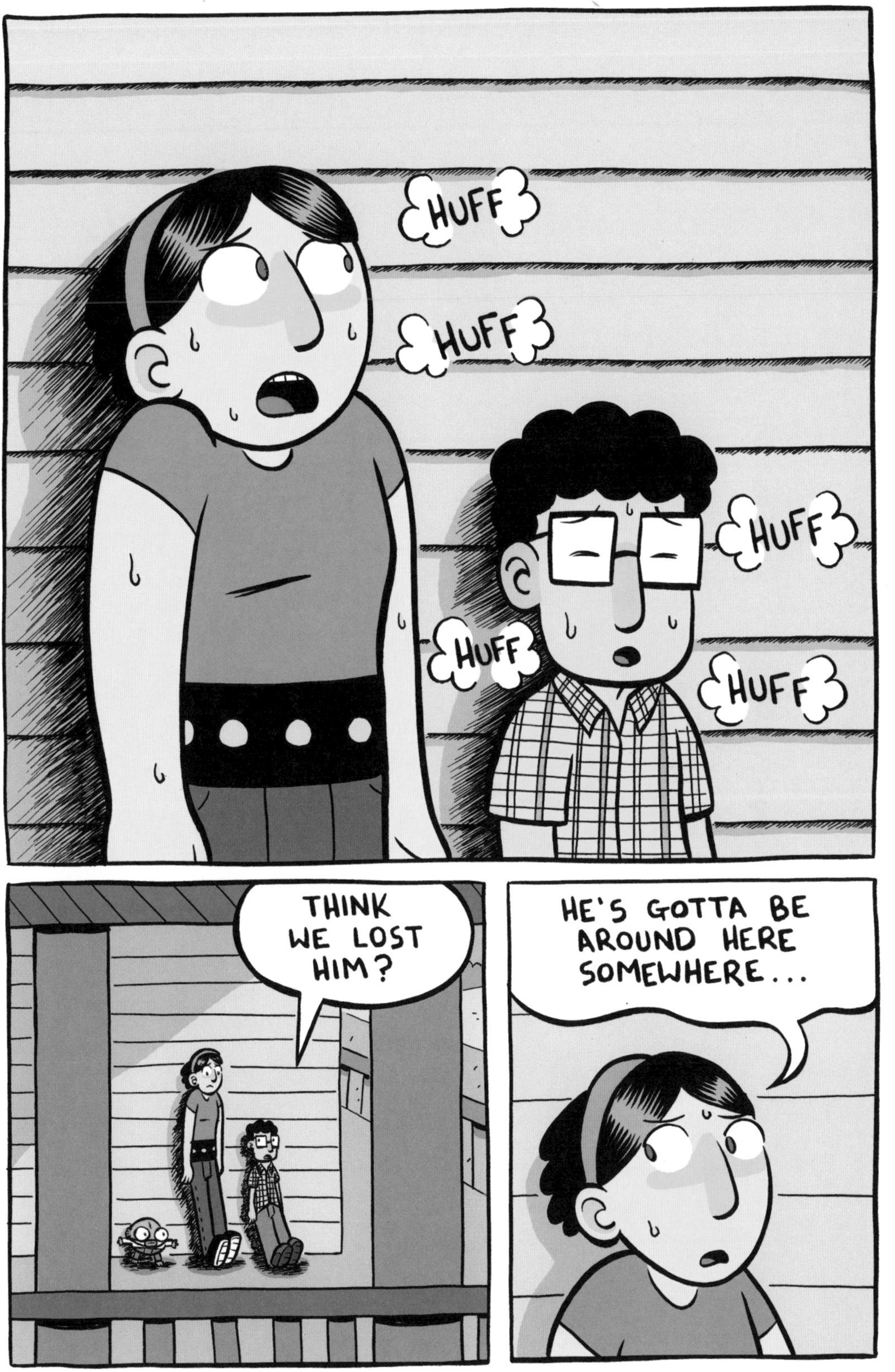
HUFF
HUFF
HUFF
HUFF
HUFF
THINK WE LOST HIM?
HE'S GOTTA BE AROUND HERE SOMEWHERE...

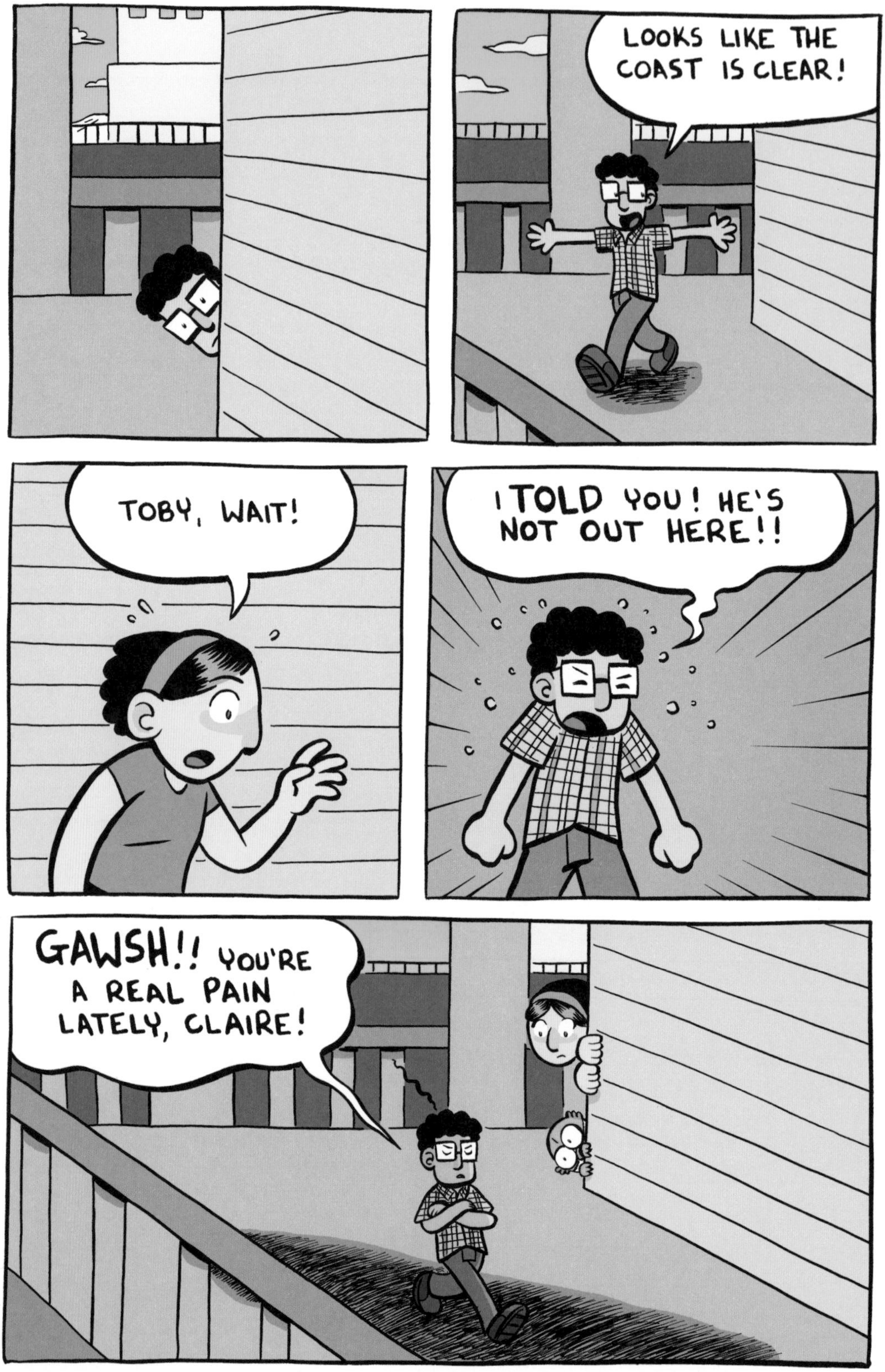
LOOKS LIKE THE COAST IS CLEAR!
TOBY, WAIT!
I TOLD YOU! HE'S NOT OUT HERE!!
GAWSH!! YOU'RE A REAL PAIN LATELY, CLAIRE!

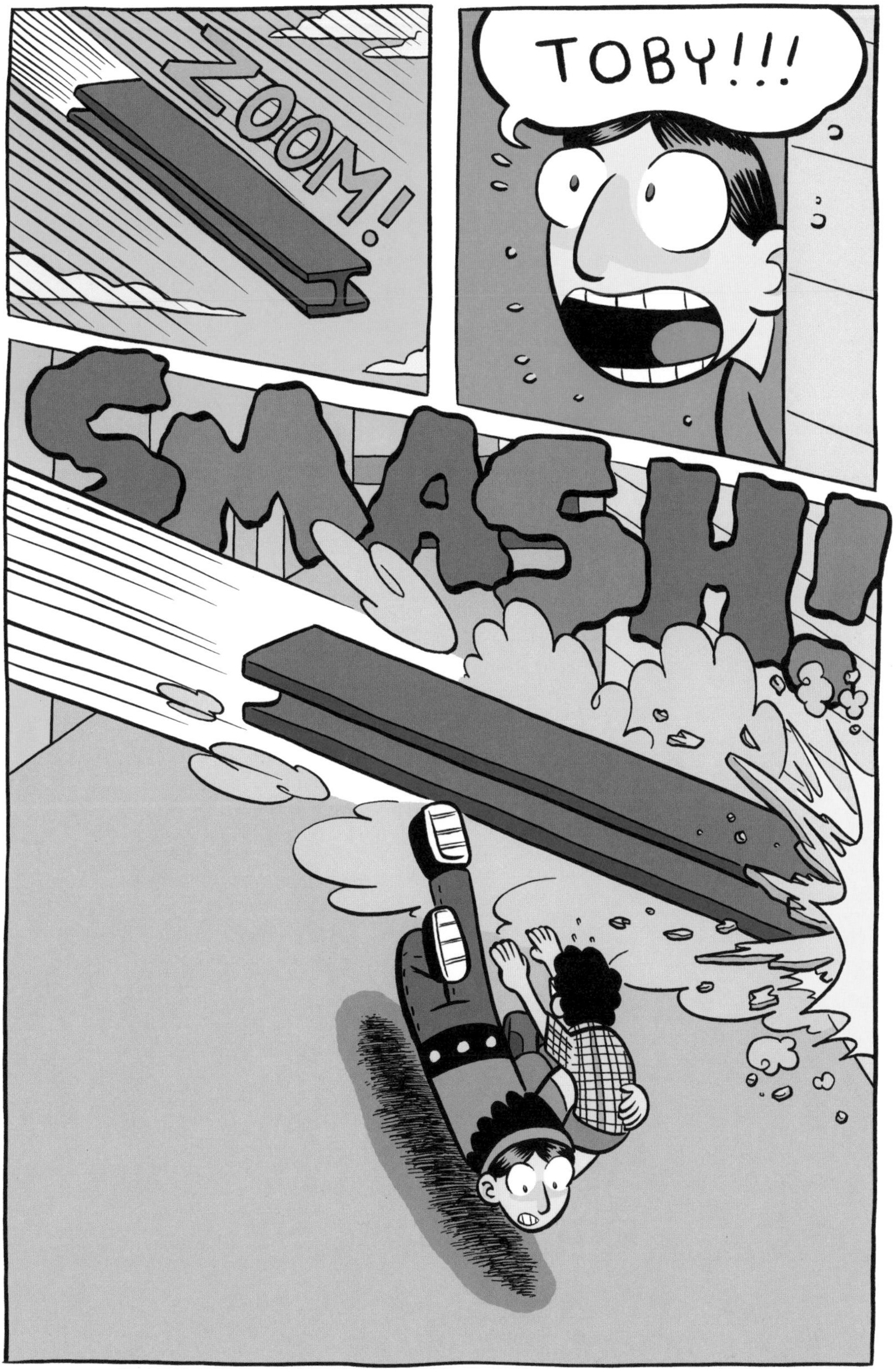
ZOOM!
TOBY!!!
SMASH!

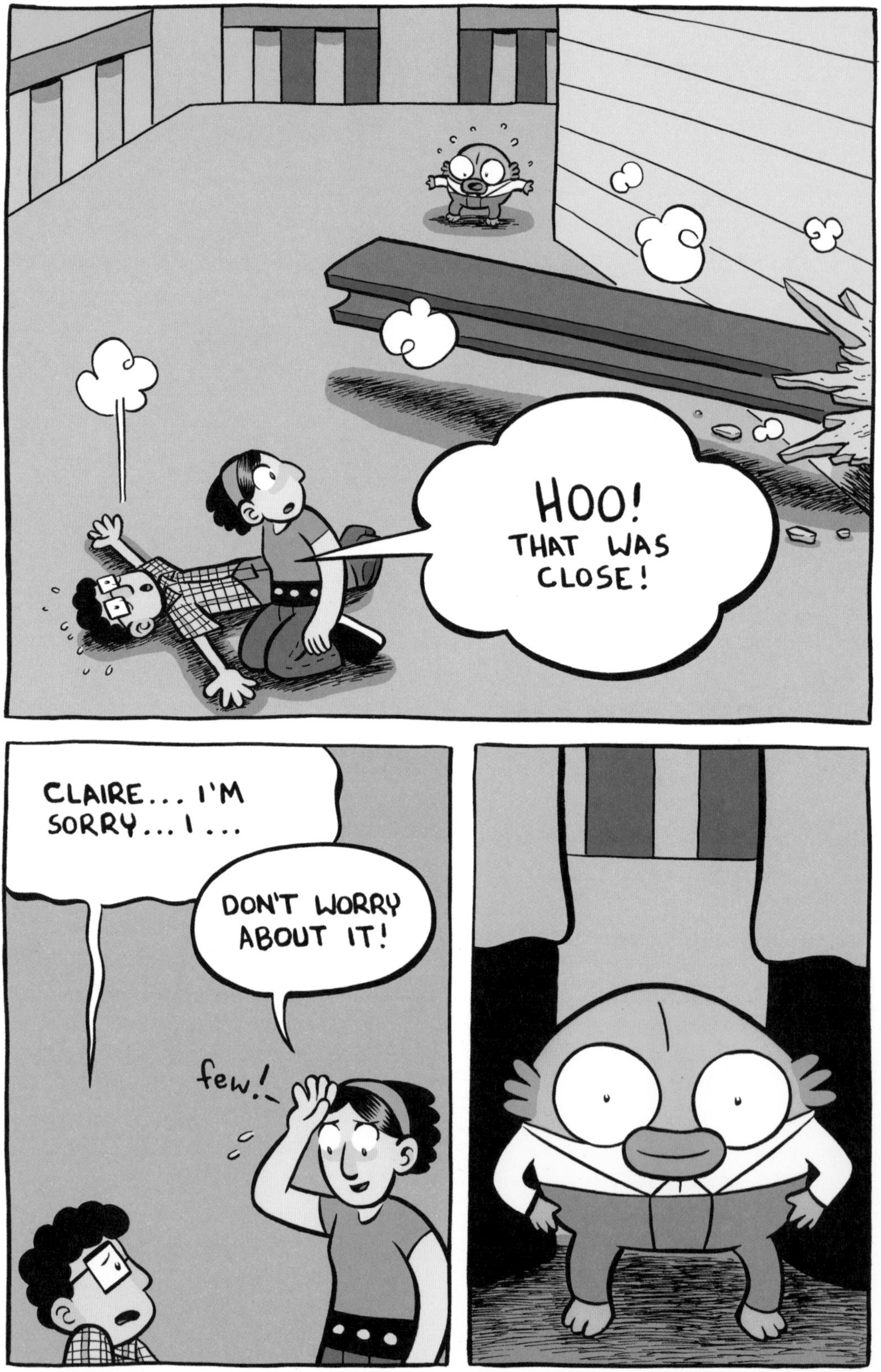
HOO! THAT WAS CLOSE!
CLAIRE... I'M SORRY... I...
DON'T WORRY ABOUT IT!
few!

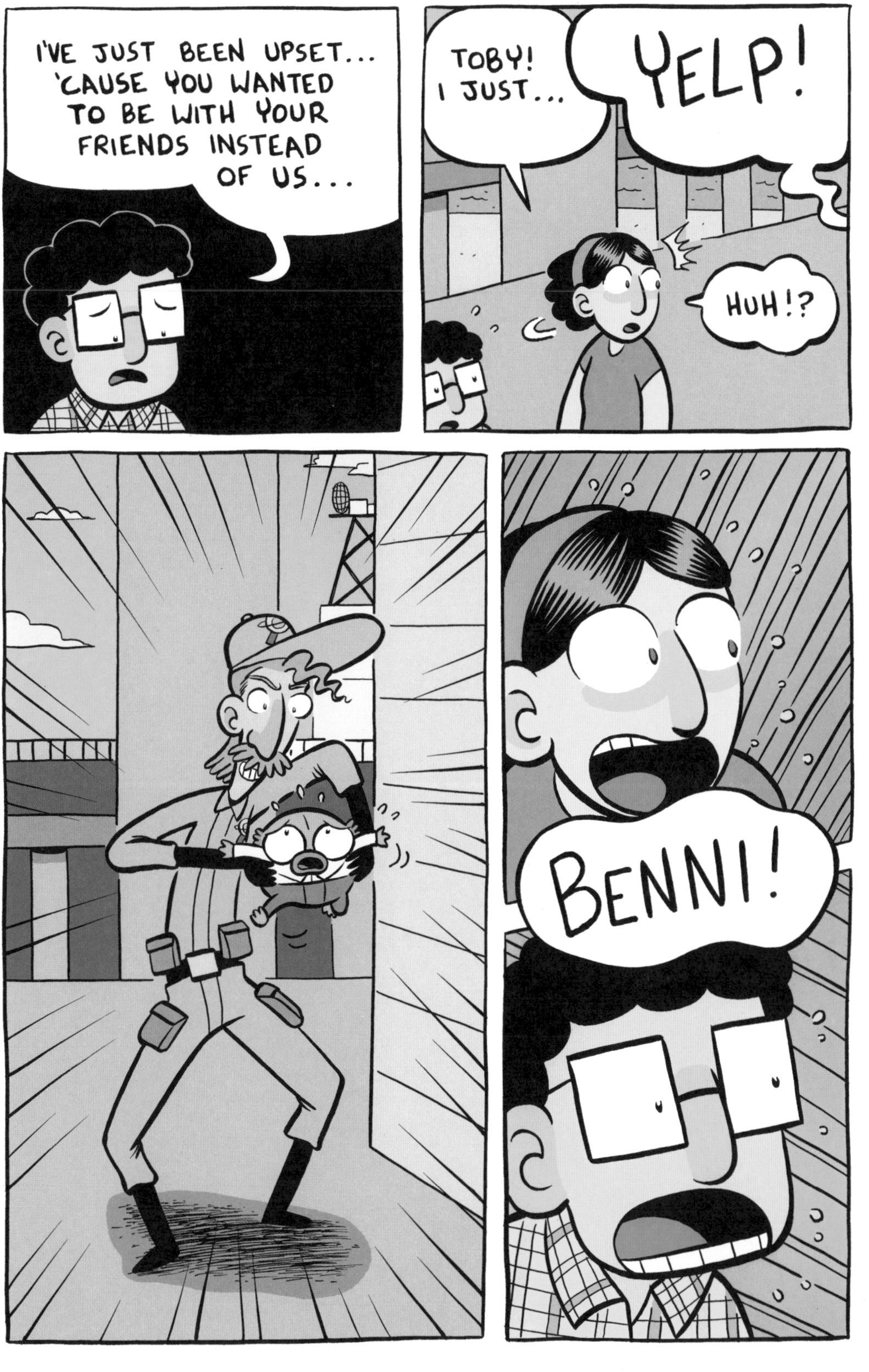
I'VE JUST BEEN UPSET... 'CAUSE YOU WANTED TO BE WITH YOUR FRIENDS INSTEAD OF US...
TOBY! I JUST...
YELP!
HUH!?
BENNI!

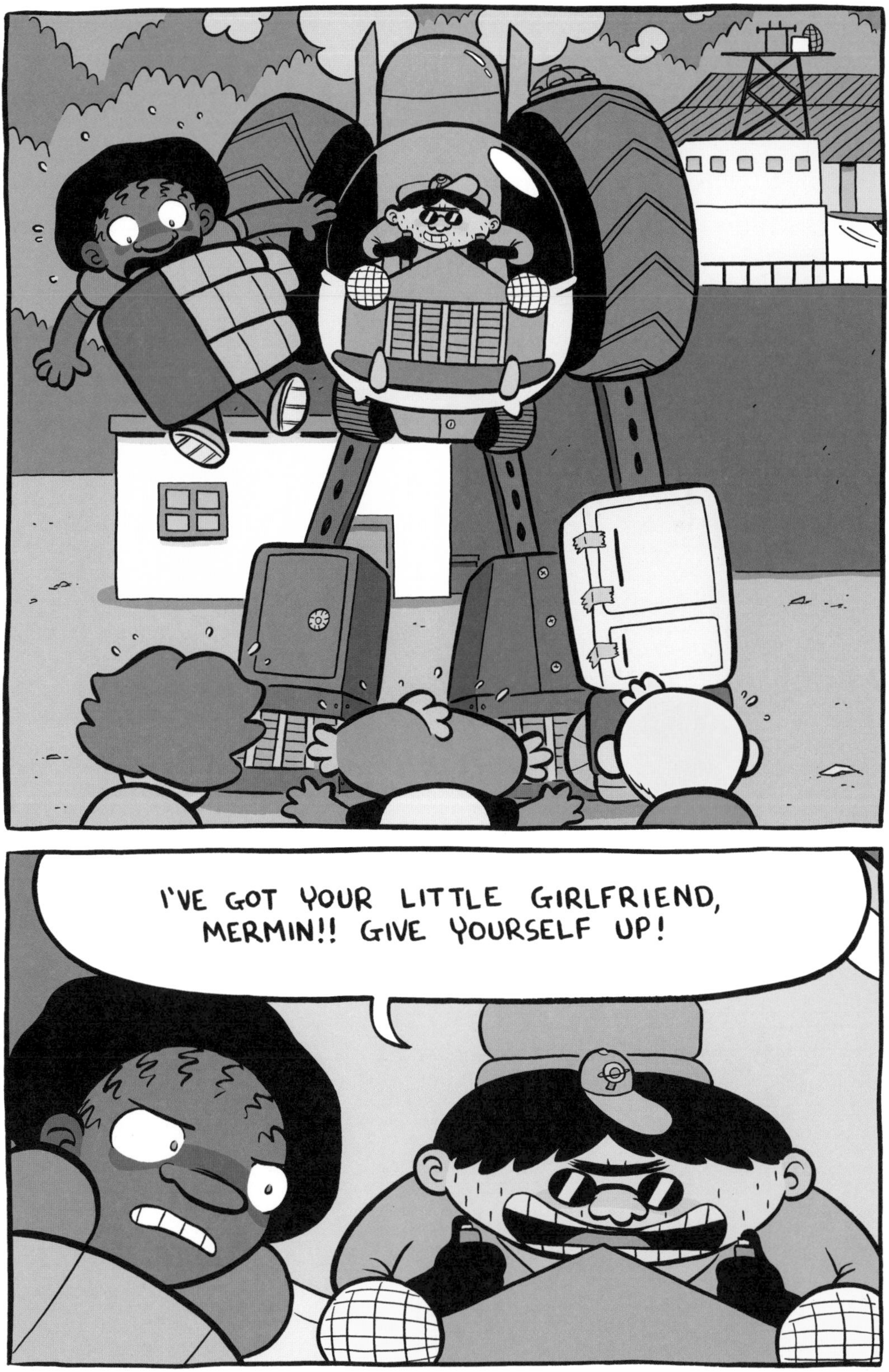
I'VE GOT YOUR LITTLE GIRLFRIEND, MERMIN!! GIVE YOURSELF UP!

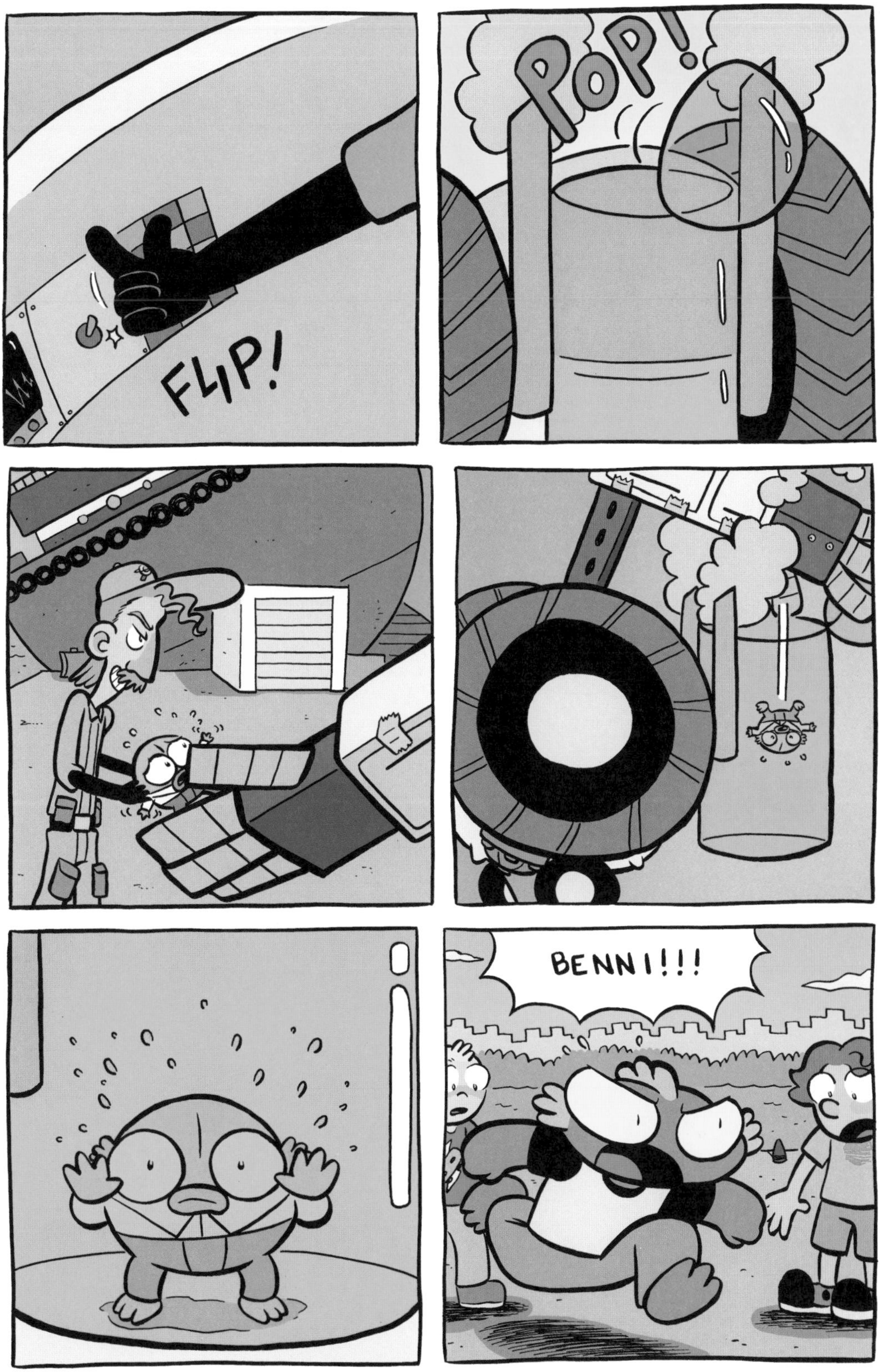
FLIP!
POP!
BENNI!!!

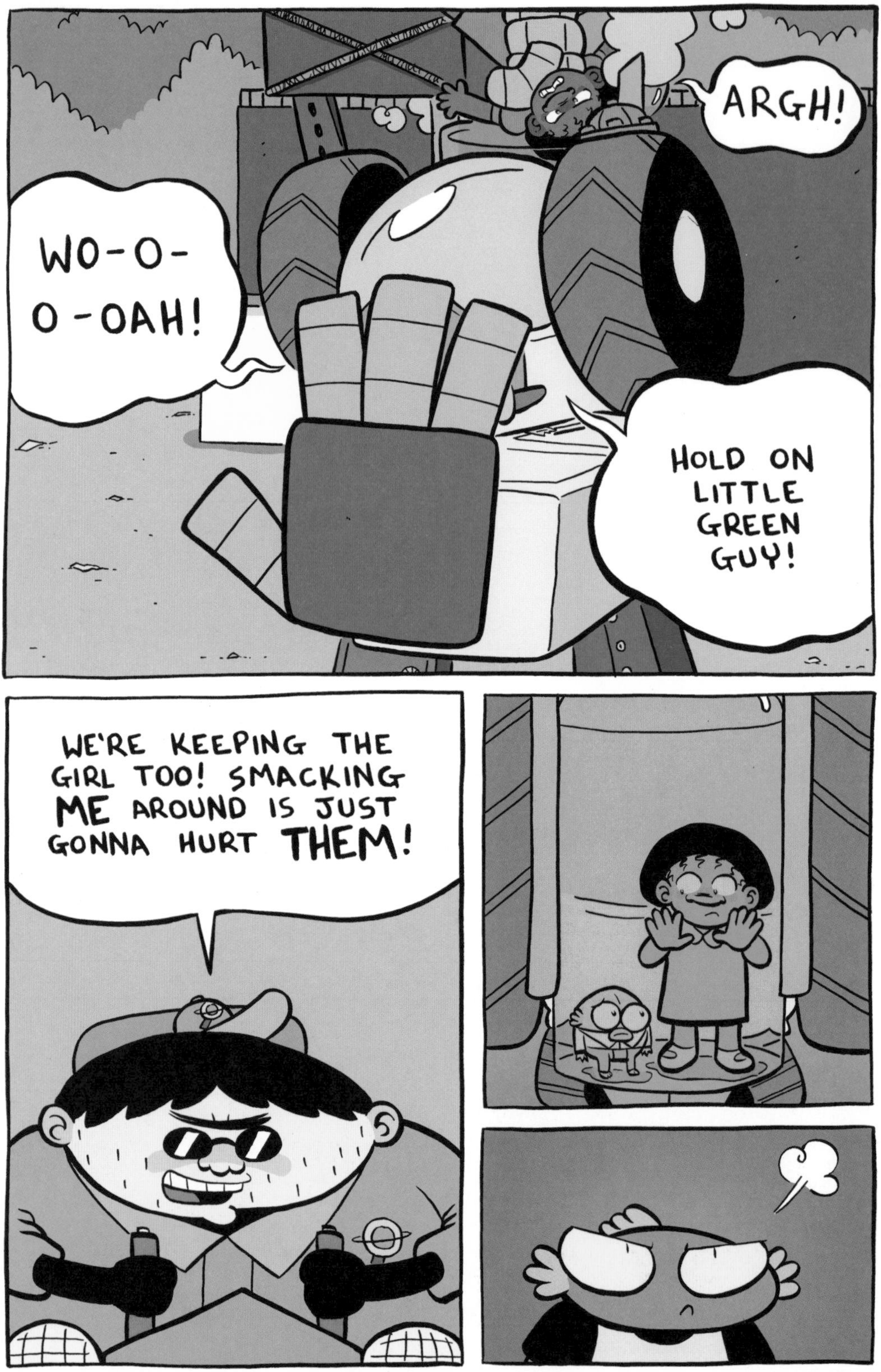
ARGH!
WO-O-O-OAH!
HOLD ON LITTLE GREEN GUY!
WE'RE KEEPING THE GIRL TOO! SMACKING ME AROUND IS JUST GONNA HURT THEM!

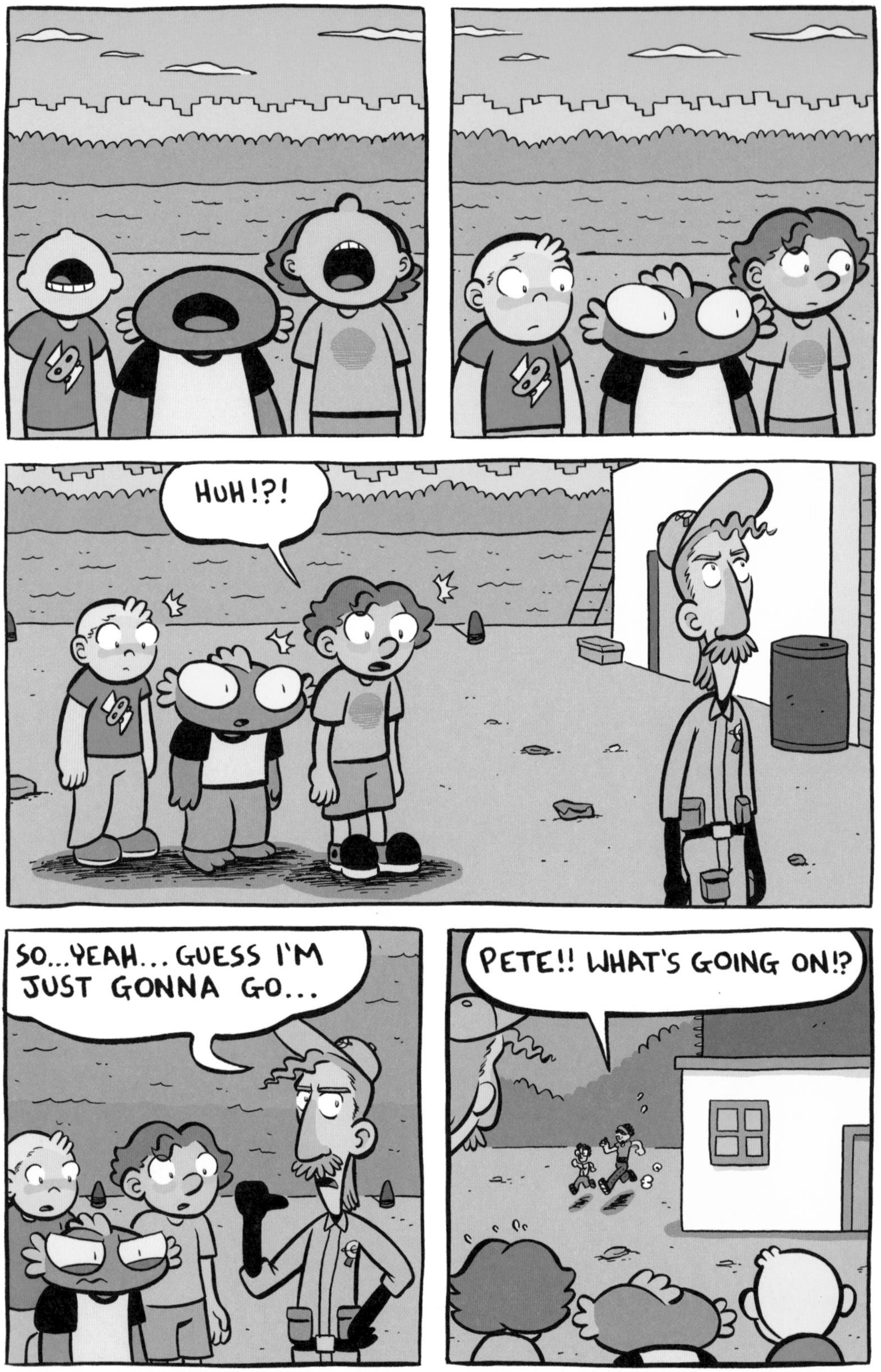
HUH!?!
SO...YEAH... GUESS I'M JUST GONNA GO...
PETE!! WHAT'S GOING ON!?

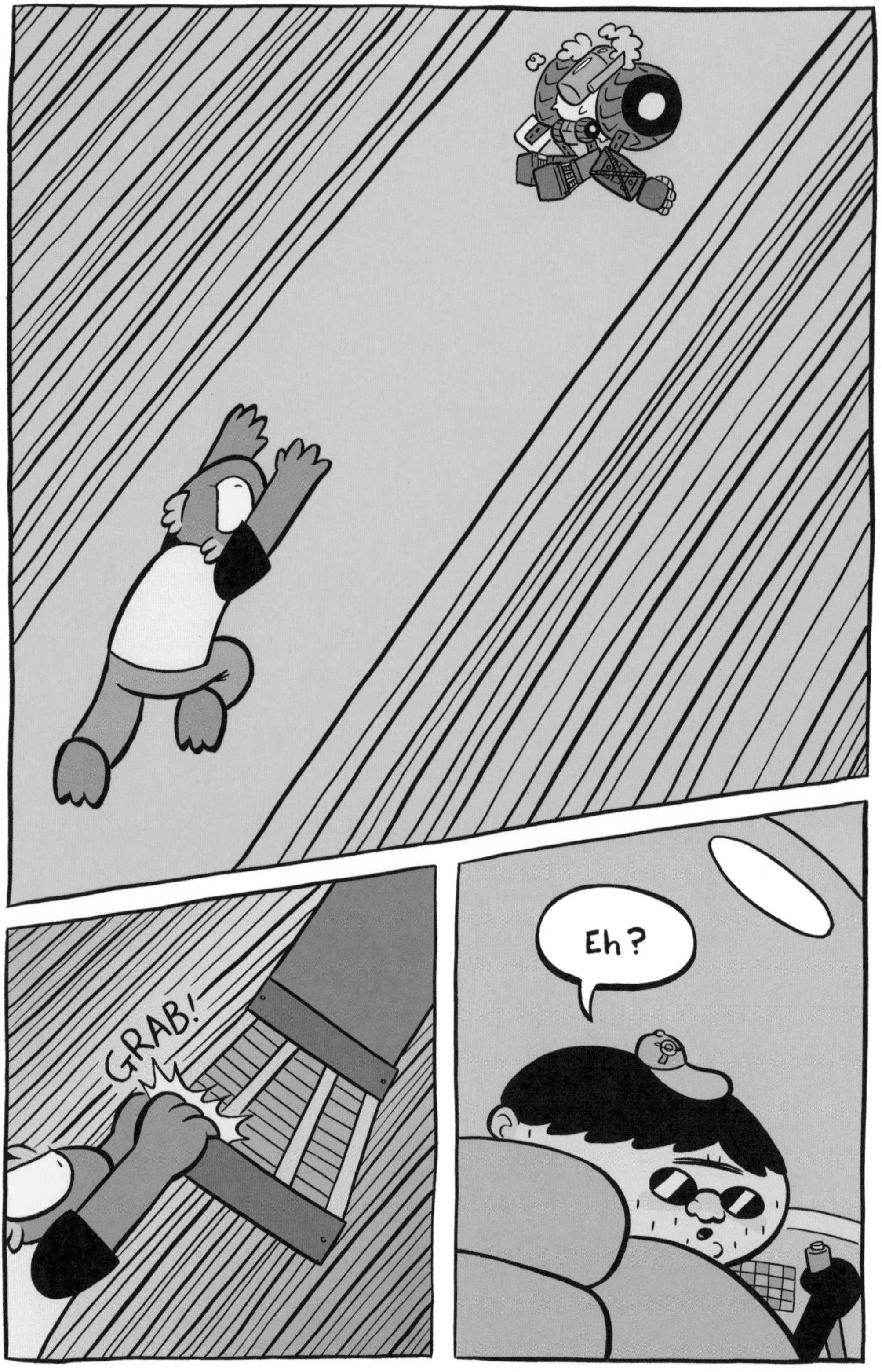
GRAB!
Eh?

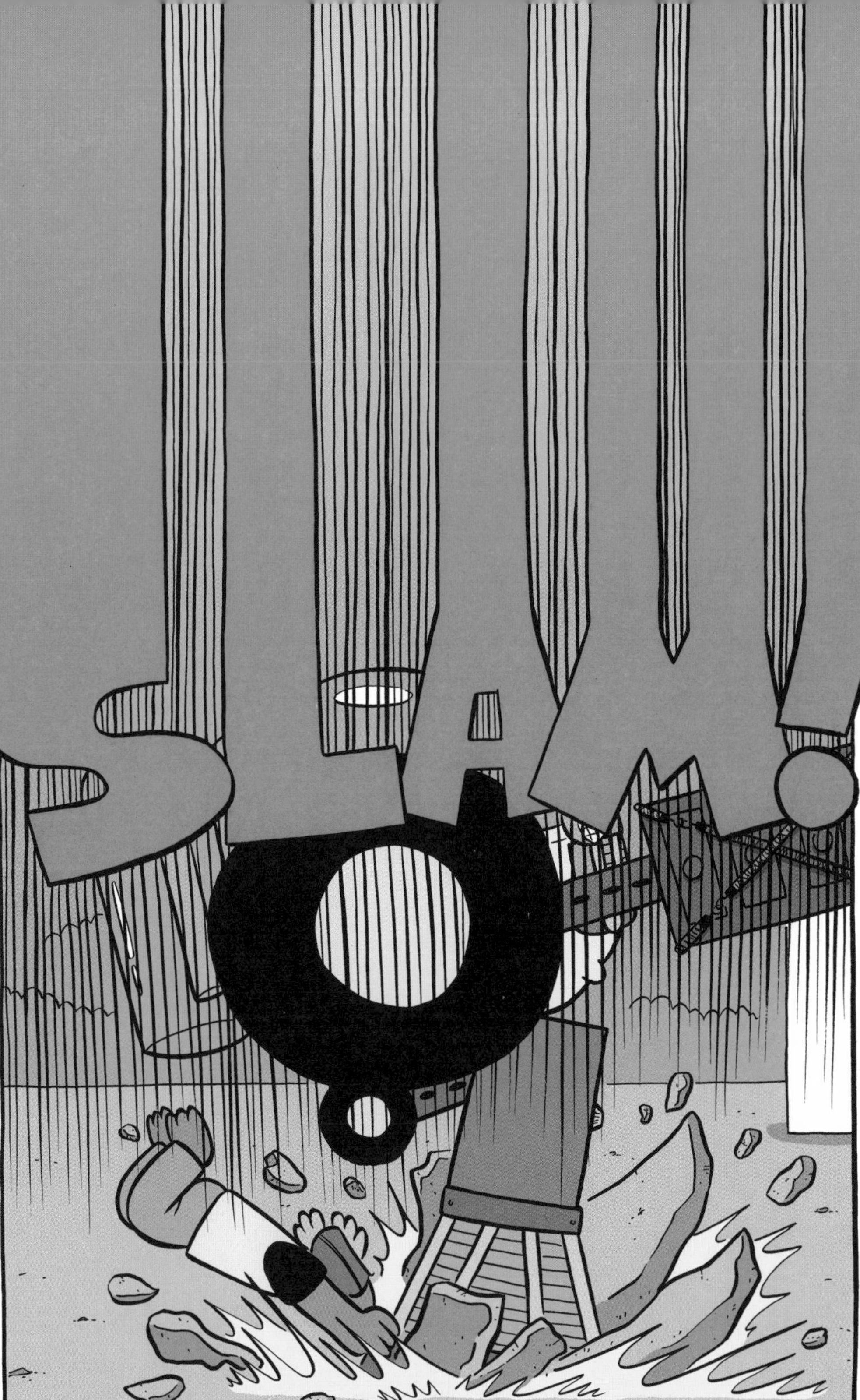
SLAM!

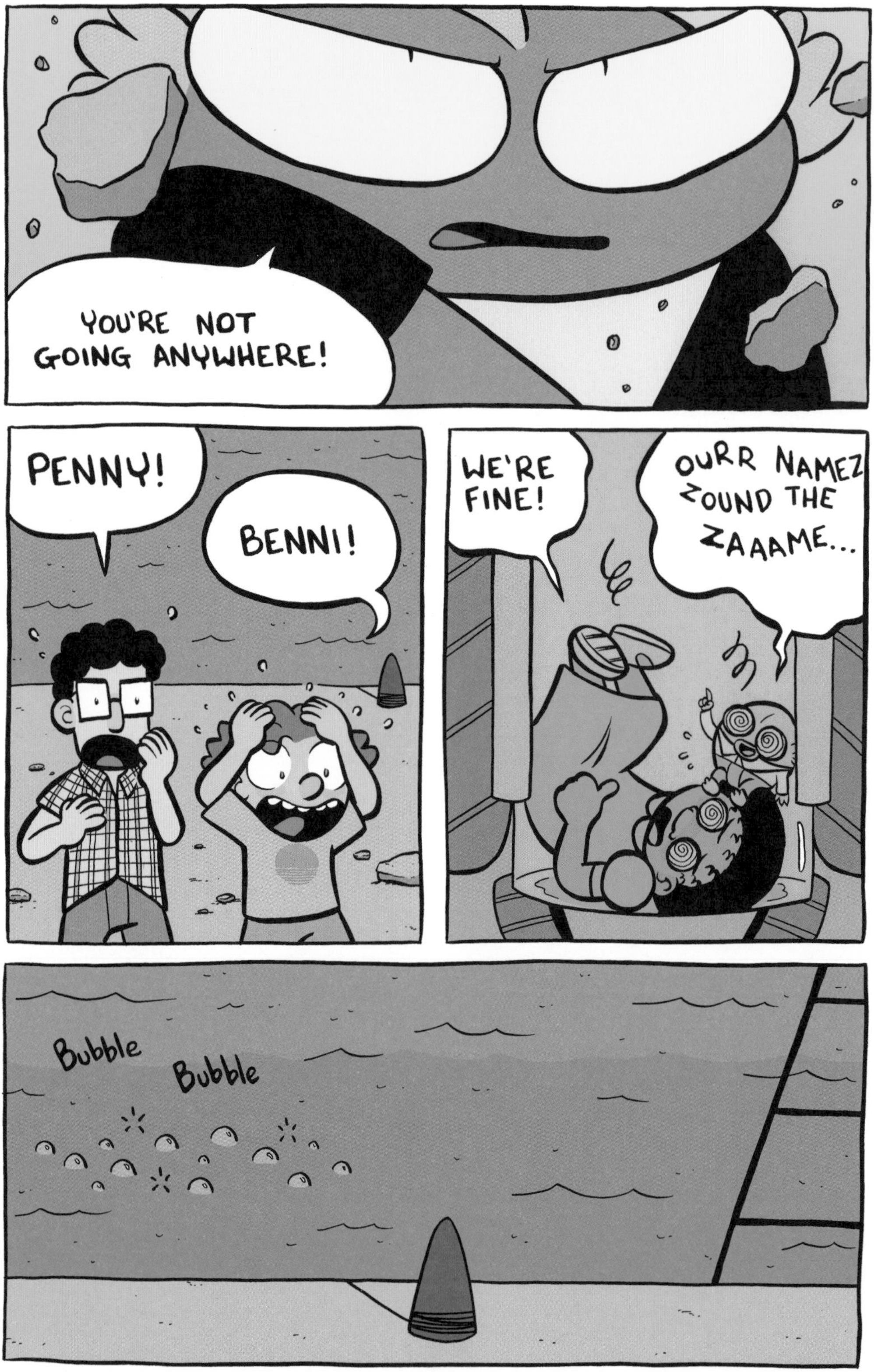
YOU'RE NOT GOING ANYWHERE!
PENNY!
BENNI!
WE'RE FINE!
OURR NAMEZ ZOUND THE ZAAAME...
Bubble
Bubble

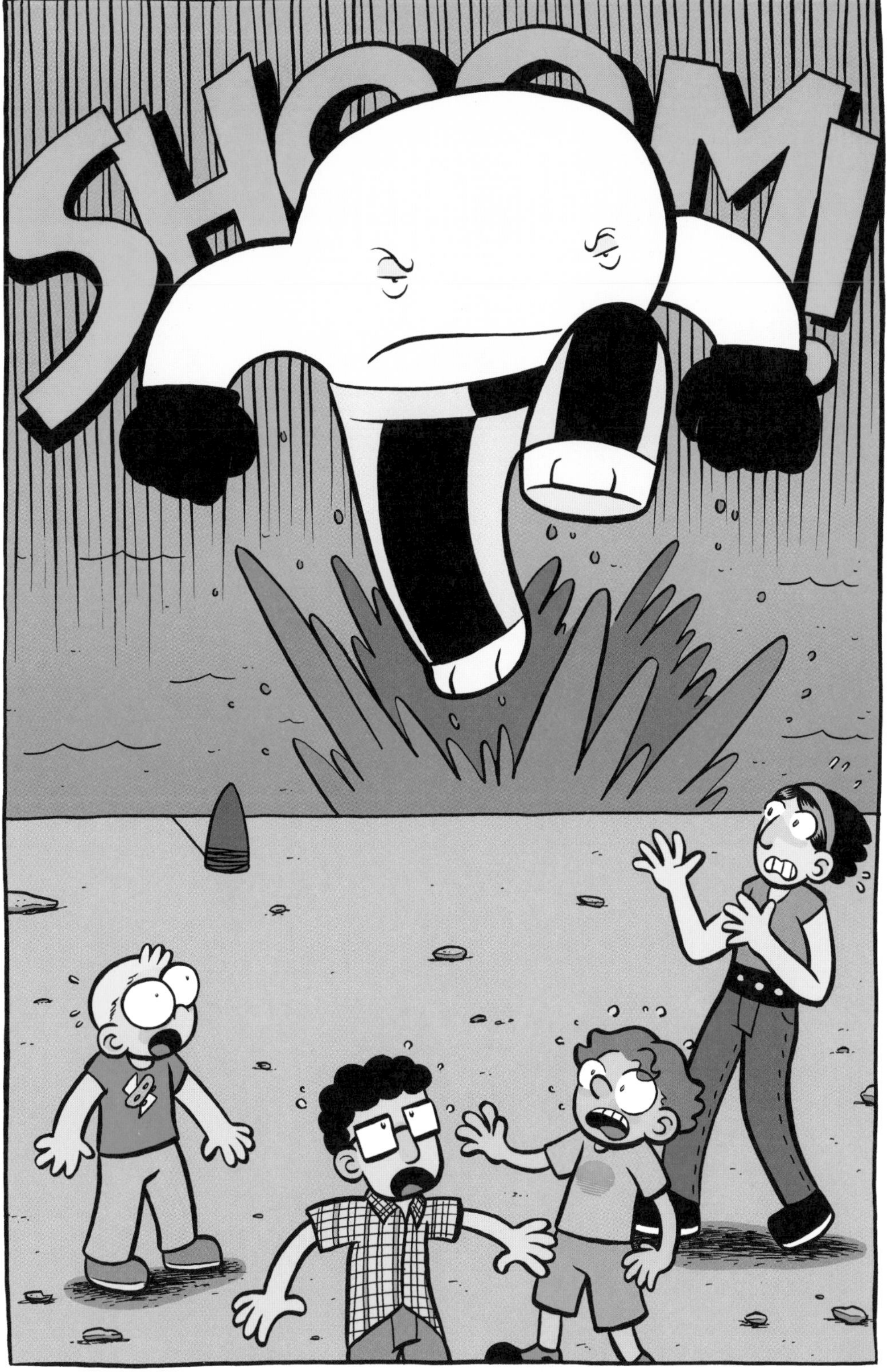
SHOOM!

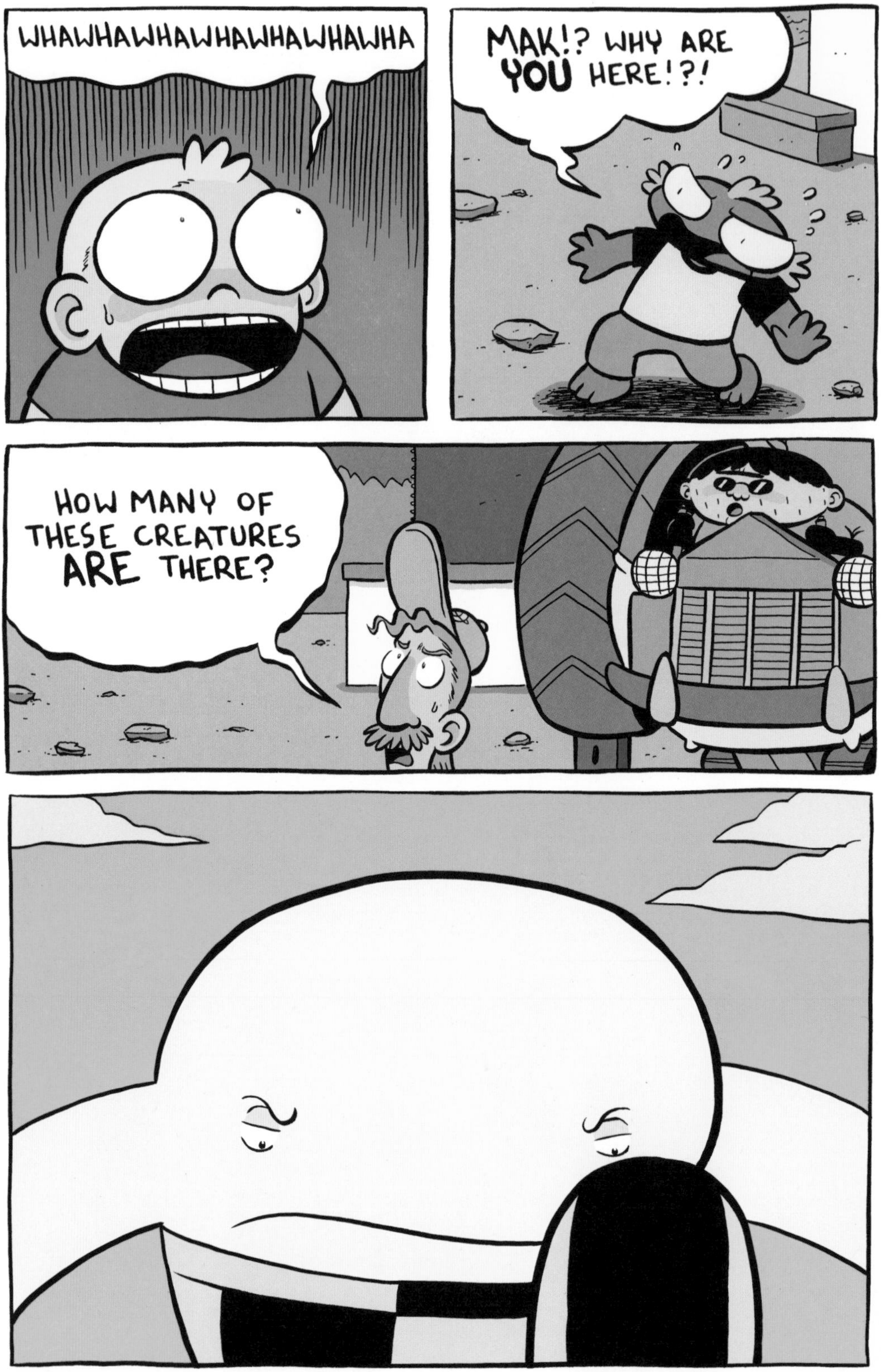
WHAWHAWHAWHAWHAWHAWHA
MAK!? WHY ARE YOU HERE!?!
HOW MANY OF THESE CREATURES ARE THERE?

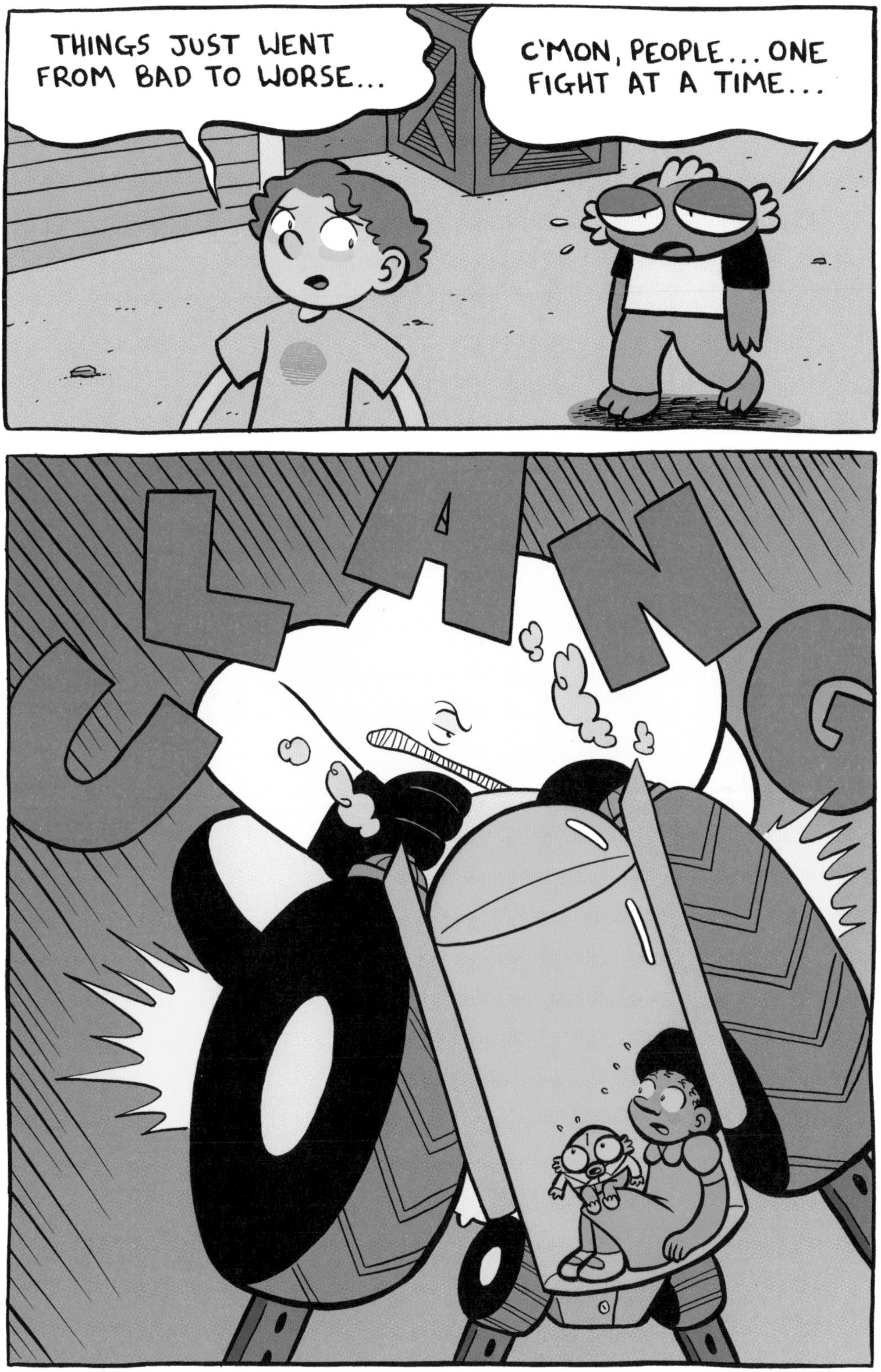
THINGS JUST WENT FROM BAD TO WORSE...
C'MON, PEOPLE... ONE FIGHT AT A TIME...
CLANG

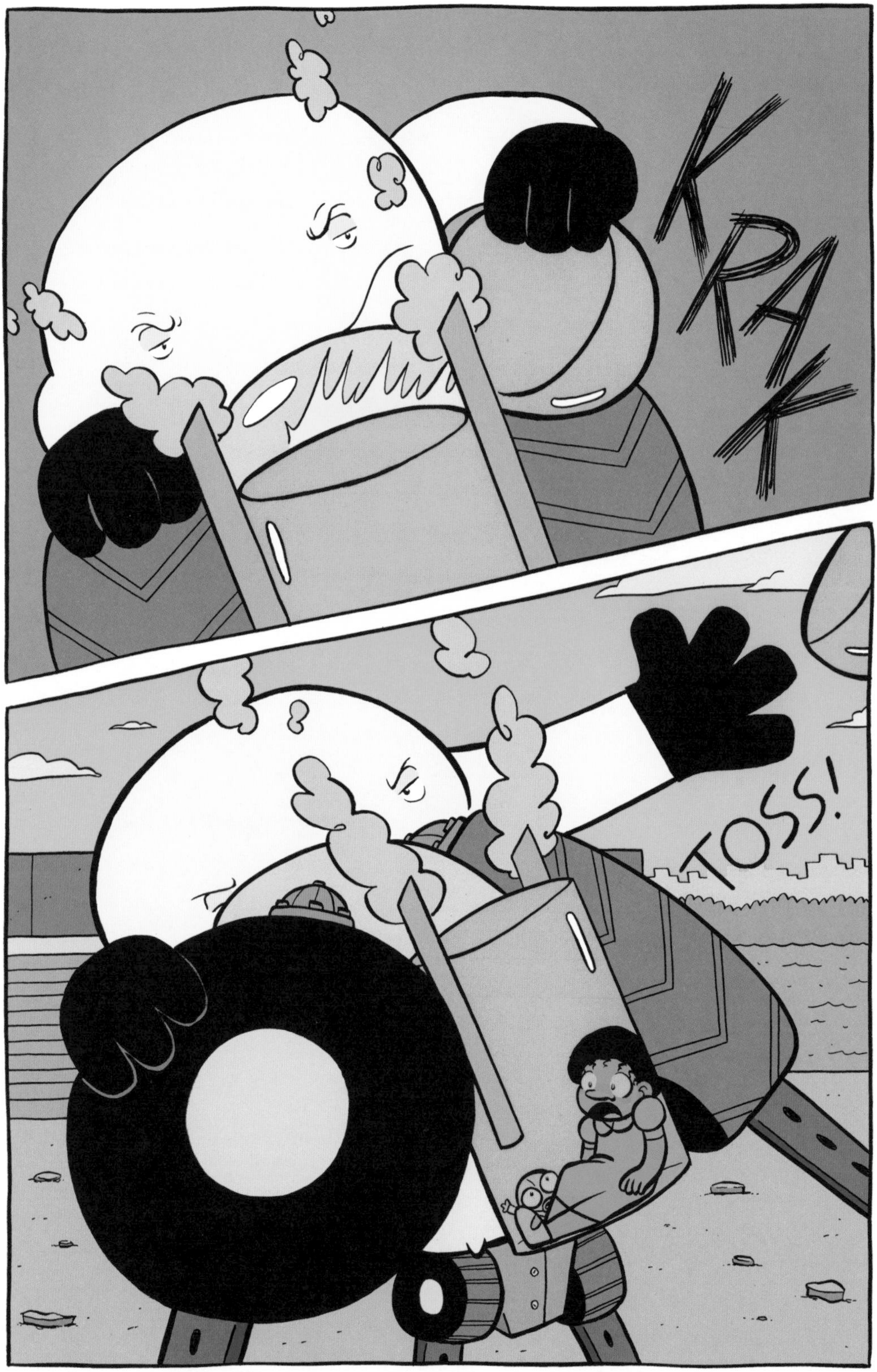
KRAK
TOSS!

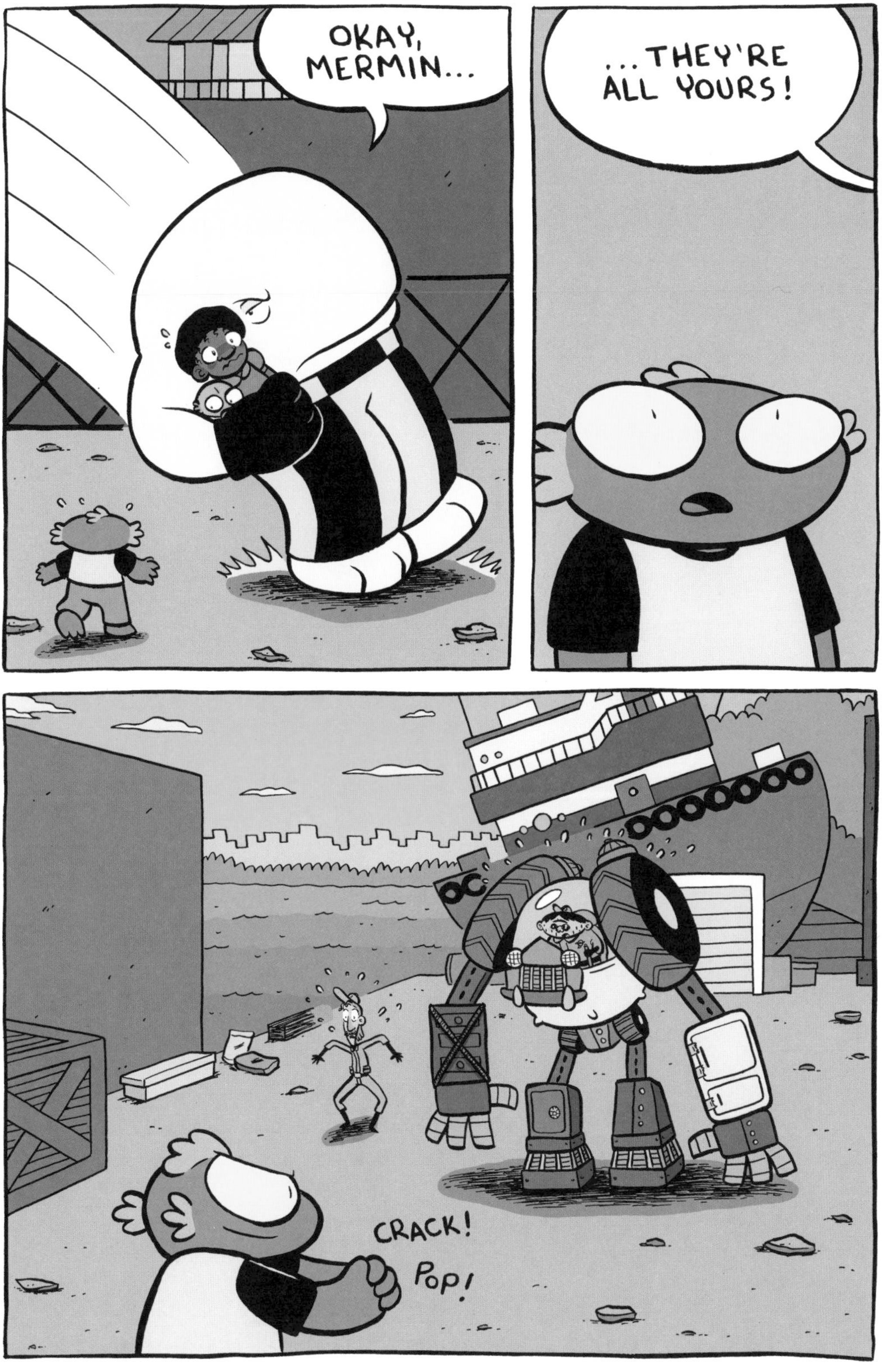
OKAY, MERMIN...
...THEY'RE ALL YOURS!
CRACK!
POP!

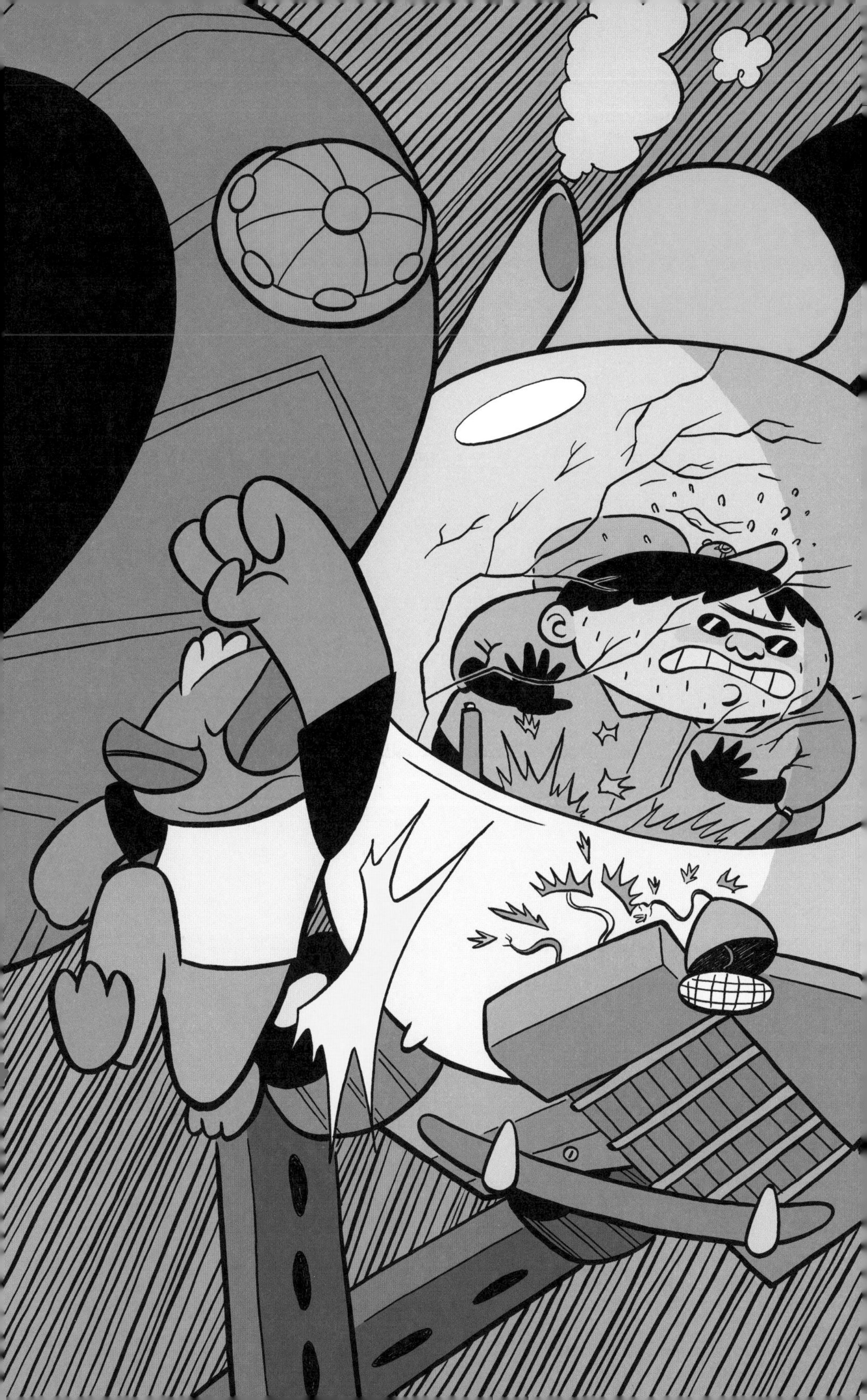

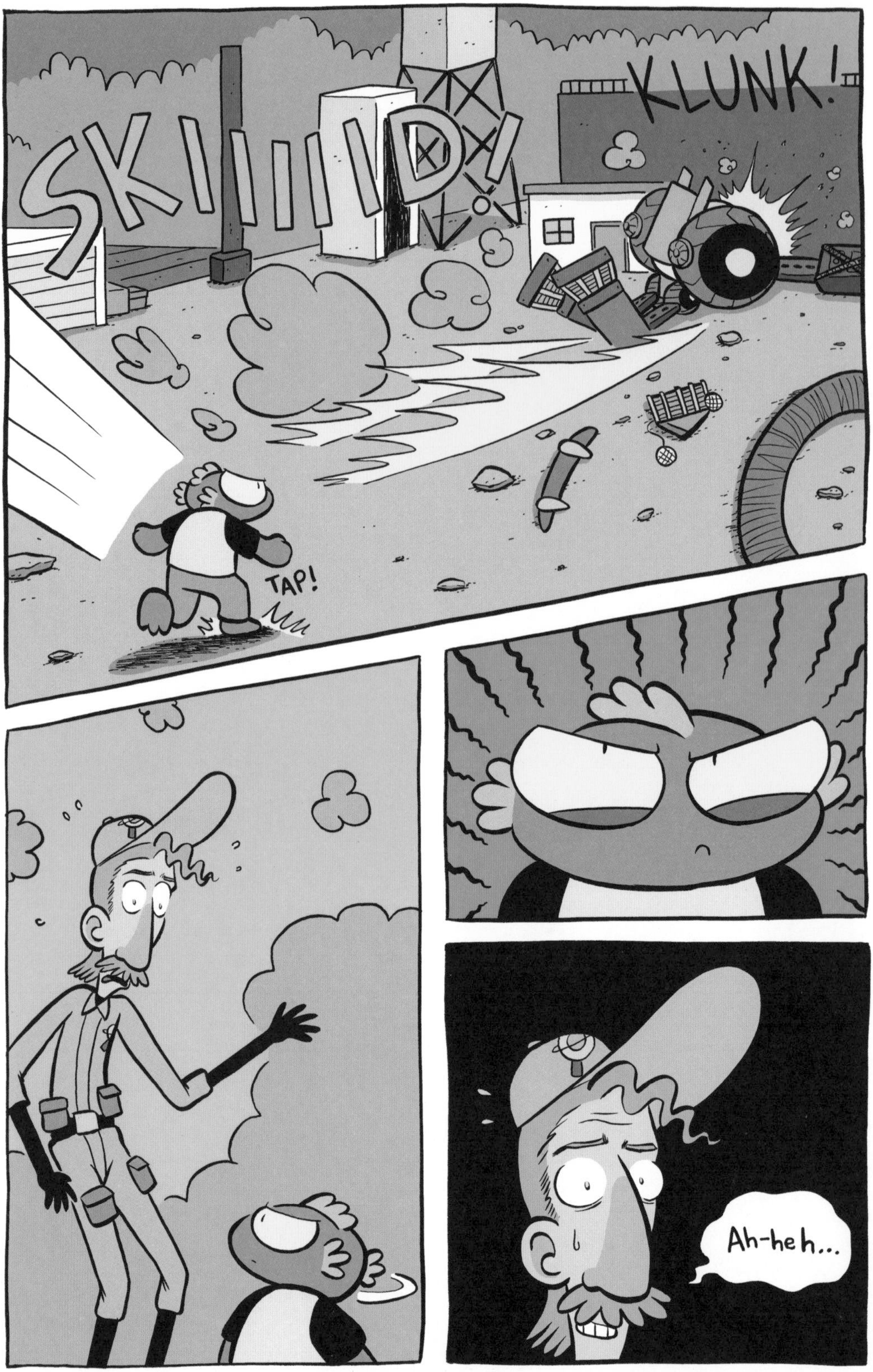
SKIIIIID!
KLUNK!
TAP!
Ah-heh...

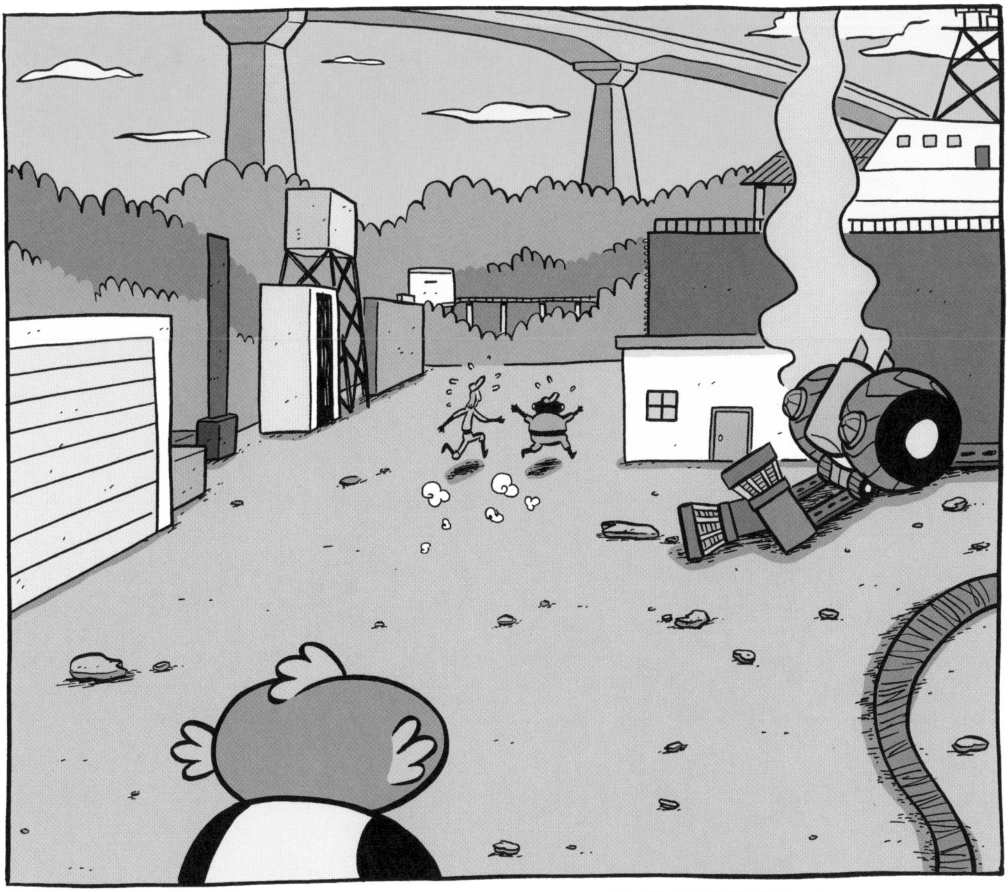

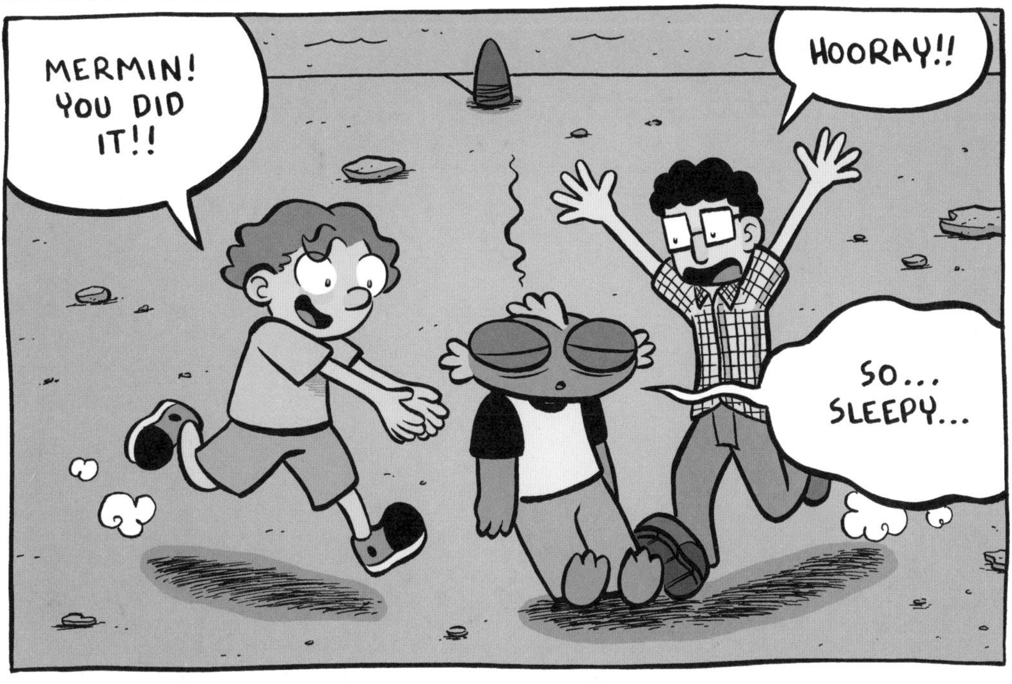
MERMIN! YOU DID IT!!
HOORAY!!
SO... SLEEPY...

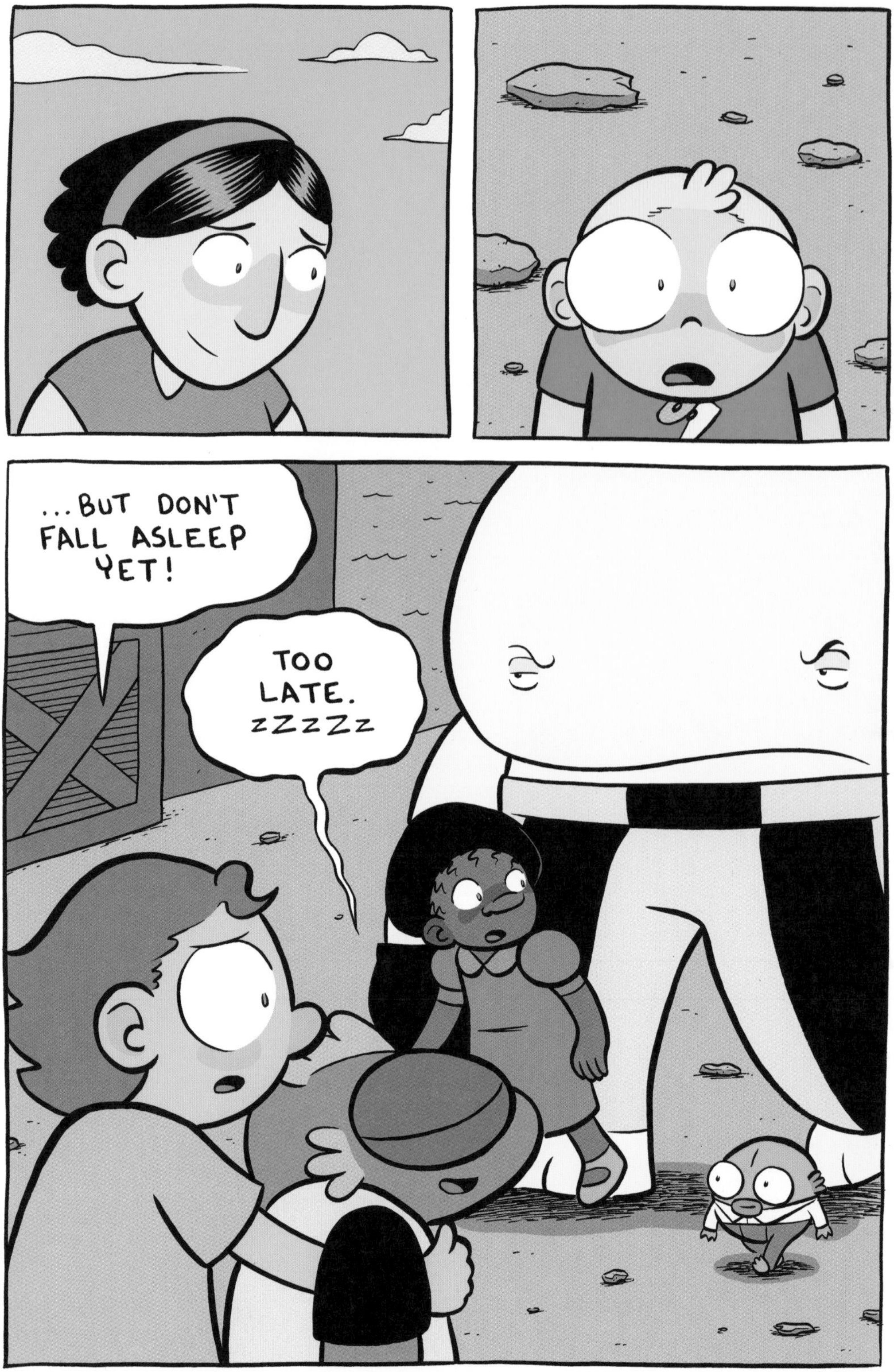
...BUT DON'T FALL ASLEEP YET!
TOO LATE. zZzZz

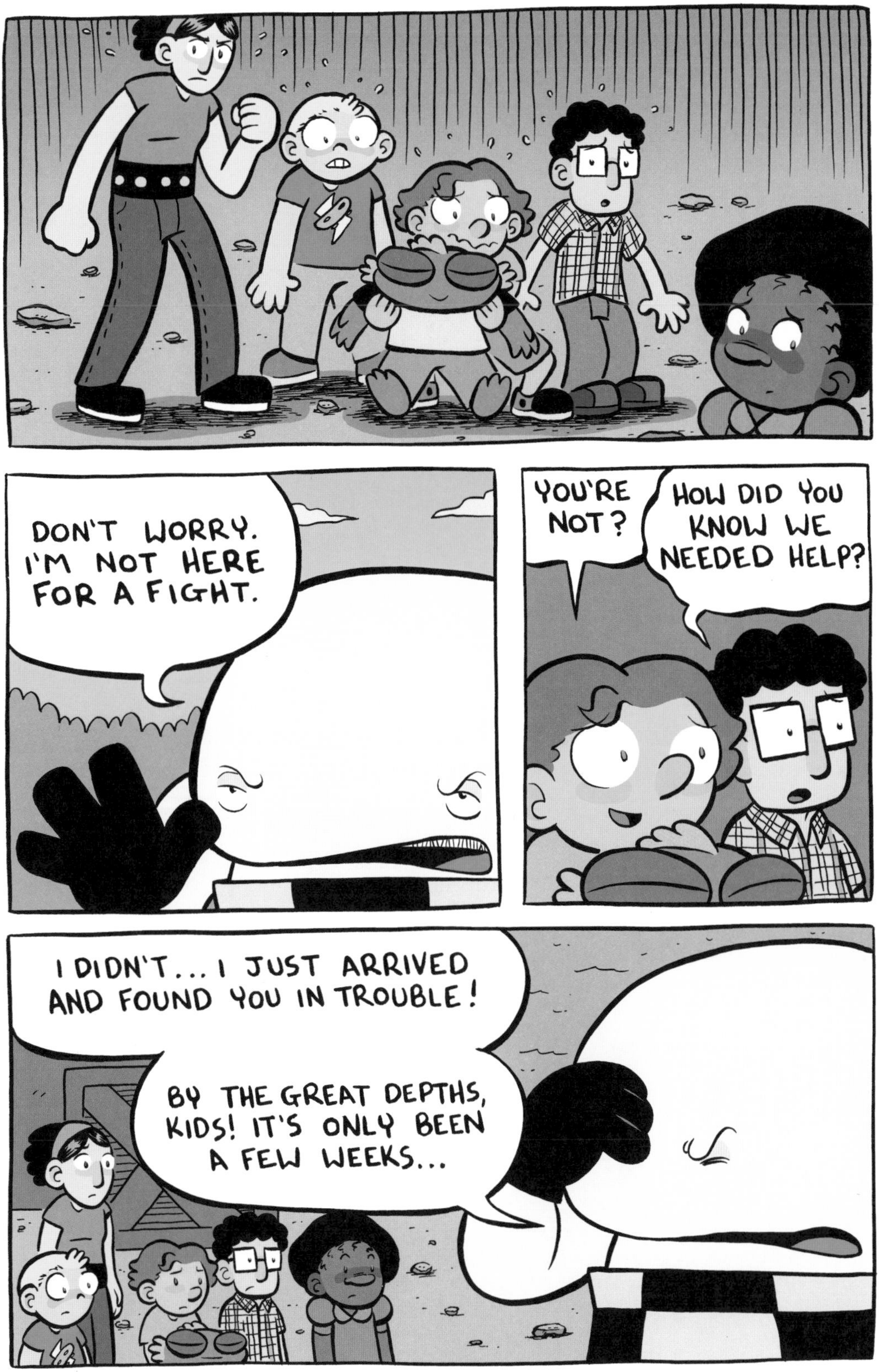
DON'T WORRY. I'M NOT HERE FOR A FIGHT.
YOU'RE NOT?
HOW DID YOU KNOW WE NEEDED HELP?
I DIDN'T... I JUST ARRIVED AND FOUND YOU IN TROUBLE!
BY THE GREAT DEPTHS, KIDS! IT'S ONLY BEEN A FEW WEEKS...

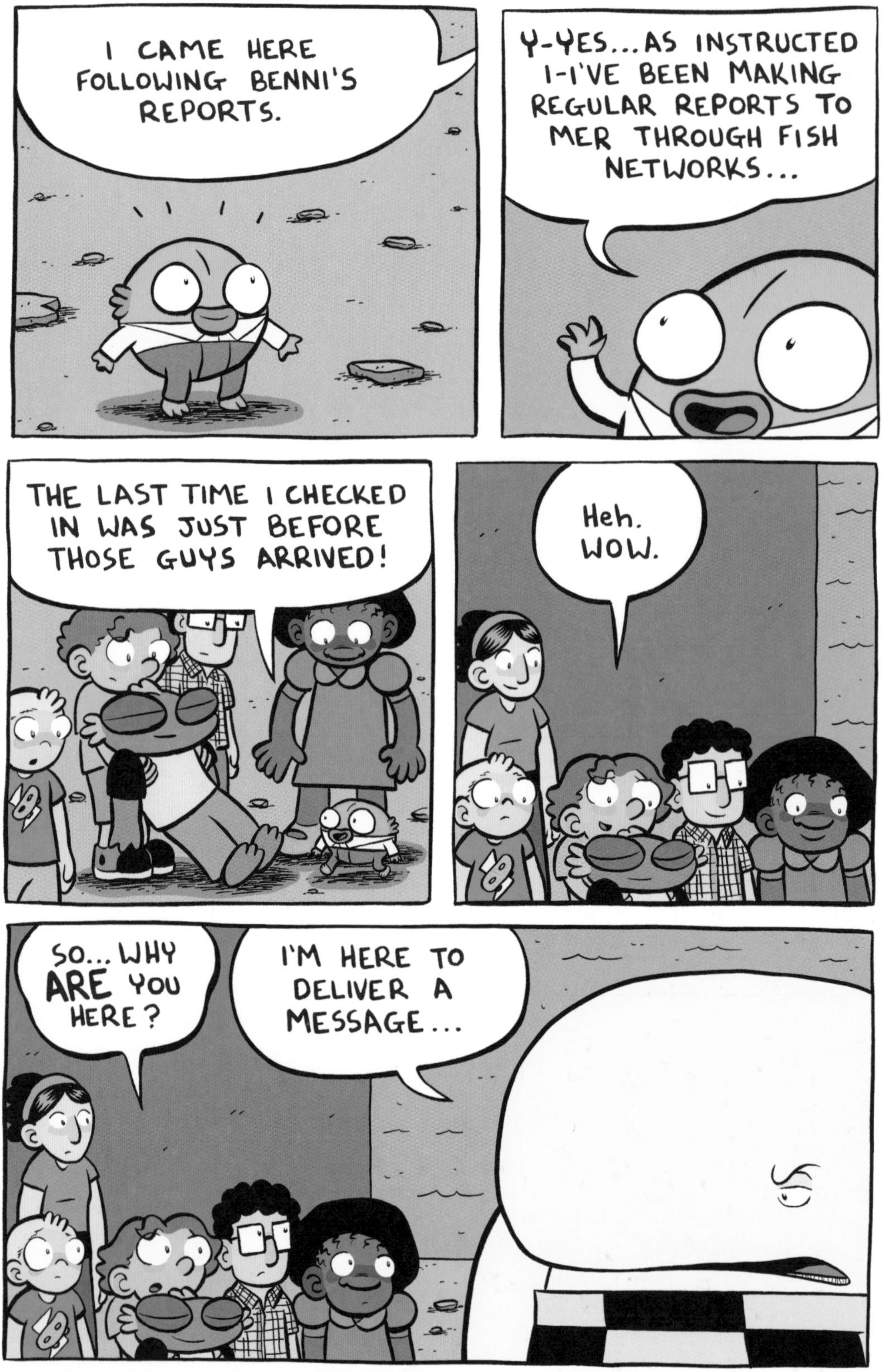
I CAME HERE FOLLOWING BENNI'S REPORTS.
Y-YES...AS INSTRUCTED I-I'VE BEEN MAKING REGULAR REPORTS TO MER THROUGH FISH NETWORKS...
THE LAST TIME I CHECKED IN WAS JUST BEFORE THOSE GUYS ARRIVED!
Heh. WOW.
SO... WHY **ARE** YOU HERE?
I'M HERE TO DELIVER A MESSAGE...

Joey Weiser's comics have appeared in several publications including *SpongeBob* Comics and the award-winning *Flight* series. His debut graphic novel, *The Ride Home*, was published in 2007 by AdHouse Books, and the *Mermin* graphic novels are currently being published through Oni Press. He is a graduate of the Savannah College of Art & Design, and he currently lives in Athens, Georgia.

MERMIN™

SKETCHES

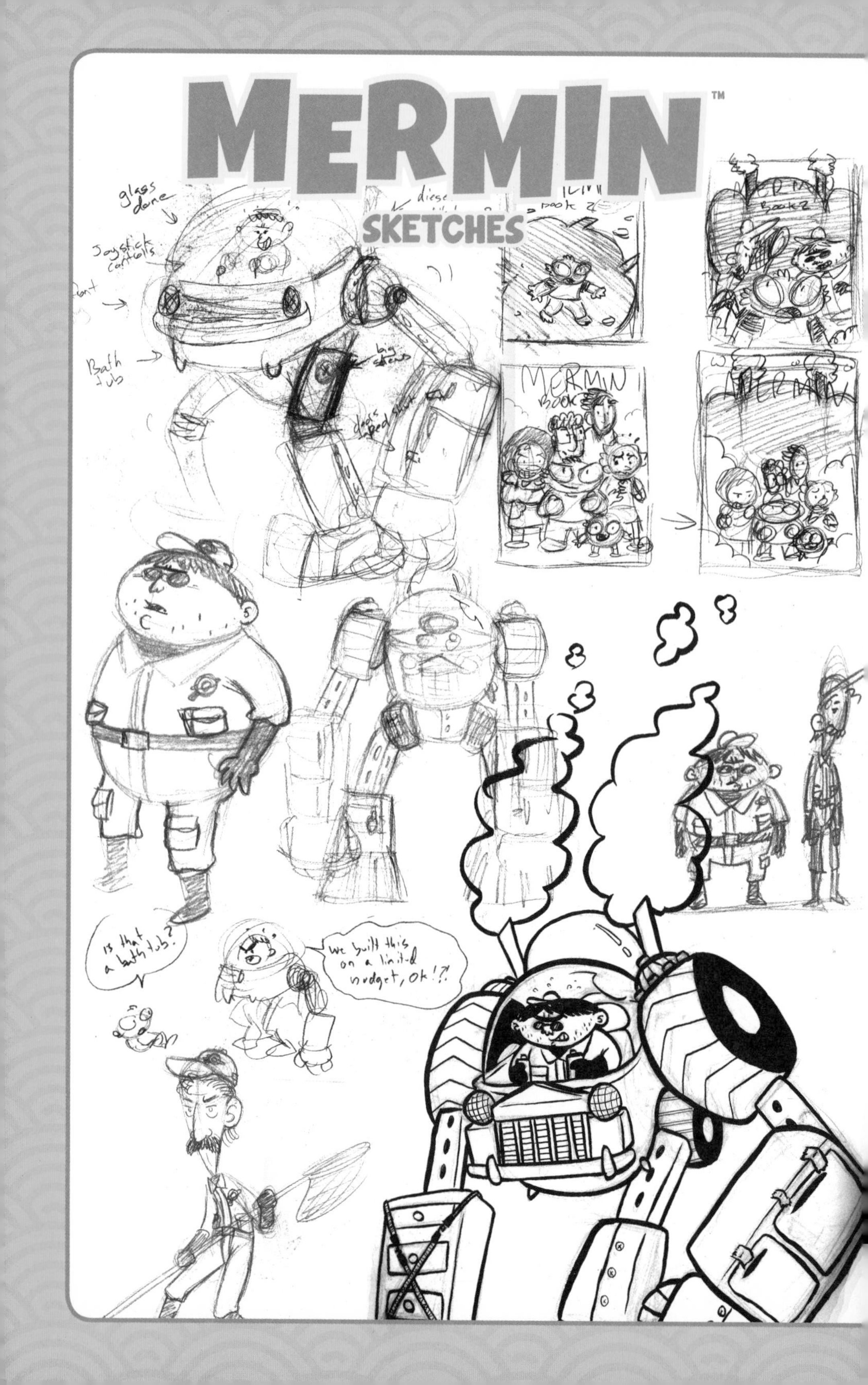
glass dome
Joystick controls
Bath tub
big screens
MERMIN Book 3
is that a bath tub?
We built this on a limited budget, ok!?

MORE GREAT BOOKS FROM JOEY WEISER & ONI PRESS!

MERMIN
BOOK ONE: OUT OF WATER
By Joey Weiser

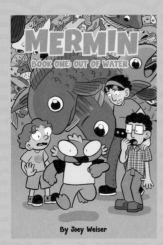

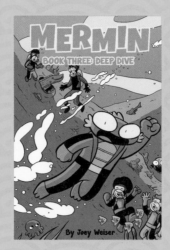

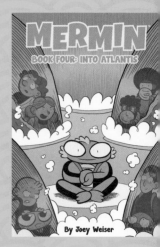

MERMIN, BOOK 1: OUT OF WATER
By Joey Weiser
152 Pages, Hardcover, Color
ISBN 978-1-934964-98-9
NOW AVAILABLE IN PAPERBACK!

MERMIN
BOOK THREE: DEEP DIVE
By Joey Weiser

MERMIN, BOOK 3: DEEP DIVE
By Joey Weiser
160 pages, Hardcover, Color
ISBN 978-1-62010-174-2
COMING SOON IN PAPERBACK!

MERMIN
BOOK FOUR: INTO ATLANTIS
By Joey Weiser

MERMIN, BOOK 4: INTO ATLANTIS
By Joey Weiser
160 pages, Hardcover, Color
ISBN 978-1-62010-258-9
COMING SOON IN PAPERBACK!

"CATFOOT'S VENGEANCE IS A MARVELOUS SWASHBUCKLING TALE. CHRIS SCHWEIZER IS AN AMAZINGLY TALENTED CARTOONIST WITH AN EAR FOR DIALOGUE AND AN EYE FOR GREAT STORYTELLING."
-STAN SAKAI, USAGI YOJIMBO
THE WEST INDIES, 1701
THE CROGAN ADVENTURES
CATFOOT'S VENGEANCE
BY CHRIS SCHWEIZER

THE CROGAN ADVENTURES: CATFOOT'S VENGEANCE
By Chris Schweizer & Joey Weiser
200 pages, Softcover, Color
ISBN 978-1-62010-203-9

"THE ARTWORK IS EXCITING AND THE PACE NEVER LETS UP. CROGAN AND HIS FRENCH LEGIONNAIRES BRING HISTORY ALIVE!"
-JEFF SMITH, BONE
FRENCH NORTH AFRICA, 1912
THE CROGAN ADVENTURES
"LAST OF THE LEGION"
BY CHRIS SCHWEIZER

THE CROGAN ADVENTURES: LAST OF THE LEGION
By Chris Schweizer & Joey Weiser
224 pages, Softcover, Color
ISBN 978-1-62010-243-5

Courtney Crumrin
VOLUME ONE
The Night Things
TED NAIFEH

COURTNEY CRUMRIN, VOLUME ONE: THE NIGHT THINGS
By Ted Naifeh & Warren Wucinich
136 pages, Hardcover, Color
ISBN 978-1-934964-77-4

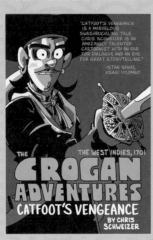

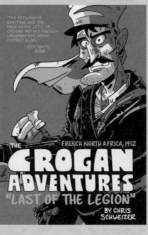

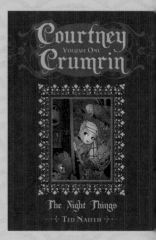

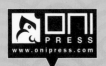

ONI PRESS
www.onipress.com

For more information on these and other fine Oni Press comic books and graphic novels visit onipress.com. To find a comic specialty store in your area visit comicshops.us.